tell me Everything

tell me
Everything

shelley a. leedahl

COTEAU BOOKS
TWENTY-FIVE YEARS

Lyrics from "We'll Go Too" appear courtesy of The Tragically Hip, from the album "Fully Completely," written by The Tragically Hip. ©1992 Little Smoke Music and Dreaming In Public, administered by TMP – The Music Publisher. Reproduced by Permission.

Edited by Edna Alford.

Cover photo: FPG International.
Cover and Book Design by Duncan Campbell.

Printed and bound in Canada at Veilleux Impression à Demande Inc..

Canadian Cataloguing in Publication Data

Leedahl, Shelley A. (Shelley Ann), 1963
Tell me everything
ISBN 1-55050-172-0

I. Title.

PS8573.E3536 T45 2000   C813'.54   C00-920157-2
PR9199.3.L394 T45 2000

COTEAU BOOKS
401-2206 Dewdney Ave.
Regina, Saskatchewan
Canada   S4R 1H3

AVAILABLE IN THE US FROM
General Distribution Services
4500 Witmer Industrial Estates
Niagara Falls, NY, 14305-1386

The publisher gratefully acknowledges the financial assistance of the Saskatchewan Arts Board, the Canada Council for the Arts, the Government of Canada through the Book Publishing Industry Development Program (BPIDP), and the City of Regina Arts Commission, for its publishing program.

The Canada Council for the Arts
Le Conseil des Arts du Canada

SASKATCHEWAN
ARTS BOARD

Canadä

city of
Regina

For Heather Rutz, Crystal Herrod,
Kirby Herr, and Ron Meetoos

and in memory of Shirley Doering
(1956-2000)

Museum's locked and it's long since past closing,
you cannot know, you cannot not know
what you're knowing

— THE TRAGICALLY HIP

The house doesn't face the ocean but it's very near, and if she fills her lungs and makes a run for it she can cover the distance between her front porch and the ragged shoreline without a breath between. When she checked this morning the ocean was raging. A wet day, the rain now soft as a mother's caress on her sleeping child, but relentless, too.

She'd been out with her resumés. Getting on with it. On the bus home she'd rung the bell prematurely and had to zigzag between the unfamiliar entries of apartment buildings, into an art gallery, under arbutus trees to dodge the rain that's seeped through her clothes to her skin. Soon she'll know these avenues that spread like arteries from the scenic Inner Harbour. Now she's feeling very much the runaway, but – she realizes in a crystalline moment – she also feels certain that inside this gentle, landscaped city, her heart's found its long way home.

She'd forgotten the umbrella, something she hadn't even owned until a week ago. She shakes the rain off her jacket and hangs it in the vestibule beside Jameson's windbreaker.

After they'd landed and he'd had his first breath of the verdant island, she'd captured his surprise with her Pentax. "Well, what do you think?" she'd asked, skipping along the tarmac like a puppy beside him.

"You're sure we're still in Canada?"

"Our home and native land," she said, though she well understood his sense of displacement.

"And it's February."

"The tenth."

They left the tarmac and waited with the other passengers for their luggage. The woman in the dirndl skirt who'd sat across from them on the plane glanced at Natasha and lifted the corner of her mouth in a half smile. Natasha gave her a slight nod before she turned to Jameson. She fingered her camera to be sure she'd replaced the lens cap. "Years from now, you'll look at this photo and you'll say, 'Here. This is where it started.'" She so wanted to hug him, but he's beyond public displays of affection now.

"Where what started?"

She saw her bag and stepped forward. "Part two."

A small village of unpacked boxes remains. Natasha squats in the core of it, sorting files. "People I Should Know By Now," she reads, and sets the folder aside. "Insurance And Financial Stuff." She's excessively organized, which takes time, but knowing that every corner of her life has its rightful place gives her comfort. "Christmas Lists." They date back to 1989 when she began keeping records of those she sent cards to, those who sent back. An inventory of friends lost and found.

It's not just the satisfaction of being organized that matters; she *needs* these records. After her thirtieth birthday she began losing names and dates. She plays little games at introductions now, repeating names at least three times, making up rhymes in her head. Mr. Kort whose pants were short. Catherine Dean with eyes blue-green. Names, numbers, appointments, Jameson's schedule and her own; there's so much to stay on top of. Even her medication escapes her. Since her thirty-fourth birthday she's had to take iron. Her doctor recently talked her into calcium. *Take pills* reminds the note on her fridge. It seems she loses something of herself every few years.

She'd recently had this discussion with her mother. Shirley'd said that of all her daughters, Natasha'd been blessed with the best memory. "You're the only one who really remembers family vacations...all those godawful summers trapped in the bush with grizzlies and man-eating mosquitoes. Well, perhaps *blessed* isn't the right word."

"Saskatchewan doesn't have grizzlies," Natasha corrected, *and God help us all if I'm the memory queen.* She sees her past as a white sheet shot through with holes and flapping on a clothesline. It changes direction with the wind and the season. Without the immediate aid of school photos or the handful of family snapshots in which no one smiled, she has only rare and fleeting images of her youth.

She hasn't come to it yet but she will soon. In a box labelled "Natasha's Treasures," there's a scrapbook of early craft collages made from whatever she could find in the kitchen junk drawer from season to season. Bits of lace, bandages, string, bobby pins, and buttons were salvaged and combined with pastel, crayon, and watercolours to create the portfolio which has been preserved through the decades.

If the scrapbook were opened and held upside down, an ancient newspaper clipping with a photo of a white-haired girl might flutter to the floor. Seeing it, yellow and brittle with time, she might carefully collect it and cradle it in her palms like a butterfly. She might blow on it, have it disappear.

The delicate wings of memory. Where it begins.

Mother Sun, Sister Rain

She awoke that morning to an explosion of sound that should have split the world in perfect halves. An airplane, she thought, spiralling through the clouds toward her. She was still closer to the land of dreams than the reality of her single bed, the grey morning light. There was another grumble overhead, then the spitting of rain against her window. Only thunder, but she was sure it signalled more than a storm.

Each day of Natasha's thirteenth summer begins with the sense that she's about to stumble onto something big, some great truth or personal discovery that will change not only her world but the worlds of all who know her. She lives for the edge and feels it's her fate to teeter there within a family of disbelievers. Where thunder is thunder.

Her parents and sisters are as static as the milkmaid in the country landscape above the couch. Natasha wills herself right into that peasant skirt. "Move," she orders the pale feet beneath the tattered hem. "Explore." Yet even as she feels the weight of the maid's basket scratch her own arms, she knows the figure will never place one delicate foot before the other, and she, Natasha, will never own the dusty secrets of the barn.

This day, with its rumbling morning of thunder, will tear itself away from the archives of her life. It's early in the season for an electrical storm. People talk; only June and already such violence. They haven't yet experienced the blistering heat that will have farmers crying for their crops, or the endless rain-soaked days that will do the same. Still, they've been fascinated by funnel clouds that threatened to kiss the earth. Wheat fields and young tomato plants have been beaten by hail stones big and hard as walnuts which Natasha and her sisters failed to preserve in the deep-freeze.

Adults discuss the temperamental climate with an incomparable passion – across fences, on the wide steps of the Royal Bank, the hard benches of coffee row – but unlike the music Natasha learns through osmosis, spiriting through the piano room's walls, she does not learn the language of weather. Showers. Sun. Overcast skies. On their own the words are uncomplicated. It's stringing these simple syllables into stories that she finds impossible. Grown-ups dress them up, disguise them in memories so deep you forget they'd begun with a frost warning. She listens to them in Wong's Cafe, studies between spoonfuls of vanilla milkshake so thick she can't suck it up a straw. Faces change. Eyes ignite, shoulders collapse, depending on mother sun.

The thunder will come first when she's taken by the hand and led back to this day, although in the unfolding of her life even the sky's fury will fade. The bike-a-thon, a Chamber of Commerce venture to raise money for an indoor swimming pool, comes second. The outdoor pool — a relic her father learned *his* lessons in — is crumbling into itself like a Greek ruin, but Natasha is grateful for it. She's grateful for the cannonballers, those bronzed boy-gods who snap bathing suit tops and whip wet towels against each other's legs. They spit sunflower seeds on the deck under a tilting sign that reads *No Spitting*. She's pleased with the wide open change room, where some breasts are oblong bags of skin and others are pliant and springy, like her own.

She will miss this archaic pool, this survivor of world wars and waterfights. And it's here where she often gets the strongest sense that all the best secrets, just out of reach, will soon be hers.

By the time Natasha and Holly slam the screen door behind them the sun is proud to be queen again. Any signs of an earlier shower have vanished. The sisters climb onto their bikes — Sportsters — new from their father's store. "See you, Mom!" Natasha yells. She follows Holly, two years older, down the long gravel driveway.

"Good luck, girls!" their mother singsongs from the top step. Natasha glances back. Shirley's head appears massive, but it's only the curlers and the sheer green scarf she's wound around everything to keep it all in place. She's twisting her hands inside the apron Holly sewed in home economics. A B+ effort, with one tipsy apple appliquéd front and centre.

Camille leaps out from behind Shirley. "Last one home's a rotten banana with worms!"

Natasha pedals through the Saturday morning calm. Clouds are pushed away and the world smells like a new, clean place. The birds still own the morning, the stores on Main just beginning to open. There's a charred vacancy between the OK Economy and Hair Now, where the girls go for their quarterly haircuts. The elder of the town's two hotels, the Empire — Natasha'd never passed it alone lest one of the town's lurching drunks stumbled into her — has suspiciously burned down.

The girls pedal past their yellow brick school, past bare tetherball poles and vacant monkey bars and the grasshopper greetings of a small prairie town. They pass through waking neighbourhoods with hopscotches chalked on sidewalks. There's the Dairy Whip, where Natasha favours rum-and-butter milkshakes; the sprawling lumberyard with its sawdust smell that gets inside her nose and makes her sneeze; the John Deere combines they've crawled around in games of Hide and Seek; the graveyard filled with plain white headstones like rows of gaping teeth; the drive-in theatre where she's not yet allowed to go; and their destination: the Highway Esso, a twin pair of gas pumps and small service station with masking tape hiding cracks in the window.

"Beat you to it!" Holly challenges.

"You're on."

Natasha's to stick with Holly and her gang *like glue.*

They arrive – Holly one length sooner – to find only a quintet of other riders gathered beneath the sailing white banner at the registration table. "We're early birds," Natasha says, fishtailing through the gravel. "Chirp, chirp."

"I guess we'll get the worm," Holly says.

The sisters are parroting their father. Peter Stensrud finds it easiest to speak to his family in quick-to-his-lips clichés. Natasha thinks his mind's often dispatched elsewhere. Where, no one imagines. He gives no clues, but Natasha knows it's not inside the knot of noise and bodies she calls her family. Her father's a mister who appears at the table at 6:15 each day with every second of his evening plotted long in advance. The scene's become a ritual.

"What do you have on tonight?" Shirley asks as she passes potatoes, their cold-room tentacles snapped off, into her husband's large, meticulously clean hands.

He almost always has something on. Natasha accepts this as the way it is, expects that everyone's father pushes away from the supper table then disappears like a spirit through the door. Many seasons will pass before she learns that her father keeps busy with Elks, the Chamber of Commerce, community sports and the church board because he has to. He has his own ghosts.

On those rare and golden nights when Peter doesn't have to charge off he sends one or all three daughters to buy ice cream treats at the gas station four blocks away. "Money doesn't grow on trees," he reminds them. "Bring back the silver."

Soon there are several fistfuls of characters balancing

bikes in the Esso parking lot, some younger than Natasha, some as old as Moses. The youngest kids have garnished their bikes with ribbons that tangled in their mother's sewing supplies, balloons from the Five and Dime. They've wired whistles to their spokes or packed mascots into handlebar baskets. The anticipation makes them itch. A boy in a Superman cape flies by with his father. A scrap between brothers breaks out. Already someone has a flat tire. Already one bleeding knee. The sun winks.

Mrs. Ledoux volunteers at the registration table. "Mother Goose," Holly whispers, using the storybook moniker shared among all the children with spice. If Mother Goose spies anyone in her crabapples she flaps after them with her prominent rear-end hanging back like a trailer, poultry neck stretched to full length. "Better check in, Tash. And try not to stare."

They approach the table, give their names, ages, and pledge sheets to the exuberant woman with the invisible eyebrows. "Thank you, girls. You're numbers 36 and 37. Won't be long now. Isn't this fun?"

Holly steps on Natasha's foot. "Yeah. Groovy."

The girls are unable to help themselves: they both gawk at the layers of chin oozing into the top of the woman's dress. Just looking at it makes Natasha think of food, of thick, vanilla icing sliding down the sides of a cake decorated by Camille or any extravagant child.

"It's a marvellous turnout," Mother Goose squawks. "Couldn't ask for a lovelier morning."

Her enthusiasm's quoted by the paper's rookie

reporter/photographer. His pictures appear blurred but recognizable in the weekly's next edition. Natasha, who catches the sun in her hair, will swallow a small seed of shock when she sees it pure white in the published photo.

Old women with crepe-paper skin clutch their hearts when the mayor fires the starter pistol. Holly spies her friends and pedals toward them. *Like glue,* Natasha thinks, steering carefully between other cyclists to stay with her. Parents clap, which embarrasses Natasha almost as much as the occasional, enthusiastic outbursts at movies, or the tentative applause after the junior choir sings in church. Peter Stensrud isn't at the morning departure, but several of his fellow Chamber members cluster on the sidelines. Natasha knows them. The young Saan store manager, whose extraordinary hands capture the crowd's various rhythms for his deaf and beautiful boy, a scene so tender and private she feels like a trespasser watching it, but it also makes her love him a little. There's the pop-eyed restaurateur, who wears safety goggles when he mows his lawn, and the new owner of Anderson's Men's Wear, whom her father doesn't trust because he wears a beard. These men swipe the backs of their necks with pressed handkerchiefs and wilt in their dark suits; the heat is unpredicted.

Natasha starts down the dull grey ribbon of road toward Marvin, a twenty-five mile trek, with Holly, Holly's cheerleader friend, Gina, and their sometimes boyfriends, Rosco and Kent. The boys weave between the girls. The blades of their bones create tiny tents beneath the thin cotton T-shirts. "No hands!" they brag, throwing their arms up as if in praise.

Big hairy deal, Natasha thinks. They get taller, fill out a little, learn to drive and take girls like her sister on dates, but they're just boys. Give them a box of Dinky toys and they'd still push them along making that "rrrr" noise.

After the first few easy miles their group narrows into a single line and Natasha respectfully takes the rear. Marvin's the nearest community, their arch rival in school sports, fastball, curling, and both men's and minor hockey; the cyclists know the road well. Natasha measures their progress by the veterinarian's farm, Benson's dugout, and the eight-mile corner, where kids a year older than Holly race their Trans Ams, Camaros, and Firebirds. Zero to something in a quarter mile.

She loses the outline of her sister's shape when Holly sails over the hump of a hill. Wherever her bike takes her is enough, Natasha thinks: on this highway, over the cracked and pitted sidewalks where they frequently break their mother's back, or down the oiled road that leads to Main Street where Natasha found a five-dollar bill and it was ice cream for everyone when Peter made her share. She doesn't see Holly's need to question or escape, if she indeed harbours the need at all. Her own need is a train screaming down a mountain – *no brakes!* – and her escapes are frequent.

In winter, when cold confines the girls to the house, Natasha time-travels to the dark corner of the basement where it smells of paint and ancient potatoes. Here, yard sale bargains and Christmas games are put to rest. A mangled *Mouse Trap* and loose *Monopoly* money. *Operation* minus the body parts. A sculpture of three-legged chairs sulks beneath musty blankets. Trunks hide photographs of people she's never met and fur coats hang like dead things from the water pipes. She pretends she's been transported to this strange world from another planet. It's imperative that she sneak her way around, hiding from the aliens who tromp like cattle above her.

When she gets tired of this game she rides the telepost; a variation on the rope climb in gym class. She does it for the burning between her legs, her shuddering release. When her limbs stop tingling, she rides again.

She's been daydreaming and has fallen far behind Holly and her friends, four figures in the shimmering distance. She stands on her pedals, body swaying with each punch; they're waiting.

"I knew you wouldn't be able to keep up." Holly's arm, tell-tale pink, is braced against the sun. She's fair, with fine features and legs that appear long for her body. She's good at gymnastics and catches on quickly to the old-time dances they learn in school. When she was eight she ranted because they didn't live in a town large enough to offer ballet lessons. "I've known snails that were faster!"

Natasha coasts to a stop. They're all looking and she melts a little under the heat of their attention. She removes her bottle from its carrier and pours tepid lemonade on her face and neck. Her collar is drenched. "Holy hotness, Batman."

"I suppose you're tired already," Holly continues, leaning on her handlebars, waiting for her to take the bait.

Natasha notes the oval of sweat beneath her sister's left armpit. Ha! She's aware of Holly's attempts to counter perspiration, the test she conducts using different brands of antiperspirant under each arm. She says nothing.

A riot of cowlicked grade six boys whiz past. "Hey! Where's the fire?" Rosco yells, lifting the weight off Natasha's shoulders. There are prizes for the fastest, the youngest, the oldest, the ones who raise the most pledge money. Natasha doesn't expect to be among the winners.

"Bet it's the hottest day so far." Rosco drags a hand across his forehead, leaving a dirty streak. He's Holly's current fling. They go out for a few weeks, break up over rumours they plant themselves, start all over again. He peels off his T-shirt and mops his sweat-dappled face. "Take your shirt off, Kentie."

Kent crosses his arms and draws his shirt over his head's nest of curls. Natasha's skin tingles in the June breeze, her perspiration a million tiny needles as it dries. Her focus drops to his feet, bare inside the blue-striped Adidas runners. Cinnamon spiders of hair take off at his ankle bones and scurry up his calves to the base of his knees. The drawstring's slipped out of his gym shorts. She swallows at the bulge where she'd like to gently place her hand if he was unconscious and could never find out. His underarms exhibit two wispy goat's beards. His chest's not yet defined, but she can see the fine shape it'll take. She grinds into the hard rubber bike seat. He has a welcoming face: toffee eyes, a tooth-filled smile, a constellation of freckles across his tanned nose. He's quiet and she's always liked him.

Rosco's another matter. "What about you girls? Anyone peeling?" He has a weight bench in his basement, barbells. The bulk of his upper body is beginning to affect the way he walks. Turning gorilla, Natasha thinks. She imagines Holly watches him work out, idly snapping her tasteless gum and stretching it into a long, sticky string to spin around her finger before she pops it back into her mouth, pretending boredom.

"Dream on," Holly says, fiddling with her bike seat. It's tipped and keeps sliding her forward, as though it's deliberately trying to dump her. "Hey Rosco, could I borrow your fat ass for a sec?"

Rosco obliges, bouncing on the seat until it's level again. "Thank me later," he says, loudly enough so that even the indifferent cows cooling in the dugout across the road can hear. He straddles his own bike again, shirt twisted and tied around the short trunk of his neck. "Let's split."

"In a minute," Gina says in her maple-sugary voice. She and Holly are swooping their hair into 1950's-style ponytails, high on their heads. Their necks glisten. Natasha's at a disadvantage with her short shag; she can't whip her hair behind her shoulders with practiced flair, as Holly and Gina do every few minutes.

Kent nudges his tire against Natasha's. "Think you can keep up?" He's radiant, smiling with his soft pink mouth, and, for the duration of these few words, hers.

"With you? No problem." She's only beginning to flirt. No one has noticed yet.

The world smells like change. Natasha feels that with each revolution of her tires she's gaining ground on the mystery that will soon reveal itself. The thunder. She doesn't know what weights the others' thoughts. The two school-free months that stretch before them, perhaps, their comic book relationships. The sun's long fingers, poking, pissing them off. Could be they're hyped about the ride and their pledges, or maybe they can't get past their ten-speeds' unforgiving seats.

She doubts that the bigger issues, like why they've been put on this planet, and by whom, are as urgent to them as they are to her. She prefers to view the world from various perspectives. Some days she defies gravity. She moon-steps through the house holding the bathroom mirror at her waist. It turns everything upside down, but her life makes more sense there, in that upside-down world where she walks on ceilings. Holly says she's a nutcracker, a fruitcake, one maraca short of a mariachi band. Camille thinks she's neat.

Natasha shares a bedroom with Camille, a high-spirited child from yet another galaxy with bluish shadows beneath gleaming, green eyes. In her half of the wide room, Natasha's cast a fishnet across the ceiling. Starfish and clam shells purchased at the local hobby shop hover in the green tangle above her bed. She can't fathom an ocean or a universe so large you can't see end to end, but she's been to Waskesiu Lake and that's almost as good. Her prize possession is a conch shell. She presses it to one ear, cups her other, but it's not quite loud enough or she can't believe enough because there's never any surf, just her own heart, crashing.

The bikers pedal past the community pasture, beside sloughs where mallards take turns doing their headless dips into murky water. They cross the Sandy River bridge where the water, though day-old-coffee brown, is swift and tempting. If anyone dared she'd be the first to dive in. Water in any form – the chlorine splash of swimming pools, country trickles too thin to be called streams, irresistible spring ditches or the white-foamed, surfable waves she's seen only on television – tugs at her chest and whispers what might be *one day*.

Gina takes Natasha's place at the rear; those strong legs that helped cheerlead a basketball team to victory do not measure up on the poorly paved highway. Natasha struggles to stay no less than five bike lengths behind Holly. *Like glue.* Pebbles wing their way back. She's mesmerized by her sister's tires, the rhythm of her heels, the slight punch of each shoulder as they climb what the prairie offers as a hill. When she grows woozy, she swerves to the yellow-lined centre of the highway and ponders the watery mirage. She thinks about deserts, cacti. She imagines herself onto a landscape of clean, clear sand the colour of skin, and sets about claiming that perfection with her footprints. Was it true that if you were dying of thirst you could split a cactus and find water? Her father's been to Arizona. He sent a postcard home. He would know. Her father, it occurs to her, knows everything.

Natasha leaves the desert. It's back to the road again, a wary hawk on a weather-worn fence post, wind, her sister's skinny bum in front of her. She tries to hang onto these simple things. Always her mind clutters up with "what-ifs?" and "could-be's," and right now she wants none of it. It exhausts her. She wishes she could learn not to think so much, like Holly, but the question of knowledge creeps back. She keeps waiting for the magic day when she'll acquire it. Dad's always had it, she thinks. It should be genetic. Maybe when I'm seventeen and carry a purse to school, like Holly, with Juicy Fruit gum tucked in the side pocket. Maybe when I'm twenty-one and sure of myself.

For now, even the easiest questions stump her. "What does your father do?" She doesn't know how to answer. It's not as easy as *farmer* or *carpenter*. *District Manager* means nothing to her peers, and little more to her. He has an office with a row of windows that overlook a store. On Sundays, after church, he stops to make sure the doors are locked by yanking on them, two times, hard. Natasha, Holly, and Camille whimper until he lets them in for penny candy. No one would notice the missing black jaw-breakers or Dubble Bubble gum, but he always leaves a silver scattering of coins beside the cash register.

"Do you know how to use that?" she asks. The machine mystifies her with all its buttons and sounds. A miniature monster.

"I'm the boss, aren't I?" he says, and she's ashamed that she asked, that she doubted him, but she never sees him ring anything in, even at closing time, or welfare day, when there are long lineups and the third till really does need to be opened. Even at Christmas.

There are few vehicles on the highway, but the intermittent drivers honk and wave encouragement as they pass. A family in a copper station wagon with terry towels strung across the back windows to temper the heat. A Volkswagon bug painted with orange and green daisies, a leftover from the previous decade, driven by strangers with Alberta plates. "Punch buggy, no return!" Rosco calls. He swerves close to Kent and raps his shoulder.

"You're an ass!" Gina hollers, but Kent doesn't lose control and Rosco only smiles harder.

Natasha hears another car behind them, a cacophony of honks. She rides as far to the right as possible before veering into the knee-high quack grass waving along the ditch. It's the mayor. His long blue arm's a lever sliding up and down through the window of a dusty sedan. He smiles, a wary expression on a slim face, and she's struck by how much he looks like Dick York from "Bewitched." She nods; he's her father's friend.

Her bottom begins to disagree with the bike seat. She alternates her weight from side to side, stands, shifts again from left buttock to right, stands again. If I survive this, she thinks, I may never sit again. Damn bony ass.

A couple she babysits for pass on matching grape bikes looking miraculously cool. The woman's hair is roped into a single braid and her calf muscles ripple. Natasha hopes she'll be like this when she's old and married; full of life, with walkers' legs. It's hard to believe old and married will ever happen, but there are pictures of her mother as a girl in perfect French braids tied with satin bows and look at her now.

Shirley's a tall woman, almost treeish. Natasha often sees that tree bend to pick clothes off the floor or sweep dust into a pan, but it doesn't bend to better hear her childhood wishes. It never whispers wishes back. Shirley smokes long cigarettes and stirs the air like a 1940s film star. Once, when Natasha was seven, her mother gave her a drag because she'd begged. Not knowing better, she'd sucked in sharply and the burn roared down her throat to her chest. After a furious round of coughing that resulted in a palm of vomit, Natasha handed the cigarette back. Not a word was spoken.

Natasha yearns for the unexpected from everyone but is most impatient with her mother. Shirley leads an endless procession of children through triads and arpeggios and all levels of *Leila Fletcher* and *Royal Conservatory*. Like the house itself, with its wide front steps and pillared entrance, polished wood floors and back pantry, Natasha's mother is always where her middle daughter expects her to be. When she gives up waiting to catch Shirley mutter more than an occasional *damn* or *hell,* she submits other words.

"Say you hate me," Natasha recently urged when they were alone, folding laundry.

"You hate me."

"No, Mom, say *you* hate *me.*"

Shirley pinched the corners of a white sheet, passed them to Natasha, grabbed the opposite corners. They met like dancers in the middle. "Why do you want me to say that? You know I don't hate you. I could never hate you."

"Just say it."

"No."

"Mom, it doesn't mean anything. I just want you to say those words."

Natasha stopped folding. Shirley balled two navy knee-high socks. Her eyes were pools of blue light. "I hate you. There. Happy now?"

A lump on the pavement ahead. Mud? A porcupine? Natasha stands on her pedals and wheels up to a flattened cat, mouth fixed in a permanent howl. Nuts, she thinks. Holly didn't even give it a backward glance for good luck. She'd like to stop and take a closer look, see if there are bugs crawling out of its twisted mouth, but presses on. If a black cat means bad luck, what about a calico? Good *and* bad ahead? Did someone deliberately hit the unfortunate animal, or was it frozen in place by headlights in the night. She pedals harder against the growing wind, contemplating each of the cat's nine lives and how they may have been spent. Rabies? Crawling into the motor of a car? Drowned in a gunny sack?

Her legs ache, and she rubs the heel of her hand down her right thigh. She doesn't realize she's been riding through the shadow of clouds.

"Is it raining?" Gina asks, beside her. She's gained some ground, and Kent has lost some. Now they are three, together. "I think it's raining."

Natasha looks up to see what's taken shape. Monster clouds swirl above them. "Look, it's just like in the movies!"

"Whoa...far-out," Kent says. He wipes a drop off his nose.

Holly yells at Rosco to stop. Moments later the leading pair swerve onto an approach. They bounce on their pedals as Natasha and the others ride up. "It's gonna pour," Rosco forecasts, face to the rolling sky. The wind pushes his long hair across his eyes.

Already everyone's skin is slick. Kent's has the gelatinous appeal of amphibians, Natasha notes. She'd like to touch it. The girl in the basement who rides the telepole would ride her tongue along the inside of his arm and taste it.

"Now what?" Holly asks. Her shirt sticks to her and she plucks it away from her stomach. "Bright ideas, anyone?"

The five cyclists stand frozen, like cows not knowing what to do with the gate left open. It's too quiet, a shattering type of silence. Natasha surveys for snake-tongued lightning; no luck yet.

"Well?" Gina sucks her index finger, pulls it out and turns it in all directions. "The wind's coming from the north. Against us."

"That's west, Einstein," Rosco snaps.

"Maybe we should ride to the next farm and call home," Holly suggests. "We're close to Gerlinskis'."

"I think we should turn around here," Gina says, "forget about finishing. No one would know."

They're still swapping strategies when a half-ton truck approaches. "It's the Pool agent's wife," Gina says above the wind. "My dad knows her."

The woman slows until she's idling beside them. She leans out the window, looks to the churning sky and says, "It's going to get ugly."

Natasha reads worry in the lines around her mouth. Beside her, a child with big eyes and a baby bottle hanging from his teeth stares at them. "Hop in! We're picking everyone up," the woman says.

"What about our pledges?" Kent calls, his voice competing with the wind. There's little to obstruct the gusts, just a lonely stand of poplars an acre too far away to matter. The cyclists shoulder into the wind, brace their legs to keep their bikes and bodies upright. "We can't collect if we don't finish."

"Doesn't matter," the Pool agent's wife calls back, cupping her hands around her mouth, megaphone style. The toddler's trying to crawl onto her lap. He steps on the horn. "Are you getting in?"

Rosco and Kent consult the clouds directly above them. "Bugger it," Kent says.

Natasha looks to the distance. An ominous grey film, like the impression left on a blurred and poorly fixed photograph, slants from sky to field – a wall pushing toward them.

"We'll keep going," Rosco decides. "We're almost there."

"What?" The woman cups her ear now and leans even further out the window. The child pat-a-cakes her face.

"I said, 'we're almost there.'"

Holly raises her palms indifferently; Gina draws out a melodic sigh and says, "Idiot."

"You're sure now?" the woman tries again. "You're positive?"

Wait! It's Natasha's voice, trapped in her throat like a

bird in a small room. The back and forth tug between head and heart. *Like glue,* her father says.

"Yeah," Kent says, slowly, as if he's been away and has just returned to the moment, the conversation, the choking wind that's fluffing his hair toward Afro status. "It'll pass."

Their potential ride begins rolling the window in fits and starts, as if it takes two hands and an incredible effort. "Okay, then." The truck clunks into first gear and mother and child drive off with grain kernels popping over the tailgate. The cyclists watch until the truck's no bigger than a kernel itself.

Kent tinkers with his bike chain. His fingertips are covered in grease, his calves are licked with it. Natasha checks the backs of her own legs and sees that her left calf, too, sports the unmistakable greasy imprint from the chain ring's teeth.

"We should have taken the ride," Gina whines, undoing the knot that lifts her shirt and exposes her midriff. "We're gonna catch pneumonia."

"No we won't," Rosco says, rock sure of himself and their physiologies. "It's just spitting. It'll blow over in no time. Let's split."

When the rain comes home hard it's almost welcome after the long miles in the heat, though the wind makes pedalling a double chore. Natasha's wrists ache from gripping her handlebars tightly. Even her thumbs hurt. Gina and Holly pair up and sing cheers:

"We're the Titans and we're so impressive, so come on team and be more aggressive!"

When the rain strikes harder, washing the highway so the yellow line stands out brilliantly against the asphalt, the drenched cheerleaders take to shouting:

"Dynamo, dynamite, let's go, let's fight!"

The wind scatters their words across the thirsty fields and they surrender to it. Their ponytails droop miserably. Holly's white shirt is plastered to her back. Natasha can see her bra straps.

A finger of lightning strikes the field ahead. "Holy shit!" Rosco screeches to a stop.

Holly steers toward the ditch, cutting Natasha off.

"Everyone – stop!" Gina's mascara is smudged beneath her eyes. It's haunting, Natasha thinks, and very effectively transforms her from girl to ghoul. "We've got to flag someone down," Gina continues, her voice weak from cheering against the opposition wind. "I *mean* it. We could get fried out here! We could get our brains scrambled."

Rosco snorts. "We're on rubber. It'll ground us."

"Gina's right," Holly agrees, shaking her pale hair out. "We should take the next ride that stops."

Rosco ogles her. "Your headlights are on!"

Holly claps an arm across her breasts. "Pervert!"

"Well...what are we going to do?" Gina's pouting like an obstinate child who's forced to share her toys. Her headlights, Natasha notices, are on dim. "I vote we wait here for a ride. All in favour?"

Three more arms fly up.

"Okay," Rosco concedes, "you wimps win." He rides into the ditch, jumps off and lets his bike fall into the mud. "We only had about ten miles left."

The passing minutes are devoid of traffic, two or four wheeled. "Where'd everyone go?" Holly asks, hunched over her handlebars, and shivering. "Guess we're the only crazy ones. Happy summer everyone."

Kent and Gina join a bare-chested Rosco in the ditch. Any chance he gets, Natasha muses. They huddle beneath his soaked T-shirt; a futile umbrella. She runs a finger over the goosebumps on her arm, the hair rising there like needles. Holly's looking beyond Natasha. She's watching the highway, rain dripping off her eyelashes. "See anything?"

"Nah," Natasha says, wiping her nose with her hand. "Nothing."

"We're royally screwed," Holly says.

"Wait!" Natasha sees lights: two holes burned into the fallen cloud. "Something's coming," she yells, making a visor of her hand. "Something big!"

The sky explodes with light and sound. Holly thrashes her pink arms. The boys cheer to the simultaneous whoosh of air brakes and the ear-cracking thunder they feel beneath their feet as the semi-trailer stops beside them.

"You kids wanna ride?"

Natasha's stomach flips.

There's a black hole where a front tooth should be and three thumbs of space between his eyes. The trucker opens his door and swings out of the cab. When he turns she sees a name, Freddy, stitched in red over his jacket's right breast. The wrist end of gloves poke out each of his pant pockets. He pulls one glove out and swipes it across his forehead. "Hell of a day for a bike ride."

Rosco is closest. "It was nice when we left," he says.

"Yeah," Gina says, the sugar sliding off her voice and leaving it cool. She inches forward. "Real nice."

The trucker touches Rosco on the shoulder with the glove. "Well, come on then." His slightly bowed legs take him to the trailer's back door. He clicks a lock and pulls apart the white wall. His fingers are pale sausages with tufts of coal black hair above the knuckles. "You boys go on up and I'll pass you the bikes. Hope you're not afraid of the dark."

Kent and Rosco climb into the trailer. They wordlessly accept their own muddy bikes, then Gina's, then the Sportsters, and wheel them toward the unknown.

The girls follow like sheep.

Little Fish

Time surrenders hours, days, weeks. Months tumble forward and further away. Winter drags his heavy feet, not knowing he's no longer welcome. Natasha watches him go, feels the days stretch, sees the snow melt into a few dirty islands, then nothing at all. She walks to school and back with her head down, watching for any glimmering in the grass or on the wet streets that could signal spring's gift of a coin. She is none the richer.

"Your dad and I are leaving," Shirley tells the girls on the first day of open tulips. They've come up in startling shades of red and yellow along the south side of the house against the crumbling foundation. The tulips' exuberance heralds the task of packing up winter clothes and exchanging them with the lighter inventory of shorts and t-shirts, slightly damp and musty now from their hibernation in the space beneath the basement stairs. "He has a conference in Charlottetown and I'm going along. We'll be staying an extra week to tour around."

Natasha gapes at this blast of news from the reticent

woman their pretty mother's become. Holly freezes.

"Where's Charlottetown?" Camille asks, clutching a bundle of warm weather clothes. "Do we get to go?" She's slung her bathing suit, a purple one-piece with a white, pleated skirt, around her neck.

"Prince Edward Island," Shirley says, splashing water from the tea kettle into the pot of her umbrella plant, "and not on your lives."

Holly takes her surprise down the hall, grabbing Natasha when they're well away from their mother's ears.

"You're pinching," Natasha protests. "What's up?"

"Haven't you noticed? It's Mom, she's –"

"Going on a trip. I was there."

"Jesus, Tash, not that!" Holly sits on Camille's bed, kneading her left temple with the heel of her hand. "She's killed every plant in the house. She's watered them all to death!"

"What?"

"Go ahead, look around. I can't believe you haven't noticed. Are you deaf, dumb *and* blind?"

Natasha sets her summer clothes on the floor in front of her dresser. T-shirts in the top left, she decides, and picks a plain blue one from the pile. *Every* plant? But her mother loves her plants, surely Holly's just exaggerating again, she thinks, folding back the amputated arms of a striped black and white T-shirt, then folding the shirt in half like Shirley's shown her. But what if she's not?

She creeps out of the room, a secret agent slinking around the corner into the hall, just as Camille comes in with another load. "Where you going?" Camille asks.

"You're not just going to leave those clothes in a mess like that, are you?"

"Getting a drink, as if it's any of your business." And so she goes, and surreptitiously inspects the Boston fern in the living room, the row of African violets swimming in the kitchen windowsill. She pushes a finger into the mud around the dining room's fig tree. Room to room, on shelves, in planters, strung up in macramé hangers – spider plants, gloxinia, Elephant's ears, philodendrons, aloe vera, dracaena, dieffenbachia, angel's tears and Moses-in-the-cradle – everything once green and growing has drowned.

"What are you doing?"

"Oh, hi, Mom. I'm just –" She pans the room, stalling. "I was looking for a button. It fell off my blouse and I thought I put it in one of these pots so I could find it later. Have you seen it? A white button, it's off –"

Shirley fingers the brown leaf of a pathetic palm, dumps what's left of her coffee into the soup of soil, letting the mug dangle from her fingers until the last drop is gone. "I'll keep my eyes open."

Natasha takes great interest in the various parts that make up her mother, including her hands, which, like the rest of her, have thinned, the veins pronounced like a topographical map. Shirley's been sick. Though she doesn't throw up or cough or have a fever, she's a shadow of the mother who'd been as predictable as the days of the week. The girls find her in bed at unusual times, her face to the window, eyes wide but unseeing. Sometimes she forgets to take her shoes off and they poke out the bottom of her blanket like a magic trick, the woman who's been sawed in half. Natasha can't put a finger or a name on what's happening. "She's sick," is all Peter offers. "Peace and quiet, that's what she needs." And so the girls tiptoe, and the house, without the usual sounds a family makes, becomes hollow.

Midnight. Natasha watches shadows branch along the wall above her sleeping sister's bed and waits for the bony fingers of her own dreams to splinter another night of sleep. Almost a year now, these dark walls pressing in on her nights, the nocturnal visits from strangers with long mouths moving but making no sounds, and it's better, she thinks, a blessing that she can't make out what they're so desperately trying to tell her. Always so close to safety. A hand pulling her up. She learns to fly in the dreams, always at the last moment, only the distance of a heel or an elbow away from being grabbed. And then? She doesn't know.

It's been a strange year all around. Late blizzards have come and gone three times before the snow decided to melt for real. Holly's been irritable. She has frequent, crippling migraines and earned a suspension for back-talking at school. Natasha's learned to stay at least one room out of her way whenever possible.

Peter's flip-flopped; he's softened. He's become more attentive, to the point of asking each of the girls about their day and even sitting down to play *Monopoly* or rummy or Snap! when he has the time, which still isn't often. He's allowed them to adopt a dog – a peppy, red cocker spaniel they've named Ginger – whom they'd been led to believe was fixed but, as the barrel of her belly attests, evidently is not. Her parents' altered states have been like a new food with a strange smell; a change Natasha doesn't quite know how to take.

She shifts in her bed, trying to get comfortable, trying to find the best position to ward off bad thoughts. Better to face the wall than the closet. Keep arms and legs well off the edge. Across the hall, a sound like weeping. It might be the elm tree in the wind, but she listens harder and knows it's not. Then someone is up. Peter? It could be, must be, his heavy footsteps. Soon the kettle will call and her father will fuss in the kitchen before he passes outside her door again, and past, to Holly's room. Natasha folds her feather pillow around her head, finds herself that way in the morning.

"*You still* haven't said what's happening to us when you're off gallivanting in Charlottetown," Natasha says, gently, though the departure's drawing near and she's anxious about her personal fate. She's helping Shirley with the lunch dishes, a chore she and Holly rotate; Natasha has even days, Holly has odd. She waves her dishtowel in front of the pregnant dog, who makes no move to snatch it.

"We're working on that," Shirley says, absently rinsing a glass as she looks out the window above the sink where the African violets have crumbled, and no one – not Natasha, her sisters or Peter – has had the nerve to remove them. "We'd planned to have Grandpa come stay, but your dad doesn't think he's up to it."

Holly, sipping tea at the table as though the previous night's headache never happened, jumps on this. "The drooler? He can hardly take care of himself, what the hee-haw would he do with us?" She takes her new, wire-framed glasses off, huffs on the lenses, then rubs them on her shirt.

Camille, also at the table, giggles behind her hand. "The drooler."

"I want to stay with Gina," Holly says. Shirley hasn't noticed the damage Holly's doing with her teaspoon, bent now to resemble a ladle. "They've got the room out there."

"What about Ginger?" Camille asks, dropping the dog a crust. "What about you, huh? What about you?" She throws both arms around the squirming dog's neck and kisses her on the nose.

"Like I said," Shirley continues, staring out but not noticing that even the garden's become a pond, "we're working on it."

That her older sister does have passions, after all, comes as a mild surprise to Natasha. Holly's passions are reserved for roller coasters, fires, skyscrapers, lipstick, garter snakes, the creatures of the ocean, her mother's negligees, stiletto heels, and, still intermittently, Rosco.

Unlike Natasha, she also has a fling with horses, but for all her hounding, Peter doesn't buy her one. What she knows of the beautiful beasts is what she's learned when Gina invites her out to ride, which, she complains, is never often enough.

She loves bouncing out to her friend's farm on a school bus named Clover Bar. Gina's place is a world of barn smells, morning chores, riding in the back of a rusted half-ton with the gate left open, legs kicking over the edge, jumping off. A faraway country of curry combs.

Since Gina moved five miles out of town and acquired horses, Holly's been bucked off, stepped on, and nipped, but she's also felt the liquid motion of a quarter horse at full speed and inhaled the crisp, harvest air up her nose. "And you should see the stallion," she says to Natasha in the lowered voice she uses to tantalize. She puts her brush down and snags her thick hair up into a ponytail once again. The action triggers déjà vu for Natasha, and the sensation of being spun on a merry-go-round. She banishes it from her mind.

"What about it?" Natasha feels precarious on the edge of her sister's bed. Even though she's been beckoned, this meeting might end with her on the floor, or pushed, literally, back out the door she's been invited through.

"His thing is about this big." Holly spreads her arms a yardstick's width apart.

His *thing?* You'd think she was three years old, Natasha muses. It's a cock, a prick, a wiener, a dink, or the more formal but infinitely more distasteful and rubbery *penis.* Surely her sister can name it. "You're full of it," she says, but she can't shake the picture of the sleek, well-endowed animal, and what Holly doesn't mention: the duet of pleasure and pain when the stallion enters the mare. Once, when the family was driving to Saskatoon, Natasha witnessed a bull and cow humping. It was just a glimpse. Her father tends to speed across the two-hundred-and-fifty miles from town to city limits, then home again, desperate to leave, hell-bent on returning. Their station wagon sings past power poles and phone lines, races Vancouver-bound trains loaded with grain. But she saw it, and that raw pleasure fixed itself into her album of erotic images.

Holly's pressing a fist to her forehead, rubbing in a slow circle. "Damn, damn, damn."

"Another one?" Natasha asks.

The migraines are whirlpools of pain that leave Holly in either a coma of misery – pale, soundless and flattened on her bed – or wild as any tyrant, capable of slamming whatever's convenient – ashtrays, her fists – into walls. Shirley calls them her "storms." When the worst ones hit, Peter or Shirley transform their suffering daughter's room into a tomb, with blankets tacked over the windows. When they strike at night one parent or the other drags their body from sleep to sit bedside with Holly, massaging the soles of her feet and the webbing between fingers and thumbs because they've heard this can help. Sometimes Holly sends them away. Sometimes she screams for them to come.

Holly falls back onto her bed, both hands over her eyes. "You can get lost now."

Natasha leaves and drifts through the Sunday house, looking for something to do. Her parents are resting, Camille's colouring in the bedroom. Dull, dull, dull. Even the country landscape she used to imagine herself into is now just what it actually is: a cheaply framed print purchased from Woolworths in North Battleford. She finally settles at the piano, where she goes through her repertoire of Beatles songs – "Let It Be," "Yesterday," "Michelle," "Hey, Jude" – all in the key of C.

"You shouldn't have quit," Peter says, surprising her because he's up now, and even more so, because he's been listening. She's still not used to the attention, after all those years of starving for it. He stands beside the piano and whistles a few bars of "Hey Jude."

"I had to quit. Mrs. Callaghan has a urinary problem. She smells. Her whole house smells. Even her peppermints smell like pee. I couldn't stand it."

"What about taking from your mother again?"

She shakes her head. "Never." They'd tried it, but Natasha wouldn't practice for her mother. Plus, her lesson was always fit in around all the other students' schedules, and sometimes there wasn't any room at all. Mostly she listened through the walls to those other pianists, training her ear. More than anything, she'd learned to create music by playing along with Beatles records, wearing monster headphones that slid over her face.

"But you're good. You could really do something with your talent. You should at least consider entering the town talent show."

"Ha!" Natasha stops playing and faces him. The

warmth that's crept into her face is consistent with her father's attention. "You couldn't pay me to enter that fiasco. If I want to make a fool of myself, I'll do it right here at home, thank you very much. I suppose you're entering?"

"Judging it," she thought she heard him say, but he'd already turned away.

"Where's Mom?" Natasha asks Camille, who's slurping an after-school bowl of Honeycomb cereal. Her dark-haired sister eats for three children but remains slight as a breeze. Only her feet seem to grow. Not even ten and she can wear Natasha's shoes.

"Outside," she says, munching. "Garden."

Natasha lets the screen door bang behind her. The ground's still wet but a week of sun has sucked up most of the puddles. Shirley's wrestling with a Rototiller that won't start. "What in the –?" Since when did her mother tackle Rototilling? She's totally engrossed, but she's no match for the machine, and the unusual twist of her mouth suggests to Natasha that she'd best step in before woman or machine turn to violence.

"Can I try?"

"It's dangerous, Tash. I wouldn't even do it myself if I had any sense, but your dad's extremely busy this week and I have to get this garden in." She wipes the back of her hand across her forehead, leaving a smudge. Her clothes hang on her angular frame, making her appear even taller than her five feet ten inches. It's almost too warm for polyester pants, but Shirley's found a pair that don't slide down her hips and she's tucked the cuffs into Peter's rubber boots. She does a few twists, then arches and rubs her lower back with both hands.

She's getting better, Natasha thinks. "How long you been at this?"

Shirley checks the sun's path. A bluebottle buzzes around her head and she swats at it. "I don't know. Too long." She frowns at the Rototiller. "Oh, what the heck. You may as well give it a go, but for God's sake watch your feet."

Natasha steps behind the Rototiller and gives the cord a yank. It whips back, startling her. "Sucker!" She tries again, this time ready for the snap. The heavy machine comes to life. She jerks forward. The Rototiller digs too deeply and stalls.

"We'll just have to leave it for your father," Shirley says, but Natasha's not finished. She steadies the machine until it's upright again and starts it with one impressive pull. She's wrenched her shoulder, but doesn't say so.

"Keep moving in a straight line," Shirley yells above the motor. "Just up and down!"

Natasha looks as though she's being dragged through the heavy soil, but she soon masters even the turns and in forty minutes she's won the battle: the large garden is sufficiently churned. "Holy earthworms," Natasha says, selecting one near her feet. She examines it, then flings it off her finger.

She desperately needs a drink. Iced tea would do nicely, she thinks, but when she looks up her mother's running across the grass with a mission and a large pail. Shirley says, "Seeds, sticks, trowel...other stuff."

"Other stuff?" Natasha checks. "Mother, aren't we supposed to use *string* to mark the rows?"

Her mother's gathered several pairs of ruined pantyhose and is quickly tying the feet together. "Couldn't find any." She grabs the nylon bundle and begins stretching it from stake to stake across the width of the garden. "See? It works."

What Natasha sees is a chorus line of beige crotches and skinny legs doing the Russian splits. "It's obscene," she says, but Shirley doesn't hear.

The sun tumbles toward the west, its sharp light reflecting off the town's five grain elevators. Natasha pulls the trowel through the earth while Shirley drops in peas, carrot seeds, onions with their funny little hats, then waves the dirt back across the seeds and pats it down. "Did I tell you? You and Holly are staying at Gina's while we're gone."

"Gina's! God, Mom, she's not *my* friend. Can't I stay anywhere else?"

"Well, I would have had you stay with the Larsons, but of course they're going to be on the trip, too. Camille's staying with the Sperlings, but I don't think you'd like it there, all those little kids —"

"But Mom, Gina's so —"

Shirley stops planting, waiting for Natasha to finish.

"I don't know."

"Well you can't say you won't have a good time, with all that room out there, the pool, and the horses —"

"Horses are Holly's thing, Mom, not mine." Not that you'd know that, she thinks, since you haven't even been on this planet for about a year. "You know that Gina has a brother, right? A *big* brother? Do you think it's a good idea sending me and Holly out there? I mean, aren't you worried about hormones and all that?"

Shirley stops again, the hand with the seeds frozen six inches above the earth.

"Well?" Natasha asks, then Ginger is there, stamping over all their efforts.

"Shoo, bad dog," Shirley says, recovering. Natasha grabs Ginger's collar and leads her out of the garden. She ties the dog to the fence with the last nylon. Ginger whines.

Shirley drops another necklace of seeds into the shallow valley. "I talked to Sylvia. David's not going to be around very much. He's got his job and ball games almost every night. He's getting to be quite the pitcher, I hear. Besides, he wouldn't ever bother with you, considering –" Her voice takes a melancholy turn.

Natasha waits. "Considering what?"

Shirley stands and wipes the dirt off her knees, halfway through a row. "Cripes, you're fourteen and he's almost nineteen. That's a –" Ginger pierces the afternoon with a litany of staccato yelps. "Shut up, dog! And Holly's far too involved with Rosco to give David a second glance."

Natasha wonders if they're done now. Her stomach's telling her it's time to eat. "What about Madge Amundrud? I've stayed at her place before and survived."

"That was luck!" Shirley spills the radish seeds and

begins plucking them from the dirt, her fingers like pincers. "I hear her father has *Playboy* centrefolds taped up all over the basement walls."

Natasha stabs the earth. "Whatever." But it's true. She'd been shocked to see the glossy photos of busty, naked women, smirking at her from every angle of Madge's rumpus room, but not alarmed. Something else in her erotic album.

"Well, what about Debbie's? You like *her* mother."

"You know her father drinks!"

She's out of options. The Gillespies? For a whole week? She remembers David as a gangly thing with dark spiky hair that implies perpetual electrocution. He used to work for her father, pumping gas. Still, she hasn't seen him for – what – two years? Maybe he's joined the human race.

The novelty of taking the school bus and bagging a lunch wears off after day one. Natasha sits alone near the back behind Gina and Holly, who seem to find everything hilarious behind their cupped hands. The bus driver, a retired farmer who sports a permanent look of distrust on his thin face, frequently consults the mirror to study his passengers. Natasha doesn't trust him back. She has purposely made him wait, and now he refuses to acknowledge her.

Life is marginally better once they're let off at the Texas gate. Gina's mother is a doting woman who often scrambles the buttons on her cardigans. She was old when she had David and Gina, now she's bordering on elderly. The house smells like a world where people have thick accents. Mrs. Gillespie always has something boiling on the wide, double-doored stove, and for the first time Natasha tastes spaghetti that doesn't pour out of a can. It took her a while to get over the pallor of the noodles; she thought they were *supposed* to be orange. The promised pool is outdoors and not yet filled for the new season. When Natasha checked, there was a foot of water in the deep end and a bloated rat – thankfully dead – lounging on top. Her mother'd been right about one thing: David is a no-show.

Sleep and comfort are as elusive as baths in the strange house. The Gillespies' water comes from a well and is strictly rationed. The girls will have only three baths in their ten days at the farm, and even then, Mrs. Gillespie strongly hints that Natasha should use Holly's water, which she doesn't.

Natasha's assigned the guest room at the end of the second floor. She's glad to be close to the bathroom. Even her mother doesn't know that when the bad dreams come she sometimes wets the bed. At home she washes the sheets without anyone knowing; difficult, but it can be managed. How in the world would she deal with it here, with water at a premium and Mrs. Gillespie always a loud voice away?

The torture of the guest bed is giving her back pains. Each night she curls lumpy, homemade quilts into the mattress's bowl-like indentation. "It's like sleeping in a crater or a den or something," she tells Holly. "I feel like a bloody bear." When she does steal a few hours of sleep, she wakes feeling wet and frantically pats the sheet beneath her. Only sweat.

There are religious pictures and Biblical quotes framed on every wall in the house. The elder Gillespies are devout Christians, though the evangelical church they attend is a mystery to Natasha. It's on the north edge of town, a huge boxy building without steeples or stained glass. The only item that marks it as religious is the gargantuan cross over the door that glows crimson, day and night.

Natasha closes the door on her temporary room. It could be worse, she thinks. In Gina's room everything's painted pink: walls, headboard, the dresser. Gina's stuck pink bathtub decals onto her ceiling, and a pink housecoat trails off the corner of her pink closet door. "God, it's like being held hostage inside a vat of cotton candy," Natasha whispers to Holly when Gina's in the bathroom and they have a scarce moment alone. "Suddenly, I feel sticky."

"I hear you," Holly says. She's folded a red handkerchief – like the ones cowboys wear – around her neck but it's not enough; the purplish hickey pokes out.

Natasha crooks a finger in the handkerchief and pulls. "Oh, *that's* attractive."

Holly slaps her hand and readjusts the disguise. From the dresser she selects one of Gina's Avon testers, a miniature lipstick called "Shame," and rolls it across her bottom lip. She rubs her lips together, then presses them on a folded tissue.

"How can Rosco stand kissing you with all that gunk on your lips? You look like a tramp."

"Don't you say that! Don't you *ever* say that!" Holly attacks. She's not much bigger than Natasha, who only meant to tease, but she manages to pin her struggling sister on the pink bed. She grabs Natasha's neck and squeezes. "I'll kill you if you ever say that again!"

Mrs. Gillespie calls "Supper!" and Holly rolls off Natasha before she gallops down the stairs.

Natasha checks her throat in the mirror and wipes her eyes. It hurts to swallow. She blinks new tears back and leaves the awful room.

The sun and clouds take turns ruling the sky and soon it's sprinkling. Mr. Gillespie, a soft-looking man with a skiff of blowsy white hair, has come in from the field to eat. "Hello, girls. Getting along all right?" He heads the long, maple table, shirt sleeves scrunched over wrinkly elbows.

"Just fine," Holly says brightly. She assumes the prayer position, at the ready. "I'd love to live in the country. Gina's so lucky. You're *all* so lucky."

"And what about this little miss?" he says to Natasha. She's noticed that he often talks to her in the third person, and she's tempted to answer in the same way. Holly kicks her ankle beneath the table, as if she knows what her sister's thinking.

"Great," she says, *if my sister doesn't kill me, boredom surely will.* The older girls have been prompted to drag her onto a horse – to no avail – and she's already snooped through the house and found nothing of interest except ten-year-old encyclopedias with missing pages. "Couldn't be better."

The back door swings open and David is there, all breath and energy, stamping toward the table. "Sorry I'm late. We had a seized engine come in at 4:30, and I – oh, I forgot –" He pulls out a chair and flips his long, auburn bangs out of his eyes, where Natasha liked them. "Company."

After "For this food we are about to receive..." the male Gillespies bow deeply toward their plates and dig into their food as if in competition. *On your marks, get set, binge!* Natasha isn't aware that she's staring at the new arrival until he looks up at her and doesn't let go. "Do you like to swim?" David asks.

He's grown into his Roman nose – even transformed it into one of his finest features – put on weight, and – she notices in his rippling forearms – developed muscle. Not bad, for an older guy. His hair, too, has lost its static quality. It gleams. "Sure," she says, and turns back to her cream corn as though it's the most fascinating vegetable she's ever encountered.

"Are we filling the pool?" Gina asks. "Can we?"

Mr. Gillespie adds more salt to his fried potatoes. "It's too early yet."

"Pretty please, Daddy," Gina pleads. "With sugar on top?"

Natasha winces at hearing someone Gina's age call her father "Daddy," even if it is said tongue-in-cheek. Who does she think she is, Veronica Lodge?

"Cece," Mrs. Gillespie starts, resting one freckled hand on her husband's forearm, "it *is* warming up."

"Well. I don't know."

"Daddy!"

"Well...only if you promise to keep it clean."

Gina and Holly hoot, and Mrs. Gillespie, startled by the outburst, upsets her glass. She jumps up and quickly whisks off her apron to dab up the damage.

"David and me'll get her pumped out after supper and if all goes okay we can start filling," Mr. Gillespie says. "Mom's right. Radio says it's supposed to be heating up pretty good this week."

"Sure thing," David says. Natasha risks another look. His teeth are white as Chiclets, and very straight.

Order restored again, Mrs. Gillespie pours half glasses of water all around, though Natasha doesn't drink it. "You girls okay in deep water?"

"We were born for it," Holly says, and Natasha can only nod.

The pool would have been enough, but school also brings a surprise. A new girl. "Beth's father is the new Faith Alive minister," their teacher and vice-principal, Mr. O'Brien, tells Natasha before the morning bell rings. She's uncomfortable walking down the hall beside him. If anyone sees she might be labelled a pet. "She's good in English, just like you."

Natasha smells a set-up. The teachers were always doing this to her, trying to make her fit into some role she didn't belong in, typecasting her with the students who got good marks, though that was all Natasha had in common with those others.

A backlit figure approaches from the opposite end of the hall. "Here she comes now."

"I'm Beth," the new girl says, leeching herself to Natasha from moment one. "But I also go by Elizabeth or Liz. I'm not wild about Lizzie, though I don't correct anyone who calls me that. I think it's impolite. What do people call you?"

Save me, Natasha thinks. Everything about Beth spells prude: the plastic, butterfly barrettes holding shoulder-length hair off a face that could never keep a secret, the powder-blue pants and frilly white blouse buttoned to her throat. Why are these people drawn to her? Natasha wonders.

At recess she sits on a swing, feet idly scuffing the dirt. Beth, beside her, begins to pump. They're being watched. Jackie and Illa, by the chain-link fence, have earned a reputation among the teachers and the greater community for being troublemakers. Jackie'd been suspended for stealing the grade eight raffle ticket money, a crime she vehemently denied although there were witnesses. Illa lives with her grandparents because her mother – who'd been fourteen when she was born – ran off with the first man who'd have her: a carny who collected roller-coaster tickets at the summer fair. Town gossips agree it was the best thing that could have happened to the one-year-old, but she's turned into her mother's daughter, sure as sin.

The notorious pair wield their power in their tight eyes, the harsh lines of their mouths, the way they bite back when a teacher reprimands them for dreaming or skipping class. They've always been indifferent to Natasha. What saves her? she wonders. Perhaps it's her own shrugging off of everything. The apathetic look she's manufactured in her bedroom mirror. The mirror sees a girl who favours hiding behind straight, sandy bangs and hair that never stays combed. Her eyebrows edge toward the heavy side, she has a strong, full mouth with a coffee table scar on the inside lower lip, and a nose sprinkled with small freckles which will multiply over the summer. Her only concession to femininity: the small gold studs in her ears. An everyday girl. She blends. Like Illa and Jackie, she's landed on the wrong side of some invisible line. They respect that, she thinks. But what now, with this new girl clinging like they could possibly be friends?

"Have you ever wondered," Beth asks, dreamily, "why the winter sky looks as clear and blue as the summer sky?" She has round, trusting eyes, like Bambi.

Natasha pretends not to hear.

At lunch, when she heads toward the trees with her salmon sandwiches and apple, Illa and Jackie are footsteps behind her. "Hey, Stensrud. Where's your little friend?"

Natasha snorts. "She's not my friend." Without turning she knows they're close enough to slam her to the ground. In the dream she'd have taken flight by now.

"So prove it." Illa grabs her arm. "We're gonna follow her home. You coming?"

Natasha shrugs. "What for?"

"Something to do," Jackie says. She's smaller, a pixie of a girl who could even be pretty with the right haircut and some new expressions, but she's generally acknowledged as the instigator. "No reason."

Natasha finds herself leaving the schoolyard with the tough girls; she's only following her feet. Before escaping completely, she spies Holly and Rosco on the ball field. Holly has one hand hooked in the mesh of the backstop. They're not all over each other, so she expects they're scrapping. When Rosco rests a hand on Holly's shoulder and she jerks away, Natasha knows there's trouble.

"There she is," Jackie says, spying Beth at the end of the block. The infamous friends break into a trot; Natasha lags behind. "Come on, Stensrud."

It's a hot day, and yesterday's rain has dried in the gutters along Main. They pass the bakery, which smells deliciously of cream puffs. Last summer Natasha stole a silver dollar off her grandfather's dresser, bought four cream puffs and ate them on the steps behind the library without a crumb of guilt. "Oh shit," she murmurs. Mrs. Sperling, Camille's guardian, is crossing the street with a baby stroller. She sees Natasha and gives a little wave but doesn't smile. Natasha says, "Hello, Mrs. Sperling," in what's meant to be her regular voice, but, perhaps because of her present company, comes out sounding snarky. Jackie smirks at Illa. They approve.

The girls gain on Beth when she swings onto Fourth Street, still unaware that she's being followed. Jackie steps on her heel, scrunching the back of her running shoe.

"Hey," Beth says, turning and hopping, trying to slip the shoe back on, "what'd you do that for?"

Illa laughs. "God you're a priss," she says, pushing Beth, who is only three-quarters of her size.

Natasha has a bad taste in her mouth. She bites her apple and finds she can't swallow.

"Did your mommy pick out your clothes?" Jackie

pulls the blue bow on Beth's collar. Natasha's afraid she might rip the bow off, or worse, tear off the entire blouse.

"I didn't do anything to you. I don't even know you. Why are you so...angry?"

Beth has started to cry. To mewl. The tears and the kitten sounds get mixed up with the bad taste in Natasha's mouth. Damn her! "What a baby," she says, jabbing Beth's shoulder.

Jackie and Illa join in, poking her in the forehead, the collarbone. "Baby, baby, baby."

Beth is three leaps into a run when Illa, who's taller than Mr. O'Brien and weighs ten pounds more, catches her and slams her to the sidewalk. Beth moans, her arms bent opposite like a chalk-outlined victim. She creeps up to a sitting position and examines her palms. Natasha sees the tiny rocks embedded in the skin, the blood oozing to the surface. The knee of Beth's pants is shredded, and there too: blood.

"Baby got a booboo," Jackie blubbers, then they back off, leaving Natasha there to stutter over her part in what they'd done.

"I'm – are you – ?"

Beth refuses her hand, wobbling to her feet on the strength of her own will. The girls stand a foot apart, contemplating each other like the strangers they are. Natasha becomes aware that she's still holding the apple. It feels out of place.

"You," Beth says.

It's the single word that gets Natasha, as if she's being marked for something like hell. The back of her hand flies to cover her mouth and the world spins in peacock colours around her.

Sleep will not come, not in any combination of bedding and limbs and not in the slow, shallow breaths Shirley's taught her daughters to take. The night's half devoured when she finally feels herself slipping toward the dark, and then it comes too soon.

He boosts her into the trailer with his sausage fingers. Did he squeeze, she wonders? Her legs radiate with heat where he touched them. The boys wrestle with the bikes and decide to lay them on their sides.

"Hope you're not afraid of the dark," the driver says a second time, closing the heavy doors. The blackness swallows them whole, like Jonah in the belly of that whale.

The pool is only three-quarters full, but it's enough. After the girls feed the horses they change into their Speedo swimsuits and race out the door. The oblong pool has a very short shallow end and is eight feet at its deepest. It's bordered by a shelterbelt on the north, and the unrolling leaves of poplar – south and east – emit a sweet, spring perfume, a fragrance so strong Natasha can almost hear it.

She sets her towel where the sun leaves slats of light on the cement deck. She tries to block the image of the bloated rat and dives in where it's deepest. The cold slams against her head and she comes up sputtering.

"F-freezing!"

Holly and Gina poke their toes in. Their skin, several degrees lighter than it will be by the end of their seventeenth summer, looks pasty against their black and red suits. Holly's outgrown the sunstrokes of her youth, though she remains wary of light. Goosebumps predominate on the cleanly shaven legs. Gina's thighs have thickened since she quit the cheerleading squad. Physically, the last year has not been kind to her. She's beginning to take the shape of a flask – her mother's design – and Natasha has no trouble adding up the years to imagine Gina dowdy at thirty, washed out at forty-five. Her moment, like the pompoms, has come and gone. Holly's two cups bigger on top and needs a bathing suit with more support than her old suit provides. She runs and yells: "Here goes nothing!" She dives with a satisfying splash that sprays the deck.

Natasha jumps back. "Holy Mary!"

Gina takes the plunge, then dolphins through the water to help her body adjust to the cold. Natasha swims from end to end under water. She challenges the older girls to try. Holly can make it almost as far, but Gina, who regularly smokes behind the barn, can only manage a length.

"So, how is it?" Mrs. Gillespie asks, balancing a tray with a pitcher of apple juice and glasses. "Cece?" she calls back toward the house. "Is this heater thing working?"

Mr. Gillespie appears through the trees in his work

boots and overalls. He doesn't look at the girls, and Natasha doesn't know if it's courtesy or embarrassment that keeps his chin near his chest. He kneels on the deck with difficulty, flitting his hand in the water. "It's starting to come," he says. "I'll have David look at it when he gets home."

An hour later, Natasha's a shark alone in the pool. She's a killer whale. A beluga spouting water toward the sky. Gina and Holly are having what appears to be a serious talk on the lawn chairs beside the pool. Natasha snatches words when she comes up for air. Holly and Rosco have split, she gleans, and this time, judging from the way her sister spits out his name, it may be for good.

"Find this," Gina says, throwing a penny into the water where the sun no longer reaches.

Natasha dives deeply, exploring the floor of the murky pool with her hands. The cement's rough, like it's been chewed, and she picks up three pebbles before she finds her treasure. She could skin her knees on the bottom. Her ears throb. She kicks to the surface, holding the penny between her fingers. "Here it is –"

David is there, in the chair beside Holly. When did he come?

"Aren't you cold?" he asks. He scoops her towel off the deck and holds it out for her. "Mom's got supper almost ready."

Natasha glances at Holly, whose eyes are locked on David. He's still in his greasy overalls from work, ball cap turned backwards, dark hair poked underneath. "Come on you little fish." He's smiling at Natasha with his perfect teeth, bending over the water. His hands are amazing. She grabs.

Friday, the girls are allowed to build a campfire and stay up late. "Not too late, though," Mrs. Gillespie advises at the supper barbecue. Natasha helps herself to a second hamburger and takes a corner of the picnic table.

"You took my place," David says, wedging in between her and his mother's fleshy hips. "I'm left handed...I need the end."

"I can move," Natasha says quickly, lifting her Melmac plate.

"That's okay." He forks beans onto his plate, exaggerating the elbow room he needs so he can poke Natasha in the ribs.

He's playing with me, she thinks, blushing. Four years older, a golden-boy jock, and he's flirting with me!

He jabs again and Natasha jerks sharply to the right. "Ow!"

"Don't be a bother, Natasha," Holly says. She picks up a potato chip and snaps it in two. "Act your age." She nibbles on the broken chip like a princess. Natasha lets it go. There's something about Holly tonight. She's not reading her clearly yet.

Natasha helps the elder Gillespies clear away the dishes and returns with vanilla ice cream and cones. "None for me, thanks," Holly chirps, and then Natasha knows. Of course she wants ice cream. She just doesn't want David to see her lick it. She'd be embarrassed to have him see her tongue. She's a funny girl, her sister. All extremes. Not long ago

Holly'd asked to sleep with Natasha. They mooned over movie star magazines and sung along to popular songs on the radio, competing to see who knew more lyrics. The next day Holly pretended not to know Natasha in the school halls. Some days Holly labours for hours over her hair and makeup, lining her eyes with a dark pencil, applying and reapplying her rouge; other times she'll regress into the porcelain paleness of the long winters. She'll forget to drag a comb through her hair at all. Natasha hasn't yet figured her out.

"Fine day," Mr. Gillespie says. Gina reaches over and wipes a goatee of ice cream off his chin. "Mom and I are going into town tonight. There's a speaker up from... where's that young guy from?"

"Assiniboia," Mrs. Gillespie says. "You kids should come along. He plays guitar and –"

Natasha glances at Holly, who's trying to bite off a smile.

Gina intervenes. "No thanks, Mom. We're just going to stay here and sit around the fire."

"I've got plans, too," David says. He dusts the hamburger bun crumbs over his plate, just missing Natasha with his right arm. "Thanks for supper, Mom. Gotta fly." Then he does something that Natasha will never forget. He kisses his mother on top of her flat, grey curls. Kisses her!

"That boy," Mrs. Gillespie says, but Natasha can see she's bursting.

The evening fizzles away. A fire's built in the traditional teepee style, with a ball of newspaper and a collection of branches snapped off by spring winds. The adults leave; David's truck rattles across the Texas gate and away. The older girls ignore Natasha. She hears a horse whinny and remembers what Holly said about the stallion and the mare. She kicks through the tall grass past outbuildings and odd pieces of lumber, abandoned tires and machine parts waiting for attention, to see what's happening in the pasture beneath the vast stars. "Hello," she says. The palomino slowly approaches the fence, hesitates, then pokes her head over. Natasha strokes the long tan nose, then smells her hand. "Are you hungry?" She curls a spray of quack grass around her hand, wrenches it from the ground and feeds it to the mare. "My, what lovely lips you have, what lovely long teeth."

It's a moon-bright night and her spirit's buoyed by the warm breeze on the open prairie, by frogs croaking their concerns in the slough. A loon calls across the sky. Behind her, a calligraphy of smoke rises above the trees. The mare lifts her nose to the wind. Natasha climbs onto the fence, throws her head back and counts the stars. A dog or coyote bays. If every night was like this, she thinks, the black sky illuminated with pinpoints of light, animal sounds. There's ample room for simple, uncluttered thought. Is she going to score well on her math test? Has Ginger had her puppies at the kennel? The questions are whole notes, forgotten after every fourth heartbeat. She's a long time, a last time, a girl on a fence in the night.

"*Yoo hoo!* Natasha! Come out, come out, wherever you are!"

Natasha turns and sees the shadowy shape of her sister long before the details fill in.

"There you are." Holly stops short with one hand stuffed in her front pocket, the opposite shoulder lifted. "Didn't you hear Gina's parents come back? We're going in. If you're not going to watch the fire, I'll put it out."

"That's okay," Natasha says, crawling off the fence, her hip suddenly sore. "I'll take care of it." She follows Holly along the footpath beside the outbuildings. She imagines mice and bats sharing the unkempt corners of these sheds, knows cranky swallows make their nests in the eaves. Her toe hits something hard and pain rockets up her foot. "Ow! Son of a –"

Holly looks back. "What's the matter?"

"I kicked something." Natasha bends to inspect her throbbing toe, bare in sandals, and sees that she's cracked her nail on an abandoned tailpipe. Damn it! She holds her foot and rocks.

"You okay?"

"Go ahead. I'll be right there." She sits on the dirt and digs the nails of her left hand into the ball of her foot. The pain's not diverted. She grabs the offending tailpipe and flings it like a discus. It clangs against a shed. She floats her soiled hand under her nose.

It smells like straw and oil.

They stumble into each other, grasping for arms and shuffling, blind, to one side, as the semi rumbles to life. "Thank God," Holly says, releasing a theatrical sigh. They sit in a circle on the bare floor, so close to each other that when anyone speaks Natasha feels their breath warm her face. Her sister's thin wet shirt sleeve brushes her own.

Kent is on her left, with Gina practically in his lap. Where Kent's knee grazes hers, Natasha's skin glows.

"We'll be back in a flash," Kent says, his tone too cheery for the darkness. The only light is thin as a wish along the top and bottom edges of the doors. "Let's relax."

They pass a comb around the circle, like it makes any difference when all they have of each other are outlines. The circle loosens slightly and they each claim their spot. Rosco is fidgety. "I'm starved."

"You can have the rest of my lemonade," Natasha offers. She wishes now that she hadn't deliberately splashed it on herself, but she'd needed it then, beneath the fireball sun. Her face feels tight and sore, as if the skin's being stretched.

Rosco reaches for her fingers and takes the bottle.

"I need food," he says, but like the poor, they have nothing to give.

Gina says, "Damn. I've got to pee."

Rosco makes a sound like a donkey.

"You'll have to hold it," Holly quips. "Like Kent said, we'll be back in town soon."

"I'll try." She sits very still and whistles a little.

The air is heavy with dust, and the mesmerizing hum of the wheels has a hypnotic effect on the passengers. They are silent for what feels like giant stretches of time, and Natasha is conscious of each move made. She has never felt so much a part of anything in her life. Then the hum deepens; gears chug.

"Is he slowing down?" Holly wonders. "We must be back. Sure hope so. I'm soaked."

The vibrations on their bottoms change tempo. Another gear shifts, their bodies veer to the right, then sharply to the left. The driver accelerates again.

"He's not stopping," Gina says. Her words hang in the air above them. Then, a few moments later: "Where's he taking us?"

"Maybe it's a shortcut," Rosco guesses.

They appear to be riding over a hill.

"To where? We should have been home by now." Holly is holding Natasha's hand; two clams, smacked together.

This is the closest I've been yet, Natasha thinks. The big bang. Her heart is insistent and she's sure everyone hears it above the din of eighteen wheels. "What if he's not taking us home?"

She hadn't meant to say it out loud.

"Natasha!"

Natasha hops toward her sister's voice, toward the thin dance of smoke and flames.

"Finally," Gina says, without inflection. She flicks the nub of her cigarette into the coals. "What were you doing?"

"Nothing. Just sitting."

Holly pulls Gina out of her lawn chair, as if she's old or pregnant. "Told 'ya. She's a strange puppy." It is not said unkindly.

Gina asks, "When you comin' in?"

Natasha eyes the dying fire. It could be revived with a little work, and she'll need it if she's to stay out much longer. The day was warm, but it's still only the tail end of May. "I don't know. In a while, soon, later." She hunches her shoulders, raises her palms. "Does it matter?"

"Not really. Come on, Holl," Gina says.

"See you, then," Holly says, staying a few moments longer, and for the first time since their parents' departure, Natasha hears the loon's claim of loneliness in her sister's voice.

The rhythm of vehicles on the highway is a distant music; familiar, like the passage of warm air through a register. Someone is slowing. Headlights sweep across the fields as a truck turns onto the long approach. There's a metallic rattling as it passes over the Texas gate, and Natasha knows David is home. She checks her watch. Two-thirty! If she acts quickly she can kill the fire and still make it to the house before he finds her out.

She doesn't move a bone. She can't see him, but she hears his truck door open and close, imagines his feet on the gravel. She waits for another door to open, holds her breath so even that won't mask the sound. Moments slip into footsteps behind her. "Little fish."

"Oh, hello."

"Kinda late isn't it?"

He sits where his sister sat, hours ago. Natasha can't focus on his face yet, but she admires the simple white T-shirt stretched across his chest. Don't be silly, she chides herself. You're a kid.

He throws a twig across the fire. It lands by her right foot. She no longer feels any pain.

"I thought everyone would be in bed."

"Surprise," she says, hoping she doesn't sound sarcastic, though she's spent so long learning to be it's hard to double back. One Mississippi, two Mississippi, three Mississippi. Who will say what next?

David scrapes his chair closer to the fire, leaving twin trails in the dirt. "Where's Gina and Holly?"

"Inside. Reading or something, I –" her voice drifts away like smoke off a match.

"It's getting cold out here. Do you want my jacket?"

Now she looks, and he's pulling an arm out of his jean jacket. "There," he says, wrapping the worn jacket around her shoulders. "Better?"

She pulls it closed. "Better." Her life has been episode after episode of fractured exchanges – between herself and adults, between herself and other kids – but now she wishes for anything intelligent to say. Even three words would do. "So."

He's smiling at her. "So, how old are you anyway? Sixteen?"

"Almost," she pauses, "almost fifteen. How old are you?"

"Eighteen. Me and Gina are only ten months apart. Guess Mom was on a roll and she decided to keep going."

Natasha laughs. "Your parents, they're really –"

"Old?"

She laughs again, and hates the way it sounds so girlie. "I was going to say *nice.*"

David adds the last log to the fire. "What about your parents. Do you like them?"

Like? She's never thought about like. Love is a given, but.... "They're okay. Dad's not around much, and Mom is around but she's not around." She fears she's lost him, but she checks and he's still there, giving her his undivided.

"You still cold?"

"Not really. Why?" Something cracks in the fire. Natasha jumps.

"I've got some tapes in my truck. We could sit in there and talk...only if you want."

Suddenly she's outside herself, watching this. She's both the girl who follows David to his truck, holding the jacket closed at her chest, and the one above, who disbelieves. His truck's parked on the far side of the garage. "Had to park out here. Dad didn't leave me enough room in the garage." Whatever becomes of this, the hovering Natasha says, there'll be no witnesses.

He opens the door for her. She crawls into the dark cave of the cab; the light from the house doesn't bend around this corner. It smells a little like beer and a lot like the unknown. Beneath her, a grey, wool blanket slips toward the floor.

"How 'bout the Eagles?" he asks, turning the key but letting the engine sleep.

"Sure."

The box of tapes is on her side, on the floor. She feels for them, finds them beneath a ball glove. He turns on the interior light and the magic dissipates. There's only one Natasha now, shivering, reckless and alone with a boy — no, she corrects, a *man* — years too old for her. David slides the tape in but keeps the volume low.

He unrolls his window, sticks his head out and whistles.

"What?"

"The stars. If I could do anything with my life, I'd study the stars. See that one over there?"

His arm's out the window. She can't see where he's pointing, much less see the star. She crouches to peer through the windshield. "Which one?"

"That bright one by the moon. On the bottom. Do you see it?"

"Yeah."

"That's Venus," he says, pulling back inside. "And what about that up there," he says, leaning so he can also see through the glass. "Do you know what constellation that is?"

"Nope." She's aware of the closeness between them, that the tape has come to an unexpected end and even the night sounds have stopped.

"Cygnus. The swan. Isn't he beautiful? And inside it, the bright stars of the Northern Cross."

"Yeah." Natasha says, though she's not sure she can make it out. She only knows Orion and the Dippers, and even they can elude her.

There isn't a whisper or a rustle. David's staring at her. It's much too quiet for comfort. Every time she has to swallow she shifts in her seat or rustles the blanket so he won't hear the real sound of her.

"Hey, know what I know?"

How long can she avoid his eyes without appearing rude? "What do you know?"

"You're going to be beautiful, Natasha, like the swan."

"Oh, please," she says, turning to the window. She forces a little laugh, touches her cheek.

He pulls her arm away. "No, I mean you are, already, but –"

She has one hand, the hand he can't see, on the door handle. The cold metal is the only thing that she knows is for real. "I should go in."

His hand is still there, on her arm, the sleeve of his jacket. It slides – slowly, painfully, inevitably – down to her hand, covering it. It's impossible to look at him. It's the longest moment, the deepest silence she can remember. "Natasha." He touches her chin. "Look at me."

She cautiously turns.

Oh, God. Their limbs conspire and she finds herself under his arm, his face near hers. He's everywhere there's space. "This is nice," he says, softly. He rolls his window up, leaving two inches for air.

Nice? It's perfect. Quite possibly the high point of my life, she thinks. Their knees touch, touch again. The body heat is palpable, yet she shivers.

"Still cold?" Now both arms close around her. His hands, somewhere at the end of them. Hands that work on cars and pitch fastballs and, Lord, she doesn't want to think what they've touched. She's caged, but it's good. She's sure he can hear her heart working like crazy to zip blood up to the tips of her ears and down to the ends of her toes. He presses his fingers to her lips and traces them as a blind man would read them, then lifts her fingers to his mouth. He kisses three fingertips. "Can I kiss you?"

She makes a sound. He takes her face in both hands and kisses her, gently, on the mouth. He pulls back slowly, waiting. "Natasha," he says again, as if tasting her name. She moves toward the warm sound. They create a kind of electricity, kissing back and forth like sparks. He twists so he's facing her, his big hand on the back of her head. "Open your mouth." He rolls his tongue around hers for a lifetime, his hands on her eyelids, her nose, her ears. She has to pull back, to breathe, to swallow saliva. He pulls her so she slides down onto the seat, one leg on the floor, the other pressed beneath him. The weight of him. He licks her neck, nicks her ear with his perfect teeth. He's breathing – just *breathing* – in her ear. She moans, which leads to more deep kisses. Heat. "Are you comfortable?" he murmurs.

"Yeah." She tastes his neck.

It changes. He slides her left knee up, her right knee toward the dash, opening her legs so he can squirm between them. "Mmmm," he hums into her collarbone.

She has to pee, but it doesn't matter. There's a rhythm to his movements on top of her. A rocking. Her head's pressed into the door. This is me, she says to herself, I am here. I am wanted here. She closes her eyes and sees the stallion and mare. She moans again, louder this time. His hands feel all over her face, tangle in her damp hair. "I wish we could stay here forever."

"Hmmm?" He sucks her bottom lip, then slides his tongue along her teeth.

Oh, God. She's going to say it again! "I wish we –"

Suddenly he's pulling away, scrambling toward the

driver's side, combing a hand through his hair. Natasha slides up. "Oh, Jesus."

Her sister stumbles away from the window.

They don't discuss it, which is the worst. Natasha fears it will be released one day like a flood, a tidal wave of threats and accusations, and she'll die drowning. Holly spends half of Saturday and much of Sunday in bed, her eyes hidden behind the cold, wet, ineffective washcloth Mrs. Gillespie offers against the pain. David's been at work or just away, so Natasha's spared the unimaginable ordeal of sitting across the table from him. She catches the back of his plaid shirt as he leaves in the morning. The sound of him in the kitchen late at night.

She consults the John Deere calendar and measures the desperate hours before her parents' return. Way too many Mississippis to count. Saturday worked itself into a spectacular thunderstorm, with lightning pulsing across the sky. Now, two days before their parents return, heat's rising again.

Natasha startles into the shocking pinkness of Gina's room. Holly's still a shape beneath the covers in bed. "Do you have anything I can wear? My tops are all dirty, and God forbid I ask Mrs. Gillespie to wash them."

Holly rolls. "Check my suitcase. There's a tank top or something. Tell Mrs. G I'm not feeling well."

Natasha looks. "It's a halter. Don't you have anything else?"

Holly slowly rises on her elbows, hair partly hiding

her eyes. "Beggars can't be choosers."

Natasha twists the halter around her hand. "Are you going to school?"

"Don't know. Think I'm headed for a doozy today." Holly takes her own temperature with the back of her hand. "Guess I'll go. I can't stand the thought of getting sick in this room. I'm afraid my barf might even come out pink."

"Well," Natasha says, "thanks for the top." The last thing she does before running for the bus is pocket one of Gina's tiny lipsticks. A shade of pink, of course.

It's stifling in the classroom, with the chickadees free and singing in the lilac outside the window. Natasha is practising her signature, thinking about how he said her name. The morning bell hasn't rung yet; there's noise and commotion. There are kids.

"What in the world do you have on your lips?" Mr. O'Brien's standing beside her. He has hips like a woman, Natasha thinks, and the beginnings of boobs, too. She pulls a tissue out of her desk and rubs the colour off her mouth. Her teacher leans toward her ear, his sour breath grazing her cheek. "I want you in my office after school, young lady. You know why."

Things change. People, too. When she was a child, Mr. O'Brien was a willow weeping in the wind. When he made the children say morning prayers on their knees he was a scarecrow. When he stalks the halls during supervision and his black shoes squeak out his presence, he's something different again.

Lunch comes too soon, then home time. The halls empty of life and sound. Natasha stands outside the office and looks through the glazed window. She can see the shape of Mr. O'Brien and wishes she could bolt to the bathroom: her guts feel like they're being stirred. She knocks.

"In here," he says. "Close the door behind you."

She stands before his desk. There is no chair. There's a fan, and now she wishes she wasn't wearing Holly's halter.

"I had a call last night from Reverend Walker," Mr. O'Brien begins, leaning back for a better perspective. He's clicks a pen. Slowly. The sound drives her. "It seems three girls followed his daughter home on Friday and gave her a very hard time."

Natasha studies her running shoes. On the bottom, in the blue rubber where no one will ever see, she's written LOVE.

"I'll be talking to Jackie and Illa later. I'd expect something like this from them, but you? What's gotten into you?"

What's there to say? The episode with Beth has paled, almost disappeared completely from her memory, *that* past a door she's not walked through. The new girl wasn't even in class today. Natasha studies the filing cabinet.

"What do you have to say for yourself?" Click. Click.

"Sorry."

"What's that? I didn't hear you."

"Sorry." There's a plant with barbed leaves on the filing cabinet. She watches it closely. When she's through here, she'll check the Gillespie's encyclopedias. She wants to know the name for this leaf shape, this very necessary plant.

Mr. O'Brien steps out from behind his desk, toward her. "You should be ashamed of yourself young lady." He's changing again, or maybe this time it's her. She feels herself shrinking before the bullets of his eyes. He points at her halter, the tip of his finger touching the strap at her throat. "Coming to school dressed like that."

She must find something else. The framed photograph on his desk. His pristine daughters, Cindy and Laurie, smile up at her. It's an outdoor photo, a large building in the background. Behind the girls, a crimson glow. Now she understands.

"You think you're pretty smart, don't you?" The loose skin under his chin quivers. He turns to his window, looks out at the trees, as if they have the answer. "You think I don't know what goes on out there? You prancing around in those skimpy clothes, teasing the boys –"

"What?" She's genuinely, knock-me-over stunned. The boys? They don't even know she exists.

He spins. She takes a step back.

"The Bible says, 'Sin began with a woman, and thanks to her we all must die –'"

His voice bounces off the office walls. She feels it, a tremor beneath her feet.

"'Keep a headstrong daughter under firm control, or she will abuse any indulgence she receives –'"

"I'm not your daughter," she whispers.

His silver glasses. Those pellets beneath. She hates him more than she's ever hated anyone. "What did you say?"

"I'm...not...your...daughter. Clear enough?"

He slaps her hard across the face. Her head flies back and she bites her tongue but doesn't cry. "Only Jesus can forgive your sins, Natasha. We're all sinners, but if we accept the Lord into our hearts, He'll take away our evil —"

Don't cry. Don't you *dare* cry. She wills her eyes to obey. It was just kissing! She didn't do anything wrong. None of this would have happened if her parents hadn't gone away. It's their fault. She'd warned her mother, hadn't she? Why's he keeping her such a long time? Yacking and yacking. His voice fading in and out. She is so tired. She could fall asleep right here, right on the floor at his feet. But no, that would be dangerous. She mustn't close her eyes, mustn't cry, mustn't look at him or look away. Where can she look? The breath of space below the closed door, and freedom, just beyond it. Hold steady, hang on to it. Words and words, that finger held high. One Mississippi. Two Mississippi. Surely she's missed the Clover Bar bus now, and her face, her face stings.

"Tonight I want you to go home and confess your wrongdoing...and when you wash for supper, take the soap in your hands and think of how Jesus can wash away your sins."

Damn the bastard to hell! Damn them all!

"Get rid of the filth, Natasha. Jesus will forgive you if you ask. Now go. I don't ever want to see you in here again."

Natasha returns, solid for a moment, and nails him with her eyes. This is her last word. Then she opens the door, clicks it firmly behind her, and crumples.

The bus awaits. Holly – her migraine averted – and

Gina are off with Kent and other friends, so it's Natasha alone on Clover Bar after the other students are dropped off. The bus driver's squeezing his eyes at her through his mirror. She knows he knows; another slap. "Rough day?"

She touches her cheek. Where David touched. What Mr. O'Brien fouled. "You could say that."

At the Gillespies' she tiptoes past the kitchen and down the hall. The bathroom is free.

"Natasha? Is that you?" Mrs. Gillespie. What if Mr. O'Brien's phoned her? They'd all know. David. "Your mother called. They've been having a wonderful time and will be flying in to Saskatoon tomorrow. They should be back around two, two-thirty."

"Oh. Thanks." Natasha closes the bathroom door. Her eyes are rimmed with everything she's held in. She runs the cold water and lets it all go. When the sink's full she drops her face into it, holds her breath until her skull aches. Finally she pulls out, gasping. She picks up the soap. She begins.

Grief

It comes to Natasha in the back seat of her parents' car while they holiday down the highway and the sun hides beneath the horizon. Grief comes and steals the candy colours of the sunset. It comes on autumn days as she lumbers home from school, alone, leaves crunching to amber bits beneath her feet, the sun still hard and bright as a fine idea, but not strong enough to ward off winter. Grief wraps its muscled arms around her on the first day of snow, and on Boxing Day, no one knowing what to do with those dead hours after Christmas.

Three sparrows fly off a line and three seasons are as quickly swallowed. What's happening? One moment she feels she could swan dive off the end of the world and never miss any of it. She could curl into a hollow, let weeds and lichen shroud her in their soft green embrace and no one would notice her missing. Other times a radio song, a poem she's made to read in school, or a child's peppermint kiss snatch her breath away, lightening her until she feels that if she doesn't reach for something solid – the piano's heavy legs, the American elm that shades the front yard – she'll pass right through the clouds. The two poles of her being are north and south: barren, uninhabited landscapes with no country in between.

She presses her fingertips to the cold window, counts ten Mississippis, then pulls away, leaving five perfect halos of condensation.

It's January. Night. And grief's snuck up again.

There's a flurry of activity in the white yard. Holly's teasing the neighbour's German shepherd with the slapping end of a hockey stick. The idiot dog lunges, then retreats, its rear raised, incisors bared, front legs flush with the ground. Beyond them, on the icy street, Camille and a team of wool-wrapped neighbourhood children chase a puck back and forth between clumps of snow.

"You should be out there," Shirley is saying, her voice breaking Natasha's concentration on the uncertain pattern her breath has made on the window. She turns away from her window art. Her mother slides out of her pale blue slippers, tucks her long legs beneath her on the couch. She touches a mug of steaming tea to her lips, as if she desires only to warm them. The woman she was, returned, Natasha thinks. The Maritimes had been good for her. Natasha witnessed the upward progression through airport to airport snapshots – brighter eyes, a hand on Peter's elbow, the light restored – but she's *sensed* it even more. The devils on her mother's back – if indeed, that's what they were – have abated. They have Natasha now.

"But I'm not like them."

"Of course you're not. No two people are alike. Cripes, look at your dad and me. But you're still too young to waste away at a window. If I was fifteen I'd sure be out there. Even if you don't join the game. Take Ginger for a walk, go build an igloo. I worry about you, Tash, sitting in here every night, watching the world go by like a widow. It's not..." she searches for a word, "natural."

Natasha knows she means to comfort. Shirley makes efforts. She's proposed a girls' school, in faraway Ontario, which she's read about in *The United Church Observer.* "Fresh faces and a brand new start," she'd said, paraphrasing the text. Natasha imagines herself in a pleated navy skirt and blue knee-highs, stiff black shoes and her hair brushed back into a neat ponytail; a carbon copy of desperation.

"I'm beat. I think I'm going to turn in early, maybe read in bed. Thanks, though...for the pep talk."

"You're sure? We could bake cookies or something. Those brownies that you like –" Shirley watches her cross the room as though she's in pain, a survivor of recent surgery. "I'll let you beat me in *Scrabble.*"

"Rain check, okay?" She's aware that her parents don't know how to take her, their sulking middle daughter. Their surprise. During pregnancy her mother'd dangled a string over tea leaves to see which way they'd spin, but the signals must have got mixed. "We expected a boy," she'd overheard Shirley telling coffee friends. The mothers were cutting fabric for a Halloween-themed school play featuring 100 percent cotton ghosts with holes snipped out for eyes. Natasha'd perched on a chair in the kitchen, talking to a spirit, the accomplice telephone pressed to her eaves-dropping ear. She envisioned her father standing outside the hospital, dark shades clipped over his glasses and disappointment, lifting Holly to peer through the window at the surprising black hair – which quickly lightened – and skinny arms. A negligent nurse left a diaper too long. A rash developed; Natasha's homecoming was delayed. "She was different," Shirley whispered, "even then."

She leaves her mother with the jangle of the television news and retreats upstairs to her bedroom. She runs her fingers over the floral wallpaper where Camille, years earlier, scribbled secrets between the roses. Her little sister, mercifully, seems to love the cold and snow; she'll remain outside until Shirley calls her in. On her bed, Natasha turns philosophical. She imagines she's the only girl this side of the moon feeling as bland as porridge without brown sugar at this precise moment in time, then thinks she's the only person *thinking* that she's the only person having this thought. A painting inside a painting inside a painting. Where will it end?

Across the room, Camille's Dolls-of-the-World look lonely, waiting for her return. Especially Miss Argentina, Natasha notes, with her purple satin dress, naughty black lace and cleavage.

As a child Natasha gathered her own dolls and burrowed into the closet or into what her parents called the pantry, a cupboard high above the deep-freeze in the back porch. It took some effort getting in. Now it's too late for the solace of dolls. Her adolescent escapes are internal journeys, departures made sitting motionless beside windows, crouched over the hot air register, or cocooned in her bed beneath layers of blankets. She gets dizzy from looking in.

If only there was someone else, she thinks. The universe is immense, there must be someone out there for her. Other girls have found their matches. Holly has Gina, and Camille has her pick of a trio of girls who rotate sleepovers on weekends. At school, Debbie has Rosalee, Illa has Jackie, Madge has Darlene. These duos seem to share a certain walk or a way of talking that rules out any hope of Natasha crashing in. And David. Had that even happened? She has no tangible mementos from the night, not a thread or a matchbook to prove it. Only Holly's face, that collision of shock and what – outrage? fear? – in the window, confirms the kisses were true.

She likes to be in the basement, in the storage room, just breathing and away from Holly's perpetual headaches and Camille's pestering; the parade of piano students who prance through her house with their shiny-covered books and their talent and their bright, promising faces that refuse even an acknowledging glance her way; and, in the long evenings, away from the monotony of television; the dizzying brown swirls in the wall-to-wall carpet; the clock that dings out each dreadful hour; the tumult of wet towels and toiletries in the bathroom; the fat, matted dog; her father's back going out the door to meet with people infinitely more important and deserving. She likes to fill her nose with the musty smell and hold it, until it becomes a taste, a meal all its own.

Her parents prefer to think it's about death. Natasha resents not being able to attend her grandfather's funeral. His heart has taken him home. Two nights in the hospital and he was away. Now Peter's father is stuffed into a new suit and waiting with his hands crossed over his chest in the United Church. It comes as no surprise – the old man had been dying for years – but now that he's officially gone Natasha feels a kinship that never existed when he was alive and living just ten blocks away. "But he was our grandpa!" she argues, clutching the newspaper that announces his death. Eighty years stubbed out in two column inches, unimpressive beside the much longer write-ups, some with unflattering photos of seniors, or, alternately, photos of faces too good to be true because the pictures were taken decades before health and youth moved on. "Left to mourn...so and so and *thirty-four grandchildren,*" she reads, about Mrs. Harold Weibe in a neighbouring column. "I bet *they* get to attend the funeral."

While her parents dress for the occasion, Natasha contemplates the imagined grey pallor of the dead, the release of energy as the soul leaves its earthly form. Would there be a popping sound, like a cork exploding off a bottle of champagne? "It's not fair! I'm fifteen. That's old enough."

Her father turns away, unties his bathrobe, and pulls freshly-pressed suit pants over his white boxer shorts. "It's not open for discussion." He fans through his closet for an appropriate shirt. He is, like Shirley, taller than average, though unlike her he's never felt comfortable with his own arms and legs. His long feet – routinely packaged in grey, brown or black Oxfords, or the hideous white on Elks nights – shoot out from beneath his pant legs as if attempting an escape. A new set of dentures don't sit right inside his square jaw and they've caused an angry canker on his gums. He frequently pops his lower plate to probe the problem with his tongue.

"Give me that," Peter says, snatching the paper from Natasha.

Shirley, black dress gaping where it has yet to be zipped, steers her daughter out of the bedroom. "Your father and I don't believe in exposing you girls to all that...unpleasantness. You'll have enough sorrow in your life." Peter shoots Shirley a look and something beyond Natasha's interpretation passes between them. Ten minutes later, within the kitchen's orange-and-pineapple-papered walls, Shirley slips in a final phrase: "Be thankful you can put it off for a few years."

But Natasha knows it will not be put off. It's not an animal that can be held at bay with a long stick; you can't sense grief coming. And they are wrong. It has little to do with death, except for the small ones she holds inside her, counting Mississippis until they pass.

She looks, and looks again. It takes her a Mississippi moment to realize she's not injured, that she's not even in pain.

"You're a woman now," Shirley says, showing her the twisty belt and the long pad that she's to fasten like a sling between her thighs, a hanging bridge. She'd been expecting a stream, not the rusty smears she's found in her panties. "You know what this means, right?"

"Yes, Mom. God! I read the booklet you strategically left on my pillow."

"Oh. Good." Shirley takes a step back and knocks into the bathroom door. "I'll go then."

Natasha checks in the full-length mirror for bulk, for any trace that these new circumstances might further ostracize her. Her blood has come on the coldest day in January, a day when the snow is banked four feet high against the house and her father has to throw all his weight at the door to open it, charging like a football player, or a bull.

She runs her hand over her slightly bloated abdomen, thankful that cramps have not gripped her as they did Holly, who, just two weeks earlier, took to her bed and moaned as if terminal. Holly's late menstruation had been a source of embarrassment; Gina and all her other classmates had been hiding pads and tampons in their school lockers for three or four years already. Shirley'd even had her eldest daughter examined, though getting her to the doctor had been light-years from easy. "I don't want some man looking at me!" Holly'd cried in the kitchen, a candle of snot hanging to her top lip. Natasha thought this absurd, as Rosco had surely been enjoying the view for well over a year, but he was only a boy.

"He's not a man, he's our family doctor," Shirley'd countered. "Ohhh...quick, throw me a towel!" She'd been giving the fridge a furious scrubbing and had upset a carton of milk in her haste. "For goodness sake, Holly, he's seventy-five if he's a day, and a vaginal exam is no big deal for him...he sees them every day. For him, it's like looking into a mouth."

Nothing was medically amiss, Natasha learned. Nature just took her own sweet course and, in her sister's case, it was the long and winding road. Even then, Holly's first time caught them all by surprise, her soprano shrieks overcoming a student's major scales on an otherwise mild and middle-class afternoon. Shirley used a three-inch common nail to open the locked bathroom door. Natasha glimpsed them crouching on the floor beside the bathtub, Shirley's arms ringed around Holly, rocking her, and both of them trying to comprehend the watery-red tips of Holly's fingers. She recalls that and the seven-year-old boy, the student, watching Natasha watching them, asking, meekly: "Should I go home now?"

She turns left and right, quite pleased with her mirrored proportions. Her sweaters address the obvious and her waist curves beneath her belted jeans. Her hair tends to limpness but responds well to the torture of Shirley's prickly curlers. She certain she's not on the verge of beautiful, as David suggested, but she has perhaps reached the point where her looks might prove useful.

Certainly, she has two facts to be thankful for: Mr. O'Brien has moved to Ontario to terrorize other innocent girls with his proselytizing, and her remaining teachers find her a quiet, diligent student – the first-called babysitter on the lists near their phones. But her luck runs out there. The invisible wall that secludes her from those her own age remains standing. It's what leaves the desk beside her empty, the invitation, always, for another.

She has long conversations with herself, her own voice assuring that she'll outgrow her alienation like she has the red velvet coat with white fur cuffs and her knee-high boots with the zipper that runs up the insides of her calves. In the way of the lonely and alone, she comforts herself before sleep, hugging warmth into her body with her own arms. Finally she clenches her eyes and prays that someone will enter her life and change all the colours of it soon. "Father unto thee I pray..." she begins, formally, then digresses into her colloquial litany of desires which always, lastly, includes the finger-crossed wish for safe sailing through the night.

Because there are no more free weeks. Because hands scrabble like crabs inside the walls of her dreams and face-less mouths suck her from sleep. Because she has no place to go with her terror. She'd feel silly crawling into bed between Shirley and Peter's long bodies, and if she turns on the light she'll wake Camille, so she lies in the darkness and concentrates on anything that will pull her back: French verb conjugations, the recipe for chocolate chip cookies. In the morning, while Camille flings herself out of bed to race to the toilet, Natasha moves with the weight of someone who's been too long in the water, too long in the cold. There are small graces; the bedwetting, at least, has stopped.

And then, as if her blood coming has opened another gate, it happens. Her life in full living colour.

"Class, this is Randy Keiler," Mrs. Philips announces in her queenly, English accent. She extends her eczema-scarred arm toward the open door, but no one walks through. Someone titters, and compassion drums in Natasha's throat. "Well, come in, then."

He enters slowly, uncertainly, and stands haloed by chalked notes on the blackboard. He looks over the tops of the students' heads at something they can't see and Natasha melts. The newcomer stuffs one hand in the back pocket of his jeans. He flips the dark layers of his collar-length hair into a centre part, like a book left open, though he's no easier to read. He has good bones, she notes, a straight nose, but a scar midway up his jaw saves him from being pretty. Someone fakes a coughing fit. He's holding his own, she thinks, a brave heart up there beneath jean jacket, T-shirt, and skin. Who is this stranger who's found their strange land? She thinks she senses his certainty of flight; he still hasn't met anyone's eyes. This is not a person her father would jump to hire in one of his stores, not a guy he'd call "the sharpest knife in the drawer."

"Let's welcome him," Mrs. Philips says.

There's a scattering of half-hearted "hellos".

"Please take a seat."

Randy scuffs down the aisle in his platform boots toward the only empty desk, a dozen steps from the door. Before he swings into it he turns to Natasha. She couldn't call it a smile, but that warm, three-beat moment of acknowledgment is there, and for the next fifty minutes she steals as many peripheral glances as would be considered legal. He's not much bigger than her, which will rule out the athletes claiming him, and a certain number of girls. His demeanour. Is it indifference or neglect? Neglect is a kite she can run with.

After class she dawdles as the other students clear out. "I'm Natasha," she blurts, extending her hand like a businessman, like her father, or at least like someone who knows what she's doing.

"Randy." His hand's a dry, comfortable shell that fits neatly around hers. "Nice to meet you."

"You, too." She's aware that the lilt in her voice might make her sound a bit too enthusiastic or put on, but the words bubble out on their own behalf.

They lurch awkwardly toward the door, both reaching for it at the same time. He holds it open and she ducks beneath his arm in a baroque dance movement. Then, as if he knows exactly what she needs to hear before they part in the cavernous hall: "Do you have time for a coffee later?"

Her heart flaps against her chest. "Yes." All the time in the world.

In a red-upholstered booth in the café at the King George Hotel, she learns. "How old are you?"

"Fifteen."

"What kind of music do you like?"

"Rock, mostly. You?"

"Same," she says, though this is stretching it. She also doesn't mind the country songs aired on the local radio station, or the classical records her mother plays at full volume when she thinks she's alone in the house.

Then it's his turn. "What kind of movies?"

"Horrors and war," she answers quickly, hopefully, trying to be honest and a mind reader, too. "Some comedies are okay."

"The old stuff is best," he says, pushing his package of cigarettes across the table toward her. "Abbott and Costello...Laurel and Hardy."

And on it goes. Connections are made all over the maps of their young lives, but Natasha believes it's more than their respect for the same movies that draws them together. She gleans that he shares her sense of being lost within some impossible maze. That hers is the greater, universal maze is a detail. For him, a new town, new school and the politics of where he will or will not fit in, but there's also the maze of family. Randy's the ghost in the middle of five siblings. Ultimately dispensable. Natasha grabs that ring.

They talk about religion. Unlike the Stensruds – or at least Peter, Shirley, and Camille, who usually make a Sunday morning showing at church – the Keilers don't seem to have any, and this intrigues her. "Swear to God?" and "Hate God if you lie?" – two standards in *her* household, the latter the only surefire route to the truth – would be lost on them.

When Randy trusts her enough to take her inside the foreign country of his home, Natasha's careful not to let her voice or expression betray her. There's a sour smell. Cats, or old food. It's hard to know.

"That's my mom," he says, by way of introduction. A drooping woman with hair the unnatural colour of

Natasha's first blood nods in her direction. No "Hello, I'm pleased to meet you." No hand stretched out in greeting. Natasha sees the kind of person who's dealt with a lifetime of not having enough: money, food, love – the whole deal. It's clear she's not wearing a bra, and the disaster of her hair implies an aversion to combs. She looks like she needs rest – a good month in a sanatorium might do it, Natasha muses. She is, Natasha learns on repeated visits, fond of a particular pair of brown polyester pants with cuffs that bell around her ankles, and a cardigan that may have once fit.

"Hello," Natasha says.

"Come on." Randy leads her into the narrow hall. A moment later they hear yelling from the kitchen: "You lazy fucker!"

Natasha spins. "Your *mother?*"

"Yeah. She and my brother, Will...they always go at it like that."

This is new to her. Open rage and foul language, parent to child. It opens strange doors. It shakes her up. Now they're inside a room with a bunk bed. There's also a tangle of blankets atop a pee-stained mattress on the floor. Randy closes the door and plunks down on the mattress. There's nowhere to look. They hear little feet outside the door. Giggling girls.

"My sisters," he says. "Don't worry, they'll go away."

Natasha finally sits on the bottom bunk, but it's low and she has to keep her neck bent.

"You wanted to see it."

She could crawl.

She learns that his father's a man of sparks and fire. His welding equipment sits boxy and heavy on the back of his truck, but he's only envisioned, not yet seen. She meets the sisters on a subsequent visit. The girls, in grades four and six, have long mops of hair – that *could* be brushed and swept back in perfect auburn ponytails – and matching, slightly pug noses. An older sister lives with an aunt in Lloydminster. The girls don't interest Natasha, who knows well the landscape of sisters, but Randy's older brothers wear intriguing faces and jean jackets left open to the wind.

Everything about Will and Gerry suggests reckless-ness: their green Charger with the pink garter stretched around the rearview mirror; their cursing mouths and the cigarettes that hang from their lips; even the way they sprawl on the couch to watch the black-and-white televi-sion, thighs bursting against the seams of their faded Levi jeans. Randy tells her they smoke marijuana, which – she remembers learning in grade eight Health class – can lead to more serious drugs like cocaine or heroin. Coke and Smack. Fun words.

The brothers are interesting, perhaps even dangerous, but they'll never take precedence over Randy, she decides. Inside of two weeks he's become the invisible hand that pulls her out of bed in the morning and puts the air in her step on the gravelled road to school.

Now she understands about fast friends.

In his apparent eagerness to be near her, to talk to her, to sit across from her in the King George – even though silences sometimes arise between them like a comfortable sigh – he seems to be signalling his need for their friend-ship, as if together they are water where before only desert had been.

In the blue dusk of after school they discover a shared respect for the roar and speed of machines. While the others gather for shinny or huddle in the rink's concession area to sip watered-down hot chocolate, Randy and Natasha charge through the season on their snowmobiles, his a beaten-up machine he's mainly pieced together him-self, hers a third-hand Polaris Peter'd bought the previous winter. They circle around the frozen pond on the out-skirts of town, leaning so their knees almost scrape the ice. They fly along the ditch beside the tourist booth or skim across the acres of hard-packed snow in the fields that could belong to anyone. They ride to the river where she learned to steer a canoe and under the wooden bridge where she's dangled a line for jackfish too sick and ugly to eat.

Natasha loves the gasoline smell, the rumble to life when she pulls the starter cord. They race down the frozen river just as day meets night, and when she knows she can't be heard, she yells at her trailing shadow and the night frighteners she seems to have outraced: "I'm free!"

It's a white world for the next several weeks. Often Natasha returns so cold she needs Camille to unzip her snowmobile suit and slide off her boots. She spends hours warming on the register, or eases into a hot bath and endures pins and needles, the painful price of quick relief. Submerged in water as hot as her skin can stand, she rests her head on an inflatable pillow and marvels at her luck.

All these weeks, right out in the open, zipping alongside the danger of the highway, and grief can't even find her.

They pass notes in English and seek each other out during class breaks. Like his brothers, Randy's a passionate smoker, and Natasha begins meeting him for quick drags at the butt-littered smoke stand. She learns to inhale on her third Export A. The claws of cold and nicotine at her throat seem a small fee for admission into this new country of renegades. Gina's usually there, throwing her hair around and swapping party tales with Randy's brothers – when they're not skipping school. Illa and Jackie, with their grudges against the world and matching leather jackets are also regulars. There are others whom Natasha's beginning to nod toward in the halls like they're members in a secret society.

On a day when the windchill factor makes it especially bitter at the smoke stand, Natasha turns from the weather to the school's brick wall. Her cigarette is finally lit.

"Boo!" Holly says, jabbing her in the spine. She grabs Natasha's cigarette and takes a turn with it, pouting at Rosco as she exhales, cigarette poised in the air near her ear. "Since when did you start smoking?" She slides a look at Randy, a small, shivering animal in his down-filled jacket against the girth of Rosco. "I'm telling Mom and Dad."

"*Quid pro quo,*" Natasha says. Although Holly's two grades ahead, Natasha has her hands down in wordplay, which gives her the edge in their scraps. She can undercut

Holly before her sister knows what's happened, or occasionally, without her knowing at all. She cups her hands and blows into the inadequate mittens – a pair of Camille's that make her hands look small – all she could find before running out the door.

"*Quid pro*...what the hell is that?" Holly elbows Rosco, and he laughs, too. "Has the weather affected your speech?"

"It means 'tit for tat,' bright one. You shouldn't be out here either."

Secrets pass between Randy and Natasha like the cigarettes and pots of dark coffee at the King George. She wants to tell him everything, to clear her head. "I've got a bombshell," she says, before they even have a table. She follows him to a table near the long, dirty window that looks out on long, dirty Main with its single stoplight. "I walked in on Holly and Rosco doing it in the rumpus room, right on the carpet! The gall. Mom was right upstairs, teaching!"

"Holy shit. What'd you do?" Randy flicks his lighter and touches a finger to the flame.

"Backed out, hoping they didn't notice me. I had to crouch beside the washing machine until they finished...I thought my knees were going to break. It was weird. Dad would totally kill her if he knew."

It's good, this telling, a release of sorts. A relief. She could never tell Randy about that other release, the way her own fingers worked inside her panties as she eavesdropped on Holly having sex, or how she felt their simultaneous passion from her shuddering shoulders to the electric soles of her feet. But that's not the story either. There's always more waiting, something that seems important and begs to be told but she doesn't know what it is.

Randy pulls a cigarette from their communal pack. He shakes the lighter and flicks it three times before striking a flame. "I want to tell you something, too, but you've got to promise not to say anything to anyone."

"Cross my heart." She almost said, "Swear to God." She leans on her elbows toward him and supports her chin with the heels of her hands. Her hair, grown well past her shoulders now, falls forward and she pins it behind her ears. Their waitress returns with a refill. Randy waits until she disappears behind the swinging tin doors to the kitchen before he continues.

"Joan didn't leave because she didn't want to move here," he confides, countering what he'd conveyed earlier about his absent older sister, "she left to get away from him."

"Who?"

"Dad. She was pregnant. When she told him he threw her down the stairs. He broke her arm."

There's a tumbling in Natasha's chest. A kind of death she can acknowledge or not, removed as she is from the victim. She's never met the sister. Never seen a picture or even imagined a face onto her. A younger version of Randy's mother? If so, *coarse* is the word that fits best. Still, it's unfathomable that a parent could do this. "And the baby?"

"Lost it."

"Oh." She swirls more sugar into her coffee. What are

the rules here? How close can she come to the edge? "Has he ever...?" She falters, wishes she hadn't begun.

"Hurt me?"

She can't look up, can't face those eyes that seem to mirror her own.

"No," he says, and that conversation is sealed. She wants more than anything to touch him, on his forearm below the bunched-up sleeves of his sweater, where the skin's smooth and darker than hers. She doesn't.

After a respectful silence she opts for the safety of school gossip. "Did you hear about Debbie Fowler's big freak-out in the lab? I guess she screwed up some experiment and trashed a microscope."

"No way."

"Probably won't even get in trouble over it 'cause her old man's on the school board. God, she thinks she's the cat's ass." *Old man?* Not a reference Natasha would have made before Randy, the smoke stand, these talks in the coffee shop haze.

"Debbie. Is that the chick with the locker across from yours? Wears jeans so tight you can hear her squeak?"

Natasha nods. His hair's fallen into his eyes – they're especially blue today, she notes – but he makes no effort to move it. He looks like a waif, she thinks. One of those poor, patched-together boys whose need makes them irresistible. You want to put them on your knee, to mother them. To love them hard.

"She's got a pretty face," Randy says through a veil of smoke, "but she's got no heart. *You* have heart."

Natasha smiles inside. She is filled up and couldn't

take more if it was offered. "Yeah? Thanks. I gotta get going. I'll see you tomorrow." She floats home, slowly releasing this joy, stretching it out with every stride until she reaches her bedroom, closes the door and rests her back against the solid frame. I have *heart*. Heart. Heart. Heart! She's never known how good a word can taste, and this one, just a sliver away from *hurt*.

They team up on an English assignment, but finding neutral ground for this is a challenge. They first try Natasha's, where Shirley watches them out of the corners of her eyes and Randy's reticence implies his discomfort with the embroidered doilies, the hulking, polished piano and the relatively uncluttered countertops. After an awkward hour at the kitchen table he remembers something he was supposed to pick up for his mom.

"Geez," Natasha says, culling their papers into one pile while Shirley sets the table around her. "I'm surprised you didn't frisk him for the family silver."

Shirley frowns. "That's uncalled for, Tash. It's just... you have other friends, don't you? It seems a bit strange, you and Randy always together. I'm not sure it's healthy."

Natasha feels wicked. "Don't worry, Mother." She pats Shirley's shoulder. "I've had my shots."

At Randy's place what Natasha notices most is that nothing matches. Not the chrome and wood kitchen chairs, the plates, not the worn plaid couch, the brown and green chairs in the living room, or even the hole-plagued socks on his little sisters' feet.

Everything is slightly short of normal, a feeling reminiscent of her years of walking with an upturned mirror in her hands, of walking on ceilings. Her head knew it was safe to step – she wasn't going to put her foot through the smoked glass of the globe lightshade, or fall through the passage to the attic, or stumble over the doorway to her room, or snap her legs falling down the sharp, surreal cliff of the stairwell – but her body distrusted. She walked slowly, lifting her knees high, placed each foot tentatively on the plaster and paint. Her world is now as it was then, as it has always been: not what it seems.

She imagines how different Christmas must have been in their two homes, with an obvious lack of the holiday season at the Keiler's. Shirley had strung garland across the fireplace mantel, anchored it with thick red candles at both ends. She'd adorned the front door with a giant holly wreath, dotted with tiny berries. Carol books were left open on the piano. They had a natural Christmas tree they'd chopped themselves – a family event with toboggans and hot chocolate – and no one swore at anyone else. Cards were strung in loops: angels, carollers, cathedrals, and reindeer danced across the walls.

Randy's mother had one tilting, half-spent candle surrounded in garish plastic ivy on the kitchen table. Natasha knows this because the pathetic display is still there, the wax crumbling. His mother wouldn't have asked, "Are you ready for Christmas?" and she wouldn't have baked gingerbread with her daughters. This woman has her own sounds and smells, the latter lingering from the home permanents she gives to women who can't afford salon prices. She has only one working lung, and she wheezes.

When Natasha finally meets Randy's father she knows her own father wouldn't approve of the man. Mr. Keiler does not consider shaving to be a moral responsibility. He drinks alone and doesn't concern himself with the snow that grows into humped white animals which creep toward the front door. He rolls his own cigarettes; a trail of tobacco shavings tell the tale of his passage from room to dreary room.

There's also the matter of the brothers. Randy tells her they've made a shrine to the gods of rock and roll in the basement, with posters and black lights.

"Is that where they hoot?" She's learning the lingo.

"Yep. They drop acid, too."

"Acid?"

"You know, LSD. Like in the 60s."

Subterranean music rocks the small house. Randy's mother grabs a pot and bangs it on the floor, right in front of her. Too wild, Natasha thinks. Nothing changes.

In the spring Natasha arrives at an intersection in her life. "I've got a job for you in the drugstore," Peter announces at the supper table. He's racing through his meal so he can get to his first meeting of the evening; he has three. "You can go in tomorrow after school."

She stares at the crumb on his lower lip. "A job? But I'm only fifteen!"

"And a half," Holly interjects. "I started in the cafeteria when I was your age. Where's the pepper?" She stretches across Natasha's plate to reach the glass shaker. "There's no reason why you can't."

So *this* is the game, Natasha thinks. Holly's told him she's smoking and spending too much time with Randy. Or maybe it was her mother. Maybe she's heard rumours in her coffee klatch, maybe someone's hinted that Randy's a bad influence. Natasha crosses her eyes. "I know, Holly. Anything you can do I can do better."

Shirley pours some coveted Vi-Co into Camille's glass, then, as Peter's trained them, she mixes the expensive chocolate milk with regular two percent to make it go further. "Maybe this isn't the best time, Peter," she says, and Natasha knows she has an ally.

"Of course it is!" Peter booms. "Teach a child to fish and she'll never...how's that go?"

"It's teach a *man* to fish," Shirley answers, not looking at any of them. "I don't think it applies."

"Shirl," Peter says out of one side of his mouth, "I think you're being a little too overprotect –"

"I'll do it, Daddy! I'll work!" Camille bounces in her chair as though she needs to use the washroom. Peter's face cracks into a smile and the crumb drops. Natasha feels that this third daughter, a child for all-day suckers and a family of Raggedy-Anns, has won first place in his heart. "You can help Mom do dishes," he says lightly, "but we'll talk in five years." He pushes his black glasses firmly onto his nose and poises knife and fork over his pork chop, ready to attack. "Now get eating everyone. Food's getting cold."

Natasha silently damns Holly, both for blazing the

trail ahead of her and for knowing how to get to her. Just when she's found someone. Just when the puzzle pieces of her life are snapping together. Her life is Simon Says and Mother May I, those games she was rarely asked to play. Mother May I take two steps forward? You forgot to say "Simon Says."

She will never forget the rubber glove odour of it. It's as if the sterile world of the neighbouring clinic permeates its wall and disinfects the pharmacy as well, but the druggist is friendly and he plays popular music on the store radio. He teaches her how to operate the till, make change, and refill the greeting card display. He shows her the list of names of those she's never to take cheques from, "Or they'll bounce like a rubber ball." Natasha scans the list. Keiler is near the top. Then her first day is done.

That night Natasha learns that she's crossed a threshold where she'd never known one existed. "So, how was it?" Peter asks, passing the peas before he scoops a helping for himself.

"Okay," she says. Then, sensing it'll please him and because it's the truth, she adds. "It was actually kind of fun."

"That's my girl."

Natasha feels herself flush at the simple, generous words from this important man who thinks she is doing just fine. Holly bursts in with an account of a woman who'd spilled her onion soup at the cafeteria. "It looked like she'd wet herself!" They laugh at that, and other things. Her father steers the conversation like he does their wood-panelled station wagon, manoeuvring it with both hands on the wheel around work anecdotes so that it becomes a triangle between Natasha, Holly, and himself.

Natasha's bedtime's bumped back to match Holly's. In the late evenings, after Peter's returned from whatever eminent events have swallowed his time and attention, the three of them watch "The Two Ronnies," hours after Camille and Shirley are already dreaming in bed.

Natasha's no longer the ghost, the wilting child with the disappearing act. She couldn't be more surprised.

Randy doesn't understand. "It's the way my family is," she explains, her hand cupping the telephone's mouthpiece as if it were a secret. "Work is sacred, especially to my dad."

"But you don't even need to work...your dad's rich."

"He's not rich, and he expects us to earn our own money. I'm sorry." She hears thrashing in the background. "I'll talk to you tomorrow." She hangs up before the dial tone meets her ear.

After one week she knows which toothbrushes to recommend and the purpose of antacids. In two weeks she has a paycheque, most of which she deposits into her savings account at the Credit Union. With the rest she buys a curling iron and blow dryer which she won't share with anyone. She tucks these treasures under the bed.

Two cheques later she buys a new jacket, warm enough for spring winds but also practical for summer nights.

There's another challenge now, but one she doesn't mind so much, not like that other, distant struggle in the land of repeated Mississippis, the challenge to escape the pale hands of her dreams. Now she must split herself: perfect daughter, perfect friend. As much as she tries to balance that scale, it consistently tips to one side.

Randy tries to make plans over the din of student traffic. "What about Saturday? There's the demolition derby at the exhibition grounds."

"I work till 6:00, then I'm babysitting for the Sperlings. They're going to a wedding dance."

"Sunday?"

She shakes her head. "Dad's taking me driving after church. I'm learning to parallel park."

"I thought you weren't going to babysit anymore, now that you're working." There's an edge to his voice, the tone he employs to berate little sisters.

"I need to earn all I can," she says, weighing her breath, trying to ease it out slowly. "I'm saving for a car." She thought she'd explained this weeks ago. "Can I call you Sunday night?"

"Sure." The buzzer calls them to classrooms on opposite sides of the hall. "Whatever."

In May Natasha makes a list. Bought: hot water bottle, heating pad, lamp with a pleated shade, Kodak camera, towels, wooden spoons, can opener. Need: dish set, good frying pan, bath mat, spice rack, coffee mugs, blanket, car. She's run out of room beneath her bed and has almost filled her half of the closet, too. "Don't touch anything, or else," she warns Camille, who's watching her add a teapot to her inventory. "Or else," has always been enough of a threat with Camille, who's eleven now, and working her way through a mean streak.

"I saw Randy with Debbie today," she says, coyly. "They were at the smoke stand when I was coming home."

Natasha's given up smoking since she's learned the value of money and has started saving it. "So?" She's not sure why she's annoyed. She's busy, employed. Their relationship has necessarily changed. Some weeks Friday arrives and she realizes she hasn't spoken to him except for "Hello" in the hallways. She feels a guilty pang over this negligence, but her hours are no longer empty vessels to fill with self-pity. There's no time to sit, stonelike, before a window while the rest of the world spins.

"So they were holding hands." Camille flops on Natasha's bed.

"And I'm supposed to care?"

"Well he *is* your boyfriend, isn't he?"

"Get lost," she snaps. "Go out on the highway and play."

That night she counts Mississippis until she loses track. She's losing him. There has to be a way to turn things around. What if Randy's all that's standing between her and grief? What if it's waiting for the ideal moment to consume her, finally, and when will that black moment arrive?

When the trees fill out? When she's on her knees at work, dusting the bottles of cough syrup on the bottom shelf?

At school she finds him searching through his locker. "Hey, how's it going?" she asks.

He's changed since that winter day when he filled the vacant desk beside her. She sees it now. He's taller, and his face has thinned, his cheekbones more pronounced. He looks raw, she thinks. Hungry. And she hadn't noticed it happening.

"Hey, Tash. Been a long time."

"What's new?"

"I'm sweet sixteen. My brothers chipped in for a birthday gift –"

"My God...your birthday! I forgot." How could she have? She has the date circled on the calendar in her bedroom. She'd even decided to buy him a sports bag, though she knows it would never hold a pair of shorts with white piping down the sides or cradle a beloved ball glove. "I'll have to get you something on –"

He puts his finger to his lips, shushing her. "Check this out." He hands her a small, rectangular tin.

"What's this?" How stupid she sounds to her own ears, how completely naive.

He touches one joint with a nicotine-stained finger. "Colombian Gold."

The pharmacist gives her a positive performance report, praising her work ethic and ability to catch on quickly, and her father approves a twenty-cent raise. She begins to sense, then *catch* her congenial boss stealing glances at her breasts, her bottom when she bends for the receipt book on the shelf below the till. When he sees her seeing him, he quickly glances away, looking so guilty she's certain he'll never try it again, but he does, and she's flattered more than repulsed. It's their little game.

In the late afternoons dust motes swim in the light from the windows above the stacks of disposable diapers. The radio plays pop songs with sax solos that make her think of the possibility of love. Her last customer, Mrs. Sperling, pays for her birth control pills and leaves with her two dirty-faced toddlers trailing behind, suckers poked in their mouths to keep them quiet.

Natasha locks the door and begins to cash out. She counts and recounts the float, then zips the remaining coins and bills into the canvas bag which is ritually locked into the store safe at the close of each day. The lights flash off as she walks down the greeting card aisle toward the back, toward the pharmacist.

He, too, is counting. Pills, four by four. "Here's the bag," she says, holding it out. She doesn't know the secret numbers that keep the money safe. She doesn't want to know; secrets are secrets. They are not her business.

"I'd like to show you how to use the safe," the pharmacist says, without losing his count. He's on the forgiving side of forty, almost married to a kindergarten teacher with a laugh that comes through her nose. A laughable laugh, Natasha thinks. Silly. "There might be times when I'm not here to lock up."

"Yeah...sure," she says, somewhat surprised. It seems

too much responsibility. Maybe he's going to take time off, she thinks, maybe there's a vacation planned. He said he had a tent. Do him good to spend a few nights in a double sleeping bag with his snorty fiancée and blow off some of that misdirected sexual energy, she thinks.

"You go on in, I'll be right there."

She steps into a storage room where there's barely space to breathe and peels back a square of carpet to reveal the submerged floor safe. It's warm in the cramped room, the air very close. What's taking him? "Oh. Hi."

He's right there, slowly pulling the door closed behind him, and he's not saying anything, and his silence is a long tail swinging slowly back and forth.

"What are you –"

He makes a noise in his throat and reaches for her. "Hope you're not afraid of the dark."

The semi slows and accelerates and takes three more turns they each fail to justify. She's read about things like this in the detective magazine she found by the burning barrel. Taking rides from strangers. The horrors of hitchhiking. She knows about the two girls who'd been tied to a tree and how their attacker took his sweet time with each of them.

"This isn't funny." Gina's voice is all waves, like a highway mirage.

"Dad's gonna flip if we don't come home." It's Holly's voice, in the darkness next to Natasha. "My God, and to think that Camille wanted to come."

Camille, safely home with her dolls. What must their

parents be going through? They'll have the RCMP *combing the ditches. Shirley will be on the phone. Peter's probably organizing the neighbours — organizing the whole town — into a search party. When did they become* Peter *and* Shirley *instead of Mom and Dad? Is this new, or have they always been people with real names?*

"You girls, Jesus H. Christ," Rosco says. "I'm sure there's some explanation."

"Let's play a game or something," Kent suggests. "What's that game you girls play where you take turns naming things?"

Natasha says, "Concentration."

"A girls' game," Rosco says, "I'm not playing."

"So don't," Holly says. "Good idea, Kent. I'll start."

"What's your category?" Gina asks.

"I'm thinking. Mmmm...brands of chocolate bars." She slaps her thighs, claps, snaps her right fingers, then her left: one, two, three, four; one, two, three, four. When all four players have the rhythm — Rosco's still sulking — they chant on the beats: "Con-cen-tra-tion, concentration now begins."

Slap, clap. "Oh Henry."

Slap, clap. "Jersey Milk."

Slap, clap. "Cuban Lunch."

Slap, clap. "Sweet Marie."

Slap, clap. "Sweet...oh, you picked mine," Holly whines at Natasha.

"We'll give you a chance," Kent says, still doing the actions. "New category...movie titles. Con-cen-tra-tion, con-centra —" The semi rumbles over a bad section of highway.

Gina stops, too. "I don't feel like playing anyway."

"Yeah, this is stupid," Holly agrees. "I quit."

No, Natasha wants to say, but she's afraid someone will stop her with, "You don't matter," so she doesn't say anything. She feels the hole in her stomach grow.

Please mister. Where are you taking us?

Natasha slaps his hand away. Is he for real? "You're supposed to stay out of the drugs." The pharmacist laughs, a forced, nervous laugh, but it snaps them both out of the indiscreet moment. Natasha squeezes past him and gets away. Idiot, she thinks. Her father has the power in his penstroke to can anyone, but she doesn't want to make a scene. Desperate, desperate man. A twig. She could beat her way through three of him. She could have kicked down that door like nothing.

At school the principal leads an end-of-year locker search and finds two joints in Randy's. He's suspended, and although he would have been allowed to write his exams he chooses never to return.

Holly graduates, but not without her own waltz with controversy. After the formal ceremony in the gymnasium, where Peter was among the community pillars who presented scholarships to the brightest of the bright, and after the dreaded and humiliating dance with parents that followed, eighty-odd teens on the raw edge of freedom beat it to the lake in fast cars. Picnic tables were burned, bottles were smashed – the usual madness – and in the midst of it, Holly discovered Rosco's pants bunched around his knees and a redhead's face in his lap. Soon she was a redhead with a bloody and broken nose.

Ballistic is the word Natasha repeatedly heard whispered on the street. Rumours mushroomed out of control on the broad steps of the Royal Bank and in smoky coffee shops, in hard plastic barber chairs and between dusty hardware store aisles, around card tables at the Legion and across the street at the busy post office where folks buy one stamp at a time. Her sister's attack was news. Too much booze, people who knew no better said. Too much night. *Holly Stensrud lost it,* they said. *That girl's a ticking time bomb.*

Holly offers Natasha details the rest of the family can only worry about. "It wasn't so much that she was blowing the one-shit-celled-paramecium-bastard, but she was doing it in our station wagon! The fucking nerve!"

Peter and his lawyer avert legal involvement, but there's damage in every direction. "When the pony dies, the ride is over," Peter says, clomping around the house with his shirt untucked, his ever-thinning hair styled in a Brylcreemed comb-over. No one knows what he means, and no one particularly cares. Holly hides behind her headaches, and no one draws a line between the convenient and the real. Camille enjoys her few classroom moments of fame via association. Shirley, who had successfully kicked her passion for long cigarettes, sneaks a few drags in the basement. Natasha tries to hold it all together with homemade pizza and rummy and crimson bouquets of peonies that Shirley pokes her nose into.

There are meetings with the school principal, the United Church minister, a counsellor who comes to their house and talks quietly – *too* quietly; even with a glass between her ear and the piano room door, Natasha can't make out a word.

Peter's careful with his phrasing. The brutal attack is called "the whole mess." The whole mess is a wide and dirty river to cross, dirtier even than Sandy River, but it is crossed, and Rosco, at the bank on the opposite shore, is finished. "Time of death, one twenty-eight a.m." Holly says. She begins going out again. She makes new friends. She picks up Everett, who's twenty-two and has long side-burns and is not likely to wander.

Her sister finally seems almost happy, Natasha thinks.

Natasha works full-time over the long, dry, dandelion days of summer vacation. Temperature records are shattered and every store sells out of fans. Camille tries to fry an egg on the sidewalk but succeeds only in making a mess. On Sundays and Mondays, Natasha's days off, she ties into a bikini, slathers her limbs and the tops of her breasts with baby oil and bakes on a reclining lawn chair. Sometimes Holly joins her, sometimes Camille, when she's not at the swimming pool teasing boys. They are brown girls getting browner. Shirley worries about wrinkles and mostly avoids the sun. Then Tuesday comes and it's back to work again. "Hot enough for you?" the shy farmers ask, rubbing their wind-cracked hands together while they wait for their prescriptions and silently damn the cloudless sky.

The pharmacist marries his fiancée and doesn't dare anything else. A Stensrud family holiday is talked about – Cypress Hills? Banff? – but it never materializes. Natasha occasionally sees Randy downtown with Debbie or some other easy girl hanging on him, but mostly he's with his brothers. Once she spies him outside the pool hall, wearing his trademark jean jacket and indifferent slouch. His hair's longer and ragged, like the cuffs of his jacket. She was going to cross the street to say hello, but then his brother, Will, came out, and she ducked into the bakery before they saw her. She wanted to tell Randy that she almost had enough saved for a cheap car. She wanted to take him to the lot and show him.

Natasha swings around the corner to sixteen and passes her driver's test on the first try. She buys a silver Honda Civic with a standard transmission and rust around the wheel wells. It takes her up and down Railway Avenue and Main with a reluctant Holly or too eager Camille in the passenger seat, and summer goes by in a green streak.

Three weeks into the new school year Holly blasts through the front door, slamming her purse on the table. "It's awful! I just can't believe it!" Natasha and Camille spin around different doorways into the kitchen. "Randy Keiler shot himself last night. He's dead. He's really dead! Oh my God, Natasha," Holly pants, the tops of her ears flushed with the adrenalin of tragedy, "Didn't you two used to be friends?"

She doesn't hear the rest until her ears stop ringing. He did three hits of acid and it was supposedly his first time. Then he'd gone home, downstairs, loaded his father's .22 rimfire, stood it on the cement floor, leaned over the barrel and blasted a neat hole between his eyes.

Natasha runs to the bathroom, kicks the door closed and vomits. She drops to the floor beside the toilet's toxic smells and weeps through her fingers. She failed him and there's no turning back. She blames herself, and his brothers, and most of all, she blames the God who could let this happen, and then it comes to her that from the first moment, the moment he stood staring over the tops of his classmates' heads in homeroom, she knew it would end badly for him, and, in his own sad way, he seemed to know this, too.

Someone's at the door.

"You okay in there?" It's Holly.

Natasha stands. The room sways as she goes to the door. She doesn't open it. She presses her head to the painted wood frame. "Who found him?"

"His mother."

She can't bear it when she hears the slap of her own mother's slippers outside her door that evening, or when Shirley slips into her room and rests one warm hand on her shoulder. Natasha, on the bed with an arm across her eyes, shrugs it off. "I need to be alone."

"Okay," Shirley says, standing awkwardly over her. "I understand. You've always needed your own space around tragedy. We all do."

"Nothing like this has ever happened before. Nothing this...bad." Natasha sniffs and wipes her nose on her sleeve.

Shirley walks to Natasha's window and closes the curtain to the moonlight. "No," she says after a moment. "Of course it hasn't."

Debbie Fowler is a mess. Everyone hears how she and Randy were so much in love, and almost the entire student body attends the funeral, but not Natasha. She knows that most of them never cared about him, never even knew him. His death is a good excuse to get out of English.

She goes to work, overcharges a woman for diapers, and has to squeeze back her grief when the woman complains to the pharmacist.

A few days after the funeral Gerry Keiler comes into the drugstore. He's been in before – to buy condoms – and just like that other time, they avoid each other's eyes.

"I need this developed," he says, handing her a roll of Kodak film. "When'll it be ready?"

"A week to ten days," she answers automatically, taking the film and placing it in the envelope to be sent away. She writes his name in the book and he leaves. His mother's waiting in the Charger. She's wearing sunglasses. It isn't bright.

The following Wednesday Natasha finds herself alone in the store. The pharmacist has gone to the King George for coffee and no customers have been in for several minutes. Earlier, while she was still in school, the photographs were delivered with the mail. She pulls out the cardboard box of alphabetical envelopes and fingers through them.

He's wearing a grey suit and a blue tie. The gleaming casket is the colour of her mother's piano. The satiny interior a rich, royal blue. His face is the wrong shade, the makeup ineffective in concealing the site where the bullet pierced his skin. She quickly slips the pictures back and refastens the seal.

Now, she could tell her parents, it's about death.

She doesn't think about their long hours of coffee and friendship, the enemy wind that slapped them as they sped across the snow on machines, or what demons he may have been racing from. She thinks about his mother with one lung. How she probably doesn't have any pictures of her son apart from school photos, if she even bought them, or maybe a few childhood snapshots, curled and forgotten in one of the basement boxes that will never get unpacked.

Now she has twelve more.

Yearbook People

Time seems to sprawl across the prairie, with moments cut and pasted together as if by a kindergarten class, painstakingly adding one day to the next and the next. All those nights adding up, too. What keeps a flashlight beneath her bed, her tiny, fifth grade New Testament under her feather pillow? So many mornings waking like someone who's sludged through fields of snow, feet dragging in the cold. Natasha's surprised to find all her fingernails chewed, the tips of her fingers burning and red. She's surprised by the maturing face in the morning mirror: it reveals nothing of the dark roads travelled across the night. The black-and-white photo-booth images stuck to her mirror portray a young woman with radiant, flowing hair and a slight smile. An illusion, Natasha thinks. The girl with short hair's been gone a long time now, but she's only ever a nighttime away.

"Camille, do me a favour." Natasha towers above her sister, an octopus of arms and legs on the wall-to-wall in

front of the television, her chin propped on a scrap of corduroy stuffed with chunks of foam, a pillow, of sorts, that she banged together on the sewing machine by herself. "If Dorry phones tell him I'm at Madge's."

Camille's engrossed in the adventures of Gilligan and his mates, who are having the time of their perpetually shipwrecked lives.

"Camille? Did you hear me?" Natasha bends and snaps her sister's bra.

"Uh huh."

"I bet." Natasha opens the front door, turns. "Hey, you want a gallbladder attack?"

"Yeah, sure," Camille says. Her eyes never leave the screen.

Natasha springs off the front steps and jogs down the wide street, fragrant with a recent oiling. Madge's stucco house squats apathetically at the end of the next block. She hasn't been inside since they were children, so she doesn't know if bare-breasted centrefolds still decorate the rumpus room walls. The girl's not a friend according to any of the usual definitions of the word. Madge dates Turner, Dorion's best friend, and the girls' relationship is based solely on this unfortunate fact. Turner's a brute. He colours Madge with mammoth hickeys and sometimes, mammoth bruises of a similar purple. The hickeys she conceals beneath turtlenecks. She has a thousand excuses for the bruises.

The girls enjoy passing a baton of jealousy back and forth. They're especially envious of the amount of time their boyfriends spend together. They curse this relationship, and, occasionally, each other. There's little joy in any of it.

Madge is painting her fingernails and singing "Dust in the Wind" along with the radio when Natasha enters her room. "Knock, knock."

"Hi. Come in. Clear a path."

Natasha sits on the bed between tossed clothes. "Have you called the restaurants?"

"Yeah." Madge, at her dressing table, fans her hands like a Southern belle suffering in the heat. She blows across her nails. The two representatives from the grad planning committee talk to each other's mirrored image. "The Capri said seven bucks a plate. They're the lowest."

"Great. So that's settled." Natasha feels a certain amount of relief with these final weeks of grade twelve sliding off the calendar, but what awaits? The universe is about to unfold, yet rather than running toward this edge as she did when a child, she finds herself dancing a strange tango: one tentative step forward, one double stumble back.

Madge squints at Natasha in the mirror. She's near-sighted and needs glasses, but she read in a women's magazine that it's possible to train weak eyes. "What are you doing with your hair?"

"What?"

"For grad. Are you getting it done?"

"Oh," Natasha shakes her head, letting her layered mane frame her face. Even the colour is leonine. She pulls it up, lets one lock spill across her eye, and pouts. "I don't know...I may just leave it like this...natural." Natural. The

All-Canadian girl next door, if she has to describe herself. A cleft chin makes her different; shapely lips turn her toward a young woman who could almost be considered sultry. She arches her back. Once, in a rare flash of generosity, Holly'd said that Natasha's breasts were exactly the right size for her shape.

Madge walks to the window. "I'm sick of this."

"You took the job," Natasha blurts. "You didn't have to." Her own directness stuns her; she's usually only this blunt with her sisters.

"I'm not talking about grad, I'm talking about...I don't know...life...this...town...everything." She turns.

Natasha searches for a safer place to look. She finds it in a shelf of Harlequin romance novels, where love between the covers never comes to blows. Everyone knows the truth about Madge and Turner's relationship, but she's not close enough to know the details. She senses this is what's coming and she's stumped. Details would bind them. Details she doesn't want.

"What are you doing after grad?" Madge asks.

The question falls like a raven at Natasha's feet, something she wasn't expecting but she's relieved it's not anything bigger, heavier. "I...I guess I'll try to find something in the city...maybe take a class. You?" Why the deliberate vagueness? She's already applied to the University of Calgary, where she knows no one, where she can begin life again, untethered.

"I'll probably take a medical or legal secretary course...anything to get me the hell out of here." Madge looks past her, or through her, and sniffs.

Natasha remembers the centrefolds. How Madge didn't even acknowledge them. "So, if you go to school, what happens with Turner?" She knows why Madge hangs on, why this young woman who forsakes her own vision puts up with it. Madge is high maintenance at the makeup counter: pretty at a cost. She's scaled walls to escape mediocrity, where the plain, plump, poor, mundane, lonely, and even, on rare occasions, the smart girls pay to enter the inner sanctum, the golden light that shines on the party crowd. To be somebody. Desired. To have their names penned into a textbook beside a heart, their phone numbers scratched into a washroom wall. They enter with their bodies, the tricks passed down from older sisters or blue books in which certain page numbers are memorized. What their fathers tack to the walls. These girls take it in the mouth. Give them a direction, they'll bend. They'll always make it fit.

Madge shrugs, then reaches for a tissue to wipe a drop of nail polish from the shag rug. "What about Dor?"

Natasha twists her promise ring: a diamond chip inside a gold heart. A thin band. She'd almost been reluctant to accept. It's only been five months since their first date – a horror movie and hours of sweaty hand-holding – but already Dorion knows her better, she worries, than she knows herself. He plays acoustic guitar and makes her name the chorus in a song about desire. He'd been to Puerto Vallarta and returned to school wearing the sun on his skin like a charm. He sings "Guantanamera" and rolls the Rs like a real Latino. He loves her legs, the arches of her feet, the hand's-width of skin between her shoulder blades. He claims he loves her completely – even the scars on her knees she has no stories for, her musk on his calloused fingers, the way she moans when he's inside her, even the nights when she says no.

She believes him. The first time he spoke of love – in the cramped back seat of her Honda – white fireworks splashed on a screen before her eyes. And he's beautiful when sleeping. She can't help kissing him, like a mother overwhelmed with tenderness for her child. Maybe it's right, she thinks. Maybe this time. It was easy to beat the blink that was her delicious interlude with David; Randy was more difficult. She thinks, often, of what that might have become. But she hasn't yet answered Madge. "No worries," she says. It's something Dorion would say himself.

Madge swings her legs back under the dressing table and returns to her fingernails. "Have you booked the band?"

Natasha groans. "I thought *you* were doing that." They're back to the roles they know best. The next sixty minutes are insufferable.

Last night, in her journal, she wrote something she doesn't understand: *It is all before them.* What is all before us? she wonders. What is *it?*

Camille sneaks up on her thoughts. "Boo!"

Natasha startles and snaps the journal closed. "What?"

"Made you jump!" Camille falls onto the end of the couch, pinning Natasha's feet. "Mom said I get to go to the lake with you and Dorry."

"Fat chance. Get off my legs."

Camille unfolds herself like a Tinkertoy; she is all angles. "Mom, I told you she wouldn't believe me!"

Shirley appears in the doorway between kitchen and living room. Piano lessons have ended for the year; they have the liberty to be noisy girls in their own house. "It's favour time," she says, wiping a glass, her strong, pianist's fingers wet with dishwater. "Camille's got nothing to do this weekend. Couldn't you take her tonight?"

Natasha scowls. "No way." The lake, a half-hour's drive away, is her refuge from the dusty town. A teenage haven for bush parties, all-night bonfires, back-seat sex, water skiing and swimming when the weather warms. "She's a kid. What's Holly doing?"

"She's in bed with a headache, and if she's feeling better later she's going to Marvin to see Everett. They're picking out their wedding invitations."

"Whoop-tee-do." Natasha plucks the inside of her cheek with her pointer finger, making a pop. Everett. Certainly a few rungs up the ladder from Rosco, but still just an electrician from Marvin. He has an apartment across from that town's only school. Natasha tries to like him, but it pains her to see a grown man drive an El Camino with dingle-balls years after they've gone out of fashion. He's into cars, war movies, country and western music, fishing and goose hunting, all of which he's willing to debate the merits of at great length. He took a course on upholstering furniture, and Shirley's hiring him to redo the Queen Anne chairs. He's making payments on a speedboat, which is something. Holly's always been attracted to speed and water. At least that hasn't died.

Shirley disappears into the kitchen, then re-emerges with a cup of coffee. "Camille, scram."

Camille pouts. "Why?"

"Because I'm your mother and I've asked you to."

"Aww....." Camille flies off and they hear the back door spring itself closed. Shirley scoots Natasha's legs over and sits. "Come on, Tash. You guys go to the lake every weekend. If you can't take your sister with you this one time...maybe you shouldn't go either." There's no punch in her voice, Natasha notes. Right lines, wrong delivery. God, she thinks, is her mother going to start murdering plants again?

Natasha hugs the pillow at the far end of the couch, wondering if Shirley intuits that her middle daughter's no longer a virgin. She's done the deed, now. The wild thing. That final rite of passage from which there's no turning back. She does it regularly, and – if the girls who whisper in the school locker room are to be believed – she probably enjoys it more than she should. She's taken care to hide the birth control pills she gets free from the town's progressive female doctor. A South African. "Why are Holly's plans more important than mine?"

Shirley presses the cup to her forehead. "I'm tired, Tash. Humour me."

She knows, Natasha thinks. Sure she does.

There's a lull between customers in the grocery store and Natasha checks her watch. Forty-five more minutes, then the freedom of Friday night. Peter'd transferred her from the pharmacy to groceries months ago, after he'd lost his two best cashiers: one to a delicate pregnancy and the other to Europe, a backpacking tour. "A complete waste of time," he'd told his daughters with a suspiciously lecture-like tone — as if this was something they might be considering in their own futures — but he publicly wished the girl well and even stuffed a twenty from his own wallet into her farewell card.

"I liked the pharmacy better," Natasha'd said, thinking out loud one Saturday as she waited for Peter to unlock the back door beside the shipping and receiving dock. "It wasn't busy. I could listen to the radio." And the sun spilled through the windows in those final hours of the afternoon, and I floated right through them.

"You needed a new challenge, and things are quite a bit busier in groceries," Peter'd said. "I'm sure you've noticed. No time to stand around mooning. It's not healthy having all that time just to think."

"You're whacked," she'd said. "Since when did thinking become a crime?" But they were inside then, and Peter was saying good morning to the cleaners who were shaking out their dust mops.

She works every weekday after school for two hours and all day Saturdays, hating every breath inside the blue fortrel uniform that effectively traps perspiration and disguises any clues that her body is blossoming underneath. She loathes the customers who don't know enough to separate their produce from their detergent on the spinning counter, the ones who ask for car service even though they're perfectly capable of helping themselves, the elderly women who want double bags and remind her, every week, to be careful of their eggs, the ones who wait in her lineup, shamelessly eating grapes.

But Peter's right, usually time zooms. Three fast months were already behind her when she noticed the young meat manager and sensed the quiet storm stirring between them. He's married, with a new baby at home. She's become shy around him, terrified that she'll make some mistake on the till when he's watching, waiting to pay for his own milk and bread at the end of the day.

One Saturday they collided, in the stockroom, and he put his hands on her ribs, just below her breasts. He held on that exploding moment longer than necessary, and she knew. It would never go further than his fingers on those bones, but his touch fueled her fantasies for weeks.

"He's here." Natasha opens the door and holds up two fingers to symbolize that she needs two minutes. Dorion takes it as a peace sign and gives it back. "Do you have any money, Camille?"

Camille displays a fistful of quarters. "Two bucks."

Natasha pushes her through the door. "We're gone," she calls.

"Sorry about this," she says to Dorion, not bothering to keep her voice low as her sister squeezes into the two-door's second seat. "It was either bring her along or stay home. Mom's on the rag again."

Dorion shrugs. "No problemo." He winks at Camille

in the rear-view mirror. "Geez, kid, you're getting tall. How old are you now?"

"Thirteen."

"Thirteen." He whistles. Natasha expects this: once Camille fills out she's going to be a looker, a knockout, possibly even a fox. She has the face for it, the symmetry, dark waves of full-bodied hair and killer green eyes, but it's more than the sum of her parts. It's what remains nameless, concealed just below the surface, that jewel. Camille is also the only Stensrud daughter who's kept up with her piano, and at one time or another – at talent shows, church, weddings, school events – most people in town have heard her perform.

They stop at the Highway Esso. "You comin' in?" Camille asks her.

Natasha looks at the building, which has grown to accommodate a long, narrow restaurant where truckers and shuffling, old bachelors mumble their orders off a laminated, one-sheet menu with typing errors, and flies buzz in the windows. It's not a nice place. It's not for her. "I'll wait."

"Do you guys want anything?" Camille asks.

"Smokes," Dorion says, handing her his money.

Camille runs in.

"Come here, gorgeous." Dorion reels Natasha in by the elbow. His eyes are bedroom heavy, mesmerizing. Since his time in Mexico even his eyes have become long-lashed and Latin-like. Natasha leans across the stick shift and welcomes his soft lips. Two quick smacks, then he explores her mouth with his tongue.

"Whoa!" She feels queasy, and breaks from the embrace to open her window and hang her head out. The evening breeze revives her.

"What's wrong?"

"My sister might see."

Camille returns with Dorion's cigarettes and a bag of sunflower seeds.

"No spits in my car." Dorion exaggerates a serious, fatherly tone and tries to grab the bag.

Camille shrieks and scrambles to shove the shiny package into her beach bag, another home-sewn project. "Not now," she says, obviously pleased with the attention, "they're for the beach."

They cruise past the drive-in and Randy's grave in the cemetery, leaving the town's sober streets to those drivers they consider less fortunate because of the anchors of age and responsibility. The sun warms them through the left windows. Remember this, Natasha tells herself. You're young, in love, perhaps even beautiful, and all the doors are swinging open. Treasure this.

Thirty minutes she holds Dorion's firm thigh, his hand occasionally cupping hers, and then this, too, becomes history. They reach the park entrance and pass the empty registration booth where the highway becomes a snaking gravel road with blind curves. They arrive safely once again, and soon they're hiking down a sandy bank to a beach flanked by giant evergreens.

"Where should we set up?" Dorion asks, looking south down the long beach.

Natasha slides out of her sandals, buries her feet

beneath the welcoming sand. "Let's go a little further," she says, "down there."

They walk another few minutes before Dorion soothes a blanket in place. "Good enough?"

She kisses his nose. "Perfect." She stares across the water's skin to the north side, to the swatches of colour that are small cabins peeking through trees. Camille skips stones, several feet away. Such a thin child, a whisper, and still, despite the bra, almost breastless. Natasha wonders if she'll ever take on curves.

Madge and Turner arrive, lugging a cooler between them. "Hey," Turner says. "That your sister back there?"

Natasha looks up. "Yeah. Why?"

"Just wondering. She doesn't look much like you."

"None of us look alike in our family. We could be strangers." This is the most she's ever spoken to Turner.

Madge drags him down to the sand.

Soon there are more classmates, the circle of bodies on the beach growing, breaking, rounding again. Maybe it's the particular light, Natasha thinks, or the water sounds. Loons, if anyone's listening. It feels like the beginning of the end of innocence. The butterscotch moon floats up over the trees; her evening turns surreal. She's weightless again, above it all.

"Great night, eh?" Dorion passes his cigarette. He says she looks sexy when she smokes and she's forever trying to live up to the compliment. She exhales like an actress, like her mother.

"Great." She drifts, snapping back to the circle when spoken to. Camille's become a silhouette on the shoreline.

For all the fun she's having, she's probably wishing she'd stayed home, Natasha thinks.

The lake's daytime blue kaleidoscopes into flecks of gold, then a dangerous green, then a black pool. Early campers who'd been strolling the water's edge return to their campsites to invoke summer with the fragrance of roasted marshmallows.

"Time to move to the firepit," Dorion says, pulling her to her feet.

"Wait...my sandals." She slips into them and grabs her bag off the sand. "Camille!" She shouts to the reeds, to the tallest one who stands ankle deep in the black lake. "We're going to the far end of the beach. Down there." She points to where a dozen speed and fishing boats rock in the water.

Slowly, without even a shadow for company, the figure that is her sister moves out of the water and makes its way down the beach, always a good stone's throw from the crowd. She picks up a long branch and appears to be drawing in the sand; letters, or designs, Natasha can only imagine.

Dorion passes Natasha a beer. It foams over the lip onto her hand. "Mmmm. Allow me." He licks it off.

She squints into the wavering veil of smoke, studies the bronze faces in the campfire's transient light, counting twelve. Her thoughts leap ahead. One day, years from this moment, this crowd she's known since the kindergarten sandbox will become yearbook people she turns the pages to, laughing at their bushy hair and glasses, laughing because she sees in their eyes that they thought they were the only ones ever to hold a claim on youth and happiness. Remember this, she tells herself again, feeling romantic. Remember you once had a boy holding his life tightly around you.

Dorion brushes her ear, whispers pennies for her thoughts. Natasha meets his eyes. He slides his hand over hers and places it against his heart. It is all good.

"I got a letter from Calgary today." She says it softly, into his neck. "I've been accepted."

She waits.

"Congratulations." He kisses her perfunctorily on the cheek. "When do you leave?"

"End of August. We've got the whole summer –"

Turner pitches his bottle into the lake. He snaps his fingers. "Another one." Madge leaps up and he laughs his raw and grating laugh. She hands him a fresh bottle. Somebody sighs.

"That's great, Tash. Good for you," Dorion says, but he sounds far away. "I'm going for a whiz." He leaves for the trees and Madge takes his place.

"How'd you do on that English final?" Natasha asks. There's so little to say.

Madge tears her beer label, rolls the bits into balls and flicks them into the fire. "Okay, I think. I got up at 4:30 to study for it."

Natasha leans away from the smoke when it finds her eyes, knowing she wears it now, they all do, a heavy fragrance in their hair and clothes. "You going to the book-burning party next Friday?"

Madge shrugs. "Maybe. You?"

"Doubt it. I may want to look at them again some-day...you know, when I'm eighty-five and losing my marbles and need something to hold on to. Those Shakespeare notes or biology labs might be just what I need."

"You're weird, Tash," Madge says, but a real smile lifts the glossed corners of her mouth.

"Thanks...I work at it."

The girls clink bottles, then both gaze at the inky lake. "So, how well can you see?" Natasha asks, feeling lucky that she didn't inherit her father's poor vision. Only Holly got that honour.

"Well enough. I see the haze across the lake that must be the cabins, I see five fingers." She holds up her hand. "I do okay. Besides, sometimes seeing is overrated."

How strange, Natasha thinks. "What do you mean?"

"Ah...nothing. Hey, did I ever tell you about my dream?"

Natasha tastes her beer. "What dream?" Dorion's returned from the darkness to the halo of campfire light. He's across the fire from her, laughing with Turner and Mark King, another of his team of popular, athletic friends. "What dream?" she repeats.

"It was really shitty. I dreamt I was on Main, by the clinic. I saw Turner across the street so I called him over and when he got close enough so that I could see his eyes —" She shivers.

"What?" A plug of phlegm sticks in Natasha's throat. Fear.

"They were Dorion's."

"Yikes, that *is* scary." But at least she knows what it is,

Natasha thinks. She takes a long drink. It's not so terrible she can't talk about it, because talking about it might make it real and that possibility is unthinkable. Madge can release this little horror and then maybe it'll be over for her. Not like her own nights. Something crackles in the grass behind her. Camille. She'd forgotten. "What's up?"

"Can I have the keys?" Sunflower seed shells staccato from Camille's mouth.

"Hang on." Natasha walks around the fire to Dorion. A twig snaps satisfactorily beneath her sandal. "We should really get going."

He nods, notices Camille walking away. "Soon. Is your sister ready?"

"Hours ago." Natasha hooks her arm in Dorion's, gently pulling up.

"You jammin'?" Turner asks. Natasha would love to smash his fat lips for all the times he's smashed Madge at parties just like this, blood on the periphery of good times.

Dorion flicks his cigarette into the fire. "I've gotta work at eight."

"And I've got to work at nine," Natasha jumps in.

"Pussy-whipped suck ass," Turner says.

"Fuck you," Natasha says. What does Madge see in him? What does Dorry? What does his own mother see, she wonders, or did he actually have some virtues once upon his lifetime? Not bloody likely.

"Testy, testy," Turner teases.

"Come on, Tash." Now it's Dorion pulling *her* away from the heat.

Mark jogs after them. "Hey, can I catch a ride back? My truck's still in the shop."

"Sure, buddy," Dorion says. "The more the merrier."

Natasha cringes. Mark's got a reputation for Russian fingers, and anyone, even her sister, still mostly bones, is fair game. She'll give up her front seat and share the back with Camille.

They catch up to her at a picnic table further along the beach. "Okay kid...time to go," Dorion says.

"What, so soon?" Her empty sunflower seed bag catches the moonlight.

"You wanted to come," Natasha reminds her. "You pleaded and begged."

The foursome plow up the sandy bank to the parking lot. Dorion stumbles where there's nothing in his path and Natasha steadies him. He slips his hand into her back pocket and squeezes.

"How much have you had to drink?" Natasha asks.

"Not much." He counts on his fingers like a toddler asked his age. "Seven...maybe eight."

"Are you okay to drive?" She's seen him drink a dozen beer and still walk a straight line.

"Is the pope Catholic? Jesus, honey. You know I drive better when I've had a few. I'm more careful then. Quit ragging on my ass!"

Shit, she thinks, now he's drunk *and* pissed off. He fumbles with the key in the lock. "Come on, Dor...let me drive." She tries easing the keys out of his fingers.

"I told you," he says, pinching her wrist, "I can handle it. Trust me."

Mark slides behind the bucket seat and Camille spiders in beside him before Natasha can intervene. If she did it now, it would be obvious, it would glare. She turns to her sister, wishing a telepathic moment, but the four years between them have always been too many for psychic energy to cross. Holly's always been the one. Holly fades in and out, a weak signal, but there. "Buckle up."

Dorion revs the engine. The noise barrels through the campground, causing children to turn in their sleeping bags and parents to curse. He checks his rear-view mirror.

"Guzzle that, buddy."

Mark tips the bottle, swallows and waves Dorion on. Wheels spit gravel. Mark hurls his bottle, smashing it to death against a stop sign.

Natasha knows each curve and hill on the ten-mile gravel stretch before the highway, engraved as they are on her adolescent heart. This is their road. She knows that if they round the corners too close to the edge the loose sand will grab the wheels and pull them into the trees. She watches for oncoming lights.

There are other dangers: deer, bears, foxes, rabbits, skunks, porcupines. The headlights blind them; Dorion could never stop in time. They'd hit a doe once, as passengers in Turner's car. Natasha remembers the stench of blood, the guys slugging a baseball bat, the doe's final twitching. They'd heaved the limp animal into the ditch for someone else to worry about. She remembers how Madge had cried without making any sounds, the watery tracks of mascara on her cheeks giving her away.

Now the road's dark, the moon's light blotted by the

tall, dense evergreens standing at attention on either side. So far so good, Natasha thinks. Then there's a light, too close behind them. She spins. "It's Turner and Madge. Let them pass."

"We'll see who's the pussy," Dorion says.

Natasha watches the speedometer climb. "For Christ's sake, slow down! What if someone's coming?" Turner's lights stay trained on them.

"This is so cool!" Camille bounces on the back seat. Mark belches, and Natasha can smell the wave of beer and garlic.

Turner pulls up beside them. Mark reaches across Dorion's shoulder and gives Turner the finger. "Get the lead out, eh!"

Dorion crushes the accelerator.

"Cut it out!" Natasha screams. She digs for her seat belt but can't find it. "You'll kill us!"

Camille cheers, laughs, bounces in the back seat. She slaps the headrest by Dorion's ears and he asks her to stop. The sounds are all enormous.

The cars fishtail around the sharpest corners, spraying gravel. Trees melt together in a dark blur; each rise in the road sends a current through Natasha's stomach. Brain damage, she thinks. I must protect my head. She curls into the small space in front of her seat, arms crossed in a shield above her. She's suffocating. Hot, dark. Oh God oh God oh God.

She wants to sleep, but when she rests her head in Holly's lap her sister pulls her up. "No sleeping, we've got to figure this out."

"What would Clint Eastwood do?" Rosco asks.

Gina guffaws. "Clint Eastwood wouldn't have climbed in the back of a semi like an idiot in the first place. Anyone with half a brain would have taken a ride hours ago, with the Pool agent's wife, or the mayor. This is your fault, Rosco. You got us into this."

Natasha feels Kent's knee press against hers as he leans toward Gina. "Listen, this is nothing. It just seems to be taking a long time to get there. Before you know it, we'll all be back at home and wishing we were anywhere else." Kent pauses. "Did anyone get the license number?"

No one.

I'm slipping, Natasha thinks. She's created a world out of memorizing license plate numbers, emergency phone numbers, the lines on the faces of the ragged men who stumbled along Main Street, just in case, so why had all that eluded her this time, when it really mattered? Her parents would be disappointed in her, their Nancy Drew daughter who played games of escape under mouldy blankets in the basement. "We thought you knew better," she heard them say.

Already she was forgetting their faces, especially Peter's. Her father goes away, often, to his stores in other towns, to cities, conventions. He returns after three or four days with a gift for each of them and always a new set of salt and pepper shakers for Shirley's gaudy cabinet display. Natasha still hopes her father will bring back a marionette or a ventriloquist's dummy, like the frightening little man she'd seen at a toy show the single time she'd accompanied him. She practices throwing her voice, but no miniature man with a painted grin and polka dot tie ever comes to live in their house and *haunt her from the closet or beneath the bed.*

And what will happen to Camille? She'll be bawling right now. She seems to cry more than most kids, Natasha thinks, and certainly more than any nine-year-old should. I'll spend more time with her, play Barbies without her having to beg, if I ever see her again.

Holly and Gina make a half-hearted attempt to sing "Kum Ba Ya," but their voices are hollow and because of the semi's vibrations they can't keep them steady through the long notes. They surrender and turn glum.

Natasha wonders which of her sins must have brought this ordeal on. The telepole?

The trucker makes a left turn.

She apologizes for the things she's made her mother do, and for sneaking change from her purse so she could buy cream soda and salt-and-vinegar potato chips at the confectionery, rum-and-butter milkshakes at the Dairy Whip.

The last time she saw her mother, Shirley was wearing her favourite halter top and a pair of yellow pedal pushers that were not particularly flattering, an apron tied over top. Holly's apron. The day before, Shirley'd failed to talk Holly and Natasha into weeding the garden which, in spite of everyone's neglect, eventually yields peas, carrots, potatoes, Red Robin tomatoes, and the occasional shocked pumpkin.

"How long have we been in here?" Holly asks. "I think we're running out of air."

"Didn't check my watch." This is Gina. "Lost it at school."

"Great," Holly snaps. "This is just great."

Natasha tries to focus on the four walls around her but

her vision doesn't extend to those edges. Her eyes, strangely, have not adjusted to the dark.

"Ya little shit!" Dorion's yelling.

Natasha crawls out from her hiding place. Turner's passed them, but Dorion's on his tail. Even the trees are screaming now.

"Whoo-hooo!"

"Eat this, you asshole!"

Above everything else Natasha hears Camille: "Boy, this is fun! Boy, this is fun!"

A *View of the* Mountains

Dawn with a twist. She's being chased across the schoolyard by a mangy black bear. Mr. O'Brien and the other teachers are scrambling to herd students inside, but the bear is faster and Natasha smells the smoke of its breath. Then –

"Good morning, Calgary. It's 6:45 and the weatherman says a fine day ahead –" She swats the snooze button, slamming her wrist bone on the edge of her night table, and wakes wondering where she is. Then the light crawls up her covers and she knows. At the end of her bed, a narrow window frames skyscrapers outlined by an almost imperceptible blue aura – the Rocky Mountains. How strange to have this hawk's-eye-view of distant peaks, and closer, concrete and glass, rather than the field, forest, and lake landscapes of her youth. Here Banff is within reach, that enchanted land of elk and ice cream cones that she visited as a child.

Much of that earlier world is a cave where bats cling to the walls. She doesn't visit often, but she remembers this game: pinching her eyes and opening them in a new country, new era, new galaxy. This time it really worked. She's leapt, and found herself here.

Peter delivered her; it coincided with a business trip. They'd decided to leave the Honda until she returned home on the bus for Christmas. She'd know the city better then and would be more comfortable driving across it. It's been two months now and the traffic still terrifies her. It's the speed of things, mostly, that catches her behind the knees. She buzzes up to her apartment in an elevator. Dialing a number can produce pizza at her door within minutes, still steaming or her money back. She has only to step outside to see an ambulance scream past.

"I feel like I'm dumping you," Peter'd said, after they found her room in the student residence and carried in her bags and boxes, the electric typewriter she'd been given as a graduation gift. One of her three roommates was also unpacking; the others had yet to arrive.

"Au contraire, mon pere, I'm dumping all of *you!"*

"Well, I guess I'll go down to the office and settle your rent. You've got enough money?"

She nodded.

"You're going to be okay?"

Natasha threw her arms up and smiled grandly. It was all she could do not to push him out the door. "Do I look like I'm going to be okay?"

"Well, I've got that meeting at 2:30, I guess –"

"Don't want to be late," she finished.

They shook hands then – two wet palms slapping – and she closed the door after her father left it hanging open, a mouth agape.

Her first class is at eight, and if she's lucky she'll beat her three roommates to the shower and get dibs on the hot water. Her general arts classes are not a chore, except English. She's at a stalemate with her paper on *The Stone Angel* and is finding words in general to be wretched. She visualizes her struggle, sees the essay as a long rope tied into stiff knots that aren't coming undone. Bram and Hagar Shipley's disastrous marriage is too many miles away; she doesn't give a damn about the octogenarian or her ambivalence toward her crude husband. They mean nothing to her.

She's beat her roommates again. She stands beneath the hot stream and soaps her suntanned arms with fragrant beauty soap. Even this – choosing her own soap rather than going with the Stensrud's usual bargain brand – has been a step up the ladder to a better place. On the shower's ledge she notes three bars of soap and guesses which roommate they belong to. Plastic-wrapped Ivory? Cherise. A half bar of Zest? Kelly's. A sliver of something blue, with an S of red pubic hair curled into its side. Unmistakably Jude's.

Jude's consistently the last to roll out of bed. A busty young woman with flames of wild, red hair, a loud and inviting laugh, a plethora of crude jokes and a fast white car, she's the most comfortable with college life, and the closest to home. Her parents' ranch, just south of High River, is less than an hour away. She knows Calgary. She leads the way. Next to her, Natasha feels like a hick. She implores Jude to take her to the airport to watch jets land, watch all those worldly people come and go. Jude whizzes her downtown past the aggressive prostitutes with their short skirts or furs, see-through blouses, red stilettos or black leather boots zipped to their thighs. They witness a man in an expensive suit approach a long-legged prostitute near the Calgary Tower. The white-wigged woman unzips him and dunks her hands – *both* of them – into his pants, and Natasha is turned on.

Kelly Wong has the best wardrobe of the four girls, and she doesn't mind sharing. Natasha's borrowed her blue velvet stilettos with laces she'd tied around her slim ankles. She's borrowed blue jeans with leather piping on the pockets, and a yellow slicker for a sightseeing trip near Bragg Creek.

Kelly's Asian on her father's side, white-bread British stock on her mother's. Her unusually pretty face keeps strangers guessing. Laotian? Filipino? Cree? In Saskatchewan she'd get asked for a treaty number, Natasha thinks. Here, all that matters less.

Cherise is the one Natasha can't figure. She takes her turn cooking and eats with the other girls, but she never sits around, never chats. She doesn't smoke, or say *shit* or *fuck,* or tell anecdotes of any nature that would give them a better insight into who she is. Studious and timid, she lives the monotonous hours of her life between textbooks and classes, and seems at once years older than the others and also years younger.

"She's the only virgin within miles," Natasha tells Dorion on the telephone. "This girl makes smiling feel like a crime. And I hate her shoes. Old lady shoes. Like grandmothers wear."

"When are you coming home?"

"Christmas. I told you."

She senses his impatience. They'd pledged to be faithful to one another this first year apart, but there'd be others wanting a piece of him now that she was a province away. He's a good catch. Next summer they'd re-evaluate; perhaps he could join her in the city. Maybe they'd break it off. The expression makes her think of a branch, cracking off a tree in an electrical storm. Their relationship is a kite flown dangerously close to high wires.

"Has anyone hit on you yet?"

"Nobody interesting," she says, then lightens it with a trill of laughter. "Just kidding. No. I've been as good as gold. And you?" There it is, tension blooming in her chest when he doesn't answer immediately.

"Same, but I miss you. Sometimes I think we're crazy trying to hang on to this thing over the miles, not that it's not worth it. You know I love you, but what about next year, and the year after that? I've got a chance for a job on the rigs."

"Dor! You never told me that!"

"I just heard. Turner's brother's getting him on, and there's a possibility...it's great money, and we'd be in the same province at least."

"It's also hard work, and bloody dangerous. Have you really thought about this?"

"I'm thinking now. I can't see what I've got to lose."

Natasha hears the apartment door being unlocked. Kelly calls, "Hello!"

"Hi," she says, cupping the phone.

"Who's that?" Dorion asks. "Who came in?"

"Kelly. Listen, I've got to run, but we'll talk about this some more, okay? And I'll see you soon. I love you."

"Yeah. Love you, too."

"Your boyfriend?" Kelly is pulling a handknit sweater over her head, its wool the soft blue of flax flowers. Her luxuriant, ebony hair falls right back into place.

"My one and only. I'm promised." She works off her ring and passes it to Kelly, who slides it over her own elegant finger for inspection.

"Cool. It's serious?"

Natasha looks at the ring on Kelly's finger. It looks good there, better than on her own skin. "You want to wear it for awhile, feel free."

She glides into a routine of staying up to watch the late night talk shows, sleeping fitfully or hardly at all, attending classes, then crashing for a solid hour of dreamless, catch-up rest after school. Afternoons are safe for sleeping. It's taken her five years to discover this.

"Natasha?" Jude pokes her head into the room.

Natasha's waking layer by layer, as if slowly leaving the soft white comfort of a coma. "What?"

"Whatcha doin'?" Jude sashays across the small bedroom to the desk, lifts one of the typed sheets off a pile beside the typewriter.

"Panning for gold...what does it look like?" She likes Jude, an outrageous, only child with thick skin. She feels she can say anything to her. She can scold Jude when she deserves it, or confess to her when she's feeling blue. Jude's the closest she's ever come to a best friend.

"Are you coming to the Highlander tonight? Some guy's imitating Alice Cooper. Everyone's going."

"Sounds like a blast, but I can't." She sits up in bed. "That essay's due next week and I'm just getting started. I don't whip them off like some people."

Jude smirks. "Hey, what can I say? I'm not knocking myself out for eighties and nineties. As long as I pass, that's all I care."

Natasha pulls one leg of her jeans on. "Try me next month."

Jude sits on the end of her bed and flexes one bare foot. "Shoot yourself, but you know, you only live once."

"So I've heard," Natasha says.

December. Still no snow in Calgary when Jude drops her at the bus terminal and her ticket is stamped for home. Natasha spends the first hour of the excruciating ride beside a grandmother with thighs like a quarterback. It appears a chicken's pecked at her scalp, leaving wisps of white cotton candy. Natasha tries to make interesting noises while she's shown pictures of nondescript grandchildren with brilliant futures. She has a blissful half hour alone, then a boy of about thirteen swings into the seat beside her.

"Want some?" He's eating long, pungent strips of beef jerky.

"No. No thanks." She turns to the window, to the

snow-meringued landscape of Saskatchewan. She takes a deep breath and holds it, another deep breath and holds it. She does this much of the way home.

She's expecting Dorion to be waiting in the town's little closet of a terminal, not Holly. "Well isn't that a fine how do you do. Hasn't seen me for over three months and –"

"Oh, he called," Holly says, relieving Natasha of her carry-on bag while she reaches for the large suitcase the bus driver's left flipped on its side in the snow. "He said you're supposed to call when you get in."

"Great." The snow is slowly spiraling to the ground. Natasha can make out the shapes of the large, sparse flakes on her sister's shoulder and has a rare, pleasant flashback. "Remember when we were little, sitting at the table with mom – I don't think Camille was even born yet – and we cut shapes from folded paper that opened, like magic, into snowflakes? I haven't thought of that in years."

"No. I don't remember. You probably don't either, but it sounds good. Very Christmasy. Anyway, we've set a date." Holly opens the car door for her, then walks around to the other side. "Easter. I've been into Saskatoon looking for dresses but haven't found anything yet." Holly's giving her a nervous, sideways look. "You'll be here, right?"

The clothes, Natasha thinks, my new hair, the tam. She's seeing a city girl now. "For your wedding?"

"No, my bar mitzvah. Of course for my wedding!" Holly sweeps snow off the car roof.

"Cripes, Holl. You're my sister. I wouldn't miss it. By

the way, boys have bar mitzvahs. Girls have *bat* mitzvahs."

"And you'll stand up with me? After Gina, I mean. I've asked her to be maid-of-honour." Holly scoots into Natasha's car, behind the wheel.

"You're not going to tart me up in some hideous baby blue dress are you?"

Holly starts the car. "Lavender."

Natasha groans.

"We're home," Holly calls, stating the obvious as she opens the front door. They let the heavy bags drop onto the disarray of Cougar ankle boots, wet mittens, running shoes, gloves, and toe rubbers that clog the entry. "Come out, come out, wherever you are."

There's a stranger in Peter's Lazyboy, Natasha notes, pulling off her tam. A slightly rugged teen with pine-cone-coloured eyes and one leg slung over the armrest, a grey wool sock dangling. New kid in town? Natasha wonders, but his casual air suggests he's always been there, filling the brown recliner in the centre of this house full of women. She pats her hair into place. "Hi, Camille," she says, "what's new?"

"Tom, this is my sister, Natasha," Camille says with remarkable nonchalance, as if Natasha's been gone a few hours, not a few months. "She's the middle one."

Natasha tries not to sound astounded. "Hello." Camille has a boyfriend?

In the kitchen, Holly explains in a stage whisper. "They don't admit they're going out. She gave me the old,

'We're just friends' line. But then you know all about that, i.e., that thing you had with Randy way back when, before he was dead."

"Can I hit you now?"

"Nah, maybe later." Holly selects a Mandarin orange from the box on the counter and begins peeling it.

"Throw me one of those, would ya?" Natasha asks. Holly does, and Natasha catches it. "When did this start? No one said anything in the letters."

"Just after Halloween, I think. Kid is kinda cute though, hey? He's got that James Dean thing happening. I think he thinks he's too cool to smile, but I catch him sometimes, and his smile completely changes his face."

"He's okay, I guess. God, I'm famished." Natasha throws her orange peel into the waste basket below the sink, then opens the cupboard above the stove and finds a Wagon Wheel behind a box of 60-watt lightbulbs. She cracks the white wrapper and bites into it, even though the chocolate's turned white on the edges due to age. "Where's Mom and Dad?"

"Mom's in the can," Camille says, joining them in the kitchen. She picks at a corner of Christmas cake, left to dry on the counter. "Dad's still at work. Late night shopping, with the Christmas season and all." Camille examines her sister's face, the brows Jude's helped Natasha shape, and stops chewing. "Have you plucked your eyebrows?"

"Wow, you have! *That's* what's different. So, dahlink," Holly says, affecting an Eva Gabor accent, "how do you like the big city?"

"It's vunderful. It's like New York or Paris compared to

this dump. The action never stops."

"Yeah, but do you get in on any of it?" Holly winks at Camille, who laughs loudly.

She's grown, Natasha thinks. My little sister's taller than me. "That's for me to know and you never to find out. I'm going to unpack."

"Did you bring me anything?" Camille asks, trailing her up the stairs.

"Cripes, Camille. No, I did not bring you anything. Who do you think I am, Dad? I hardly have enough money to live on let alone spend any of it on junk for you."

Camille throws her hands in front of her face and steps back, but she can't hide her dejection behind the defensive comic move. "I meant for Christmas. I meant did you get me anything for Christmas?" She's a younger girl again, Natasha sees, and she wishes she hadn't been so severe. It's Dorion making her feel this way, making her lash out. Her little sister has nothing to do with it.

"I'm shopping tomorrow. And you can even come with me, pick out something you want. Okay?"

"Uh huh." Camille leaves Natasha in the stairwell with one bag in each hand. Moments later Natasha hears her launch into a stormy tarantella at the piano.

"Natasha?" Her mother's voice, behind the bathroom door.

"Knock, knock," Natasha says, standing outside.

Shirley unlocks the door. She has a terry towel turban wrapped around her head. "Hello, honey!" She squeezes Natasha's shoulders. "So good to see you!" She points at her turban. "I was hoping to be finished this before you got home. How's my college girl?"

"Fine. Tired. Remind me never to take another bus as long as I live. You look good," she says, meaning it.

Shirley pulls the towel off and touches the back of her freshly-dyed hair, lighter than it's been for years.

"Your hair!"

"You think it looks okay?"

"Yeah! A little like Shirley MacLaine or the mother on 'The Partridge Family.' Or were they the same person? Nope, I think that was Shirley Jones." She touches her mother's bangs. "Hey, we'll catch up in a minute, I just want to use the phone in your room so I can call Dorion. Okay?"

"Sure. I'll put the kettle on. I want to know everything about school and Calgary and your roommates and –"

"We've got three weeks, Mom. I don't want to get all talked out on the first night."

"Okay, but hurry. We missed you!"

"I'll hurry." In her parents' room she flops on the bed, closes the door with a foot and dials Dorion. They missed me? When did they even notice I was here, she wonders. Dorion's mother calls him to the phone.

"Guess who?" Natasha says, keeping her voice low.

"Hey, how was the trip?"

She hears it right away, a snag. "Long and boring. Are you coming over?"

"Yeah, I'll be there in about half an hour. I'm just helping Dad with the washing machine. Stupid belt slipped off."

"Is something wrong?"

"No, why?"

"You sound...different, that's all. I can't wait to see you."

"Me, too," he says, with less than half the enthusiasm she'd anticipated. Just a teaspoon. "See you soon."

Natasha finds the other Stensruds and Tom at the kitchen table, their hands wrapped around mugs of hot chocolate. A bag of pastel-coloured miniature marshmallows is spilled between them. Camille dunks one into her drink and sucks off the chocolate.

"How's Dorion?" Shirley asks.

"Kinda weird, but good, I think. He's coming over in a bit." Natasha pops a pink marshmallow into her mouth.

Holly pushes away from the table, knocking everyone's cocoa. "Oops."

"Hey!" Shirley says. "Slow down."

Holly looks at Natasha for a long moment, scrutinizing, Natasha thinks, as she did at the bus terminal. What's up with her curious sister now?

Dorion takes her to one of their favourite spots: the hill at the top of the airport road, where the bright, sweeping light keeps time in the sky and the town lights are blinks in the distance. "So who was it?"

He's crouched against his door, smoking. "Tash, it doesn't matter."

"No, I want to know. At least give me that much."

"Debbie. Debbie Fowler."

"Bastard!" She grabs handfuls of his hair and smashes

his head against the window, the steering wheel. "Bastard...you fucking bastard!" Over and over she screams and smashes him and he lets her do this. He doesn't even protect his head.

In the week that follows she feels herself wilting.

It was a merry fucking Christmas, she writes in her journal. The whole thing leaves her totally dry, like the skull of an animal bleached by the sun. She buys a bus ticket back to Calgary four days earlier than planned, then cancels it and drives.

West of Medicine Hat she gets trapped in a wolf pack of vehicles travelling below the speed limit and she hovers precariously close to sleep. The sky is a bowl of grey milk. The car's heater is at full blast, and no radio now. Just highway sounds, wind where it leaks in the back window. The imperfections of the road beneath the wheels.

A stomach growls, long and low. Then Natasha's answers, like an echo. Nobody laughs.

"The police must be on it by now," Gina says. "Do you think we'll be on tv?"

"Our pictures, maybe." Kent bumps Natasha's knee again, but she knows it's just the motion of the semi. "They'll probably use our school pictures."

"Oh God, not that!" Holly cries. "I hate it! My hair was screwed-up and I looked like a freak."

A freak. Just last week their father was watching the news and had commented on how the world was full of them. Natasha makes a mental list of ways she will improve the world, or at least the tiny planet of their home, when the truck driver returns her to it. She will tell her mother something that will make her happy. She will tell Shirley that her classmates think she's pretty. They do. She is.

Are they speeding up again?

"Christ, I've got to whiz," Rosco says.

"Do you have to do that? Do you have to always take the Lord's name in vain?" Gina asks. "I've got to pee, too. I can't hold it anymore. I'm going to have to go." She stands up and rubs her knees. "Holly, come with me."

"What? Where are you going?"

"Back there," she points to a corner. "On the floor."

"It's going to stink," Rosco says.

"Gross me out," Holly says loudly, but she gets up with her friend and soon they hear the water tap sound of Gina releasing her bladder, but nobody looks and it's too dark to see anyway. And nobody laughs. And nobody teases or makes any sound at all when the girls return to the circle and Gina rests her head in her hands and bawls.

Second-term classes are not going well. It's too much, juggling this new life and all its possibilities, these new people, the daytime hours filled with lectures and poorly hand-written notes on the board, the life with Dorion behind her now but not erased, and that other, beastly world of darkly dreamt hours that leaves her damp and mumbling – something about the highway – in the morning light.

Natasha drops philosophy and geography and finds herself with three free afternoons a week. Her naps stretch out, her nights get later. Jude introduces her to friends from High River. They go drinking in bars that play heavily on Calgary's cowboy persona through western decor and drink specials like the "Tequila Two-step" and "Bronc Buster." She gets sick in a public washroom while Jude holds her hair away from her face. The men Jude calls friends drive 4 x 4 trucks. Natasha squishes in to sit on someone's lap and thinks, momentarily, that this is where she needs to be. No one's attached to anyone else. They all make the rounds, though Natasha slips through the loose net of arms and legs weekend after weekend without getting snagged.

One Sunday morning Natasha passes Jude's room enroute to the bathroom and spies a man's naked ass in the tangle of Jude's sheets and a hairy leg slapped across Jude's waxed thigh. It's more than she needs to see, but she doesn't close the door. Maybe Cherise will see it, too.

Kelly takes a part-time job at a furniture store and when another opening arises, Natasha – who still feels a charlatan in her classes and a visitor in the city – is there with her resumé.

"Have you ever worked in commission sales?" the razor-haired woman in Human Resources asks, splaying her hands across Natasha's resumé. Her androgynous glasses have slipped to the end of her nose. Natasha would like to reach across and push them up, or pull them off altogether.

"Well, no. But my father manages a chain of stores in

Saskatchewan and I worked for him in different departments when I was in high school." She points to the items on her resumé. "I know how to sell."

"And what about interests? It says here that you like travel, astronomy, swimming, and East Indian cooking. That's an interesting combination."

"I guess." Travel, if you counted the family camping disasters where Peter could never relax. Too many ants, mosquitoes, black flies, moths; too much sun; not enough sun; too many obnoxious people on the beach; too long a wait at the golf course where they charged too much for a round; too much horsing around with the campfire; too many campers playing loud music in the sites next to theirs; and too many babies bawling anywhere they went. There was trouble with the hitch and the propane stove exploded. The outhouses were hideous and the girls got too hyper. Bears were an ongoing threat and rain was a death sentence. The astronomy was her short flight across the night sky with David. Swimming? Well, she did have her Intermediate badge from the Red Cross and she had enjoyed the cold shock of Waskesiu Lake on a day when the sand was too hot for human skin. East Indian cooking was Jude's idea. "You've got to appear well-rounded. Well, you know what I mean," she'd said.

"And what would you consider your major faults?"

"Well, I work too hard. My co-workers were always telling me to slow down, but I don't know. I couldn't. I've got business in my blood. Comes with being a manager's daughter, I guess." How unusual. There's not even a seed of fear in her voice.

She's hired, but it's someone else who drags her bones to the store and attempts to sell smoked-glass, gold-chrome, and wood veneer furniture on commission, another young woman who listens to lectures and studies for exams because she's promised her mother she'll try to salvage what's left of her year. Neither venture is what even the most ardent optimist would term a success. Natasha's name will not grace the dean's list and she'll never get the "Employee of the Month" award. Ever.

In March there is a barrage of phone calls from home. Holly wanting her measurements, her shoe size, her opinion on hymns for the wedding. "Like I would know, or care?" Natasha tells Shirley. "Why doesn't she ask you?"

"You're her closest sister. She wants everything perfect, and she doesn't want it to come down to the final hour without you having been involved at all. Plus –"

"Plus what?"

"She doesn't want you and Camille snickering about her choices behind her back."

"No need to worry about that. I'll snicker to her face."

As her sister's wedding creeps closer, Natasha's increasingly thankful for the provincial border between them. "Spared making those stupid Kleenex carnations," she tells sisterless Jude.

"Matrimonial traditions are a gas," Jude says. "You should be elated...I would be."

"Would not."

They're in Jude's room, sharing a bag of chips on her bed and not minding where the crumbs fall. They can hear Cherise typing through the wall, and the tap of a knife in the kitchen where Kelly's slicing vegetables for a stir-fry. Jude crunches through another handful of chips. "Did Cherise ask you to go to the forum?"

"What forum?"

"Some chastity thing put on by the campus Bible thumpers."

"No, thank you God!"

"I guess she knows you're a lost cause."

"Me! What about you?" Natasha pushes Jude, who falls back on her pillow. "I bet you've slept with more guys than you can count on two hands." Natasha reaches over to Jude's desk for a pen and paper. "Here you go."

"What am I supposed to do with this?"

"Make a list."

"Get out."

Natasha puts the pen in Jude's hand. "Go on. Let's see if you can do it. And I don't just want names. You get bonus points if you can write one memorable thing about each guy."

"You want the details?"

"Not necessarily sexual. A middle name, maybe. Where so and so was born. Just something to prove each stud was more than a piece of meat. I'll give you a dollar for every name and another for every detail. The only rule: you have to tell the truth."

Jude smiles. "You're on." At the top of the page she writes: *Allan. Liked to tongue my ears.*

Natasha leans over the page. "That's good. Keep going."

Allen. Wrecked three condoms before he finally got one on right.

"Two guys with the same name?"

Jude picks up the pen again. "Just wait 'til I get to the T's."

"Incredible. You're going alphabetically."

Billy. Liked wrestling, semi-professionally and in bed.

An hour later Natasha hands fifty-six dollars of her store-earned commission over to Jude. In her journal she writes that it was worth every cent.

An "A" on a term paper. She calls Shirley collect.

"So things are looking up?"

"It's just one mark. Don't get your heart rate up."

"But you're going back next year, right?"

"I don't know yet. Maybe. We'll see how I feel in a few months." She lights a cigarette. "So two weeks until D-Day. How's the mother of the bride?" She's skirting. She's already decided, or, rather, it's already been determined that this, too, is not where she belongs: with the chinook winds, the panhandlers on Eighth Avenue, the prostitutes and businessmen and a dozen radio stations on the dial. She's waiting for it to end. She's enduring.

"I'm fine, but your father's a little off kilter. I think it's the expense of it all, mostly. Three hundred dollars to have some friends of Everett's play two guitars and an accordion at the dance? I mean, come on. And of course there's the decorations, the reception, the booze. And Holly's making these little candle things, with lavender lace wrapped around them, and these tiny gold bells she found at the craft store. Did I say *Holly's* making them? I meant *we, we* are making them. All that work for a memento that'll be lost or forgotten before the weekend is over."

"Before the *night* is over," Natasha corrects.

"And you know how I hate handiwork."

Natasha's heart is as light as a birthday balloon; her mother, absolutely, positively, one hundred percent back from the Twilight Zone. "I remember. You'd buy me a new winter coat before you'd replace a zipper."

"That's not true!"

"The red velvet coat with white, fake fur cuffs. I loved that thing, and you passed it off to Good Will just because of the holes in the pockets."

"You kept losing things."

"Used Kleenex, a few nickels and dimes, lint-covered candies."

"Oh well. It is nice to see Holly happy. I mean, she deserves happiness, if anyone does."

Natasha counts three Mississippis of silence after her mother's sigh. Why does Holly deserve happiness more than her, more than anyone? "Because of all those years of squabbling with Rosco. The migraines. Is that what you mean?"

"Yes, all of that." Shirley clears her throat. "I've got to run, kiddo. I've got Davie coming up the sidewalk for his two o'clock. I wish his mother would just pull him from lessons. He obviously hates piano. He never practices and

I swear he's allergic to rhythm. Oh well."

"Talk to you later –"

"Yeah. Wait! Tash? How are you sleeping, honey?"

"So-so."

"Well don't be afraid to take a sleeping pill every now and then. You won't get hooked."

"Geez, Mom, really? I'm kidding. I know. Say hi to everyone for me, okay?"

"I will. See you in a few weeks."

"A few weeks it is."

After she has an argument with an Australian couple about the quality of the chocolate leather couch, after she finds a parking ticket tucked beneath her windshield wiper, after she gets held up in Friday traffic on 16th Avenue and then learns that the elevator in the residence is under repair, she tramps into the apartment with all the weight of her day to find Cherise a virtual zombie with her eyes on the bare wall. A female police officer is there, too. Jude has the teapot in her hands, but it's Natasha who lifts the singing kettle off the burner.

"Hey, what's up?"

"Are you the other roommate?" The officer's heavy around the hips. Her uniform is not flattering.

"One of the other ones. I'm Natasha Stensrud." She doesn't know whether she should extend her hand or raise both arms stick-em-up style for some crime she may have subconsciously committed. Cherise is still as a statue on the couch. "What happened?"

"Your roommate, Cherise, was walking home from the campus library and she was sexually harassed."

"By a flasher!" Jude rasps. "He was jerking off!"

Natasha feels her hand fly to her mouth. She feels like she is falling, tumbling down a dark tunnel. She knows there is more to ask, that the answer might be devastating. "Did he...did he do anything else?"

"No," the officer says, looking at the pages on her clipboard, "not as far as I can make out. She's not revealing much. Maybe you can help."

Natasha shakes her head. "No, I don't think so. She doesn't talk much at the best of times." It feels strange to be speaking about Cherise as if she's not just ten feet away. She lowers her voice. "I-I don't really know her that well." *But I've been wishing something like this on her. Just because. My God, I'm a witch!*

"I was the one who called it in," Jude says, handing Natasha a mug. Natasha takes it with trembling fingers and sips. Her friend has forgotten the sugar. "She could hardly spit out a word, and she was white as a sheet. Said some guy showed her his 'private parts.' Poor kid."

"She's older than you," Natasha whispers. "So what happens now?" she asks the officer. "Will you ever find the guy?"

The officer shrugs. "Not without some help here. Tall, with dark hair and plastic-framed glasses. That's not much to go on. The only other hope is that he's done this to someone else and the girls can ID him together." The officer walks back to the couch and squats in front of Cherise.

Natasha feels weak. She falls into one of the straight-backed chairs at the table. "A repeat offender," she mouths. "That's her *hope?* And what kind of description is that. My God, Jude, that could be my dad."

Jude remembers sugar and stirs some into Natasha's cup. "Never met a man yet who wasn't an exhibitionist. They all leave the door open when they pee."

"Not all," Natasha corrects. "Dorion didn't."

The countdown is on. In ten days she'll drive back to Saskatchewan and stand — bedecked in lavender, awash in flowers, wobbly on her heels — beside her sister in the United Church.

Today's a workday. She calls in sick, pours a glass of orange juice and skims the *Calgary Herald,* deliberately neglecting articles with doom in the headline. She unscrambles the word puzzle and reads the Pets column before reluctantly returning to her essay on regional poets. Four hours later, she's slogged two pages closer to her conclusion.

The room is stifling; a Hollywood car chase rages in the space between her temples. So this is how it is for Holly, she thinks, massaging the stabbing pain. She opens the window and hopes inspiration will ride in on the night. Instead, the muted music from the campus pub is ushered in on a breeze. TGIF. Thank God it's Friday. She closes her eyes. Someone's singing about love, an emotion she vaguely recalls, like one remembers a vacation taken long ago in a foreign land. Everything's different, if not new, and half the time you suspect you're not even really there.

Translation is slow, and usually too late. She conjures Dorion smiling at her across two rows of desks with his out-of-season tan; waltzing at the grad dance in his tight shoes while her parents looked on; his warm mouth on her neck; the blades of his shoulders; the way he looked softer, vulnerable after sex; his lips slightly parted in sleep. How long did it take him to betray me? she wonders. Hours, days, a few weeks?

She doesn't pick up until the fifth ring.

"They were drinking," Shirley says, in her housecoat, light-years away. "I hope you're sitting down."

"I'm sitting," Natasha says. She takes a deep breath.

"Turner died instantly and probably felt no pain." Shirley's voice softens. "Dorion shot through the windshield. He'll live."

"Oh." A word so small it barely travels through the lines.

Shirley continues. "You know what those lake roads are like after a good shower. He's lucky."

She doesn't know how to feel. First the separation, his infidelity, now this. There's nothing to say.

"Tash...are you okay? I mean —"

Natasha knows what she means. It's about death, stalking once again. "I will be." She pictures her mother, her mouth shaping sympathetic words into the black wall-phone while ashes fall onto her housecoat. She says goodbye and returns to her room, creeping past the smell of department store perfume at Jude's door.

She's drawn to her window and beyond, to the mist

that hangs over the city like a shroud. The architecture of browns and greys and the budding trees below merge into a Monet canvas. She stares until she sees nothing, like Laurence's stone angel staring over Manawaka from her towering graveyard position. Everything washes away as if it were chalk art in a relentless rain. Only sound remains. A single voice that hammers against the drums of her ears. It's Camille, before there was a Tom, that summer of the end of innocence. "Boy, this is fun. Boy, this is fun."

Gina's *body-wracking wails quiet to sobs, then hiccups, then a few thin sobs and she is done.*

Kent surprises them. "Maybe we should pray."

"What?" Rosco asks. He, too, has not been able to hold it and has taken his turn in the corner.

"Maybe we should pray." Kent fingers his Saint Christopher's medal. "It can't hurt."

"Okay, Catholic boy, pray away, as long as you do it in your head."

"Rosco, do you have to be such a jerk?" Holly asks.

Only then does Natasha recall that Kent attends the separate school and comes from a whopping family of Catholics. They even have their own softball team, comprised solely of cousins and uncles. She can't imagine it.

It seems to her that many of those sprawling, Catholic families have a distinctive look, so that even without names, one can glance the shadows beneath the eyes or the shape of a jaw and say, "That's a Gerard," or "There goes another Maloney. Is that number eight or nine?"

"My turn now," Kent says. He wobbles when he stands, and puts his hand briefly on Natasha's head to balance himself.

"What are you thinking about?" Holly asks her as Kent's stream hits the floor in the corner.

Natasha is embarrassed for him. "Catholics. Actually I was thinking about the Gerards. And the Maloneys. I always see them hanging around the war memorials in the Elks Park. Saw them there last night."

"Bunch of jerks," Rosco says.

"God, you never cross the Elks Park at night, do you?" Holly asks.

Natasha doesn't. "Sometimes. Why?"

"It's...it might not be safe."

"Why?" She thinks she knows what her sister's implying, but wants to give her a run.

"God, you're ignorant," Holly whispers. "They're... you know —"

"Catholic?" She keeps her voice down, but Kent is still in the corner. He really had to go, she thinks.

Holly rolls her eyes. Natasha can see the whites of them, but not much more. "Horny."

The final English essay is scrapped. The year itself is packed into boxes, her dorm key turned in.

"You're quitting? Now?" Jude watches Natasha pull sweaters and jeans from the dresser drawers and stuff them into a box with the blow dryer, sheets, the toaster, an iron she rarely used. "But school's almost finished, Tash. We've got a measly month and a half. You'll lose all your credits."

"Is that genuine concern about something as mundane as school? What about 'You only live once'?" She wraps tea towels around four tall glasses and sets the bundle on top of a box already too heavy for her arms.

"I'm serious. Don't throw this year away." The sky, a gloomy palette of bluish clouds for a second day now, seeps into Jude's voice. "Is it this place? You and I can get an apartment together." She lifts her feet when Natasha tugs at the nightgown beneath them. "We don't have to live on campus."

"It wouldn't work, Jude. I'm going back."

"To what? That asshole boyfriend who's doing the class slut? Your family? Come on, you said yourself that you and I are more like sisters than you and your real sisters are. Why are you doing this? Shit, I haven't even taught you to ski yet!"

She wishes she could explain, or that someone would explain it to her, speaking slowly, carefully, the way those who don't know better speak to the deaf. It has to do with history somehow, with what's been left unsaid. There are holes everywhere. How can she possibly move forward when she doesn't know where she's been? At least once a week she gets a glimpse of the mirage. All these years, swimming against the current of her dreams. No more.

"One last look at the mountains," she says, leaning out her car window at the moment of their final goodbye. "I'll write."

Jude squeezes her hand. "You better."

Hollywood Legs

But no doors open. No light leaks through the windows when she circles home like the runaway who slinks in the back only to realize no one's noticed her missing. No one explains the cryptic night travels, the peaks and valleys of her emotions. Shirley's evasive, Holly hides behind her headaches, and Peter, even when he is home, is away. Natasha's whisked out of her teens on a carpet of not-knowing.

Two-and-a-half years are swallowed by time, two-and-a-half years without sex or even holding anyone's hand in a movie theatre. Six months of unemployment. Seven episodes of watching Dorion and Debbie parade down Main with Nikki and Nigel, their twins. One nasty case of tonsillitis. A complex ovarian cyst. A sprained ankle. Two consecutive bad jobs – laundry duty at an old folks' home and tending bar at the golf course clubhouse. John Lennon's death.

She's twenty-one and coming to grips with the fact that she'll never be an interior designer or a psychiatric nurse working with the criminally insane or a private investigator or Jodie Foster's best friend. Twenty-one and terminally desolate, while her mother is forty-four and finding herself.

Natasha blames Mrs. Podhorovski from home ec for putting the home-decorating seed in her head, and she blames her father for everything else. If living at home isn't enough to test what's left of that worn-out dress – her spirit – she's now facing the deathly prospect of working in one of his stores again. She favours the lumberyard, because of the sawdust smells and because she appreciates men like Dorion, and even David, who were handy, but the choice isn't hers to make.

"You can work in groceries," Peter says. He talks and chews simultaneously, then washes his words down with milk.

"Swallow your food, then drink," Natasha says. "God, that is *so* disgusting." They bully each other, nightly, over beef and turkey TV dinners. Neither of them has learned to cook, home economics or not, and Camille spends more time at Tom's than at home.

Holly, a Lundquist now, is still sore at Peter for getting up on stage at the wedding dance and doing his soft-shoe routine. At the reception Everett blundered through the typical drunk and inarticulate thank you to Peter and Shirley, "For raising such a great daughter."

The Stensruds agree he's a decent enough guy, if a bit of a Clydesdale. Across the dance floor his family sized them up, too. They're Norwegian, at least, so Holly can't be too far wrong, though they'd wished for a Lutheran wedding. Everett's blonde, blue-eyed sisters tossed blessings like confetti on the steps of the United Church, hoping for lots of blonde, blue-eyed children to call them Auntie.

Holly's learned to make lefsa and a sugary pastry called rosettes. She's deliriously pregnant. She calls Natasha frequently from her home in Marvin, where Everett's a busy electrician with two men beneath him. "What do you think of Lief for a name, if it's a boy of course?" Natasha hears crochet needles clicking. "Or Svend."

"You'd call your kid Svend?"

"So you don't like it then."

"I just think you're getting a little carried away with this Norwegian thing, Holl. It's not like we're even third generation. What's the big deal?"

"It's important to Everett."

There's nothing more to say. Holly's hypersensitive where Everett's concerned. She resents Camille and Natasha because they aren't wildly ecstatic about their new brother-in-law. He has lovely long eyelashes, but the memory's fresh: Natasha had to work up to touching him in the receiving line.

Peter washes down another forkful of tinny peas. "Well, do you want the job or not?"

"I hate that store. No offence, but I hated working there in high school and I'll hate it more now."

Her father chases a sliver of roast beef around the foil. "At least it's a job." His voice is a mosquito at midnight. Buzzing and pissing her off.

"Did you know," she begins, ready for battle, "that

when I started I couldn't figure out the produce scale so I used to make prices up?"

"I don't want to know this –"

"Three-fifty for a bunch of bananas. A buck for a head of lettuce. I never knew how far off I really was, but no one ever complained."

"Do you think you can figure it out now?" Peter pushes his chair away from the table, an old gesture that used to mean he was off and running to the first of his nightly commitments but now establishes another kind of distance. He's down to old-timers' hockey and the Credit Union board. He looks tired, and, since Shirley's left for university, battered.

Shirley's apartment in Saskatoon is five blocks from the university, with low lighting and lots of dusty ferns. Natasha thinks it's funky. Her mother's taking first-year arts classes and she drives home every other weekend. All this school business has, as far as anyone knows, erupted within one volcanic year. Prior to this it had always been the piano, those eighty-eight keys, that safe ivory. The metronome counting her through Holly's headaches and brooding, Peter's times away. She was a good teacher, with several students. One of the Sperling girls – Natasha'd babysat her and now she was all grown up herself – had taken lessons from Shirley and told Natasha, from behind the till in the Saan store, that Shirley'd been an inspiration. Natasha wouldn't have guessed.

Her mother is home on one of her weekends. Natasha's

thankful that she still cooks, but where before she'd scramble to clear the table as soon as they'd finished eating, she now moons over tea while food particles barnacle onto plates. The bathroom sink becomes a wasteland for Peter's whiskers, slugs of old toothpaste and the small blue coins of soap that get trapped in the drain. The vacuuming, general room-to-room straightening and laundering of Peter's dress shirts fall upon Natasha. Even when Shirley *is* home.

There are other changes, too. Shirley had never given her appearance much thought, often wearing Peter's dowdy cardigans or thin brown socks, so when she returns from Saskatoon in a new jumpsuit with a red scarf draped artistically around her neck, her lips glossed pink and eyes like skylights opened wide with mascara, Natasha smells something rotten.

She comes across her mother packing for another two weeks away. Several colourful islands of clothes sit on the bed's white comforter. She folds each article before setting it in the suitcase and smoothing it with her long fingers. Her back's toward Natasha, who watches for a few moments from the doorway. Something black shimmers in Shirley's hand.

"What's that?" Natasha plops onto the bed. The suitcase hops and her mother does a half-turn toward her, as though her neck's stiff.

"Panties." She holds them up. Bikinis with a tiny black bow sewn onto the waistband, front and centre. "Like them?"

"Nice." Natasha flips through the wrinkled pages of a *Time* magazine, glossing over an article on the world's

first test-tube baby. The issue's several years old. *Very* nice.
"So...how's school going?"

Shirley shrugs. "I study a lot. At my age everything takes twice as long to sink in."

"You're not that old."

Shirley seems not to have heard her daughter, because when Natasha looks up from Louise Brown's photo her mother's already left, her feet dancing down the hall.

Moving back was meant to be a bridge, but the weeks caterpillared into months, months metamorphosed into years. This is how you get old, Natasha thinks. The basement, once her launching pad to mythical worlds, has become another rug to vacuum. The place beneath the stairs a campground for cardboard boxes and old sheet music, the musical accoutrements her mother received from students at Christmas and never had a spot or desire for. Natasha feels the life being sucked right out of her. There are moments when she still believes there's a place for her somewhere in the world, she just doesn't know where to start looking, which rock to turn over.

She dials Holly. "I loathe living with Dad. He doesn't even realize when he farts! And the store is sheer drudgery."

"It can't be that bad. And the price is certainly right. Wait until you have a mortgage, and groceries to buy, and —"

"You remember what it's like...the boss's kid has to work twice as hard as anyone else. The other employees talk behind your back. And that blue fortrel uniform. I feel like a target wearing it, like a sniper's going to pick me off from the top of the cookie shelves. And don't even get me started on those nurses' shoes we have to wear. White soles. Oh, my God. You know what I hope for? A holdup. Some guy in a balaclava to come in and –"

" – we paid four hundred dollars to get our furnace fixed. You can't even imagine…what's a balaclava?"

" – the customers really piss me off. The other day I snapped at Mrs. Gillespie because she didn't put her grapes in a bag. Sweet Jesus. Mrs. Gillespie!"

"Of course when the baby comes there'll be diapers and food. I'm thinking about going disposable. We got the crib and stroller from Everett's sister, but we'll have to buy a highchair and dresser. Say, you don't know of anyone who's got a playpen they're not using, do you?"

"But it's not like I have a lot of options at the moment. The metropolitan persona didn't fit. I was lost in the street lights and sirens, and my heart was never in selling beds, although I guess it was as close as I'll ever get to a career in interior decorating."

"Tash? You never answered me. A playpen. Do you have any friends who might want to sell one?"

Friends? She's trying. She's made attempts to see Madge and other former classmates, but all those swears they'd shared on the school lawn at graduation – I swear to stay in touch, I swear not to forget you, etc. – haven't held. Many of her old schoolmates are already mothers. Even Jude, still in Calgary, is expecting soon, and she gets her share of *those* conversations with Holly, whose gaga land she can only tolerate at intervals.

Camille and Tom are hot and heavy in their final year of high school. "I can't believe what that girl gets away with. You never let Holly or me stay out all night," Natasha says, accusatory eyes aimed at a small tear in Peter's white undershirt. He's eating Bran Flakes. Then he'll have two slices of toast with raspberry jam, a cup of coffee with milk, and a quartered orange. Nothing changes. The sticky mess around the top of the jam jar where he scrapes his knife, despite her threats, reappears each day. "It's not bloody fair." She wonders, briefly, what day it is. One morning seems to bleed into the next and she never really knows.

Peter slurps another spoonful of milky cereal. He's reading the newspaper and has slopped Bran Flakes on one corner. Dolly Parton's warbling through the transistor radio, the music far too loud and lively for the hour and the audience. "What?" He continues reading.

"Camille. She gets away with everything." Natasha scratches her scalp. Her hair's an angry snarl to her shoulders. She'll slap it down with water just before she leaves for work. She doesn't care about impressing the meat manager now.

Peter pouts at Natasha over the paper. "She doesn't attack me every chance she gets."

It's an old argument that's run out of steam. Camille is going to graduate with honours and a music bursary. She also works, in the pharmacy, where Natasha served her time years before. The leering pharmacist's gone and Camille claims to like her job. She also has four young piano students. They adore her.

One Sunday afternoon after another Saturday of late night movies and over-salted popcorn, Natasha corners her mother in the bathroom. Shirley's preparing for another departure. She's curling her hair.

"I was thinking about moving to the city," Natasha says, testing.

"Mmmm."

"If I do, could I stay with you for awhile?"

Shirley clips two white hoops onto her ears. "I thought you hated city life."

"Bad timing, I guess. It could be different this time. Saskatoon's smaller, closer. I'd know people. I could get a better job."

Her mother unplugs her curling iron and coils the cord. She's taken to wearing sweaters that accentuate her bust, this one a peach colour cut low and wide enough so that her collarbones are revealed. Forty-five now. A college student. Looking better than ever, Natasha thinks. "So...could I stay with you?"

Shirley hesitates, as though she's catching her breath or her nerve. "I hope you don't mind, Tash, but I'd really rather be alone."

"Just a few weeks? Until I find a job and get my own place?" She closes the toilet lid and sits.

Shirley's sigh is a descending scale. "You can't keep bouncing back and forth between your father and me. You're twenty-one —"

"Twenty-two. Last month."

"Right. Anyway, you know what I'm saying. It's time you found your own way. Do something with your life. You're making money, why not save and take a trip?"

"I don't want to go anywhere." Not quite true. The idea of a long vacation to an exotic locale interests her; it's having no one she likes well enough to go along that's depressing, and she's lost the part of her that could move to Calgary alone.

Shirley seems to read her mind. "You and Camille could have a great time together."

"I'm not going on any trip, with anyone." The toilet paper roll's empty but she doesn't fill it. The toilet likely needs a good scrubbing, too, but she can't keep up with all of it. There's too much.

"Okay Miss Woe-Is-Me."

"Oh, please."

"Someday you're going to look back on your life and you'll see this grey area of wasted time." Shirley gathers her makeup and earrings and scoops them into her cosmetic bag. "You'll think about it when you have a million things to do and no time and would do anything to have this precious time back." She opens and closes a few drawers. "Have you seen my toothpaste?"

"Look under that towel in the corner." Who'd know better about wasting time, Natasha thinks, vaguely recalling the ghostly period where, save teaching and making hot dog, hamburger, or spaghetti-from-a-can meals, her mother was little more than a lump in a bed. "Is that what happened to you?"

"What?"

"You know, you started running out of time."

"I just know how precious time is. I don't want to

waste a minute of it." Shirley lines her brush with tooth-paste.

"So you move to the city and take arts and sciences. And you're fulfilled."

"You don't understand."

"Hey, I'm proud of you, remember? I was the daughter who was behind you all the way."

Shirley removes the toothbrush, her mouth full of paste. "You don't sound behind me all the way."

"I'm just down."

Shirley spits and rinses twice, then pats her pretty mouth with a face cloth. She steps toward Natasha, gently squeezes her shoulders and kisses her forehead, something she hasn't done since Natasha was a child. "Your ship, my dear, will come in. Trust me."

"*You drove her* to it, Dad." Peter's just returned from a meeting and has found Natasha, as usual, watching television in what was formerly the piano room. Shirley's grand has been moved into the living room, where it sits like a ship on dry land when Camille's not teaching students that every good boy deserves fudge. No one else touches it.

"I never drove her to anything. She wanted to go to school. What could I do or say to change that?" He cracks open a beer and sits, heavily, on the opposite end of the couch. The theme from "Hawaii 5-0" blares against the winter walls. "Where's Camille?"

"With Tom," Natasha says, "where else? There's

another beer in the fridge, if you want one."

"No thanks."

Natasha plans her next attack while an embezzler leaps from a speeding car with a suitcase full of crisp cash. "If you hadn't been so...stereotypical, she wouldn't have felt compelled to leave." It's the first time she's put it this way. It's always been a going away before, not a leaving.

"Your mother's never been satisfied with anything. She always wants more but doesn't know what." Peter talks without losing the thread of the televised crime.

Natasha listens with her eyes on the same program, head and heart far from Honolulu. "What do you mean she's not satisfied?" She doesn't swallow this. On the contrary, she's always felt her mother was the picture of contentment, teaching all day, spending her downtime in quiet ways. Long hours over coffee and dainties with her closest friends. "This family is so screwed-up I can't stand it." She reaches over and turns the television volume down. "What I want to know is why?"

"Turn that back up," he says, punching out each word.

She leaves it. "Take last Christmas."

"What about it?" Peter's peeling off his socks.

"Ever since I can remember, Mom's prepared a huge meal...turkey and the works. Okay, she never gets the gravy right, but at least she tries. You eat, then hit the couch. You're snoring before we've even got the table cleared."

"What has that got to do with your mother going to university?" He rests his long, white feet on the coffee table. His yellow nails need clipping. Natasha tries not to look at them.

"Everything. Don't you see?" She throws her hands in

the air. Too much television; she's more melodramatic than usual. "Women aren't falling for that cult-of-domesticity shit any more."

"I can't figure you out," Peter says. "Who are you mad at?"

There's a commercial break. They could get to the guts of this now, but the possibility terrifies her. Three minutes. Three minutes to dig back through the bones of the years to see what skeletons dwell there. During the car ads, the beer commercials, he could answer her questions. Everything could change, starting now, if only she could leap, if only she knew this man, if only the right words would calmly come. "What happened to Mom before you guys left for the Maritimes? Something happened, I know it did. She was a basket case."

"She was sick."

Further, she dares herself. "I found tranquilizers in her jewellry box. Hundreds of them."

"It was a long time ago." Peter doesn't flinch.

"Talk to me, damn it!" She jumps to block the television. "Why does Holly have headaches that'd knock an elephant to its knees? Why've I been having nightmares for as long as I can remember? At thirteen I was popping sleeping pills like others kids popped candy hearts! Tell me, Dad. Is that normal?"

He steadies his eyes on her and in the parenthetical lines around the odd angle of his mouth she sees a stew of bewilderment and sorrow, but nothing slips through. "I don't know."

"You're lying! Something's wrong, something's always

been wrong and we just go on pretending that we're okay, that Mom was okay when she killed every goddamn plant in the house and Holly was just fine when she beat the living shit out of that girl in high school. Was that okay, Dad? Was that *all* okay? Or how about the fact that I've crept through my whole life not knowing why the hell I'm such a mess?"

A pounding. Natasha's surprised that it's not in her head; Peter hears it, too. "The door," he says. He slides her out of the way like she's catatonic or one of the pointy-boobed mannequins in the clothing department of his store.

Natasha slumps onto the couch. Fuck it all. Her three minutes are up.

"What was all that shouting about?" It's only Camille, kicking off one leather ankle boot, then the other. "You guys locked me out. I was knocking on the door for ten minutes!"

Peter hasn't returned.

"Do *you* know?" Natasha asks.

"Know what?" Camille shrugs out of her thick sweater to a black turtleneck underneath. "What's happening?"

"This family is completely fucked. Nobody talks. We creep around like there's a baby sleeping in the room down the hall and God help us if we wake that baby up. There's...I don't know...a hole somewhere."

Camille crosses her legs on the coffee table. "You were fighting with Dad."

"Perpetually, but I'm talking about our whole lives, yours and Mom's and Holly's, too. They're hiding, Camille. I know it. I walk in on Mom and Holly sometimes and they shut right up." *Listen* to me!

"Tash, I hate to break it to you, but this is normal. *We're* normal. Every family is screwed. Why can't you just let things be uncomfortable. You're always digging and prying into everything. God. We're not that deep!"

Peter creeps back into the room with a bowl of cashews. He holds them out to Natasha like a peace offering. "Wonder what Mom's doing right now."

He has no idea, Natasha thinks, and she'll be damned if she's going to tell him. "I'm going to bed." She leaves Peter and Camille in the blue television light with Dano and a Taiwanese drug dealer. In the hall she turns up the thermostat. The furnace protests, but soon the comforting sense and sound of hot air pulsing through the register hums her to sleep.

Like a mother.

Like the highway.

She resorts to one of her old tricks. She'll count to three hundred, slowly, with Mississippis in between, and when she's finished they'll be safely back home. When that mark doesn't work she makes it four hundred. Then a long, drawn out seven hundred and fifty. Another two hundred, with double Mississippis and the alphabet between each number. She keeps losing track and starting again from scratch.

Gina begins to whimper again, which sets Holly off.

Natasha can't help herself in the tight darkness of the travelling room. She lets it all go. It's happened before. That bizarre time at Bible camp after a born-again counsellor's campfire testimonial. Slowly, after the revelations, a presence they believed to be the Holy Spirit moved through each of them and the circle of kids sobbed, hugged, and praised the Lord in eerie unison. But this time there's no joy. Natasha squeezes her eyes so she can't see, can only hear Kent's weeping, accompanied by deep, sucking breaths, and Rosco's awful whimpers punctuated with long sniffs and curses.

Look what I've brought on, Natasha thinks, with my lust for true adventure. Maybe with my lust, period. Five young lives might be lost and no one will ever find us.

Suddenly there's a swerve in her thinking. Maybe the trucker isn't even human. Really, she hadn't had a good look at his eyes. Maybe they've boarded some kind of UFO and are being shuttled off to the Twilight Zone. Her arms and neck prickle. Then she remembers that this is what she's always wanted. The great truths revealed.

In the same year that Camille heads to Montana for an abortion, Holly's pride and joy turns one. Shirley misses the abortion but makes her grandson's birthday, although each member of the family thinks she'd rather be elsewhere. It's too cold and wet to sit in the backyard, but the late September air is sticky in the house and they feel trapped by it. Their words get stuck. It's Shirley's idea to take the festivities outdoors where nature helps obscure the long silences.

Everyone's home for the party. Camille and Tom slouch in lawn chairs, a respectable distance from the picnic table and the rest of the Stensruds. They're living together in a trailer park. Common law, Shirley says.

Shacked up, according to Peter. Tom smokes incessantly. As soon as he finishes one beer he gets another from the Coleman cooler in the grass. Beside him, Camille chews on a strand of long hair and reads a paperback. She drops it twice.

Everett, Holly, and Shirley toss a ball to Nels. The birthday boy is magnificent in a pastel green sweater and matching cap. Natasha snaps pictures. Peter's taking an incredibly long time to bring out the cake.

"Camille, go check on your father," Shirley directs. Camille sets her book face down on the lawn chair. Natasha watches her sliver-thin shape disappear into the house. She's lost weight since the abortion, and hadn't had much to spare before it. She's quit teaching. Even her own hands seldom find the notes these days.

Nels loses interest in the ball toss. "Come to Auntie," Natasha says, coaxing him to sidestep around the picnic table. "Tell Auntie what a kitty says." He sucks on his pudgy fingers and ignores her. "Meow," she tries, "meow."

"I don't know why he won't answer," Holly says, defending her blessed boy. "He talks a mile a minute at home."

"They're always like that," Shirley says. She's doing something different with her hair again. Frosting it. "You guys were like that."

"You can't tell me you remember," Holly says. She unsnaps her jeans beneath her bunny hug and loses some of the pinch between her eyes.

Natasha feels they're talking to the ghost of their mother.

"Sure I do." Shirley smooths Nels' wild blonde hair.

"Who's Grandma's boy?"

Footsteps rustle in the dry, amber leaves behind them. "Mom." Camille rests one white hand on Shirley's shoulder. "Something's wrong with Dad."

Shirley bolts for the house; Camille stands there, trembling, her dark hair falling forward over one wet, green eye.

"My God," Natasha says, shivering. "What's wrong?"

"His face – I think he's having a stroke." Camille starts to cry, and then Tom's there, holding her and rubbing slow circles on the bony middle of her back.

Natasha and Holly find their parents in front of the bathroom mirror. The right side of Peter's face droops like melted wax. He touches the sagging skin with hesitant fingers. Natasha steps closer. "Dad?"

"It's okay," Shirley says, steering her daughters out of the narrow room. "Everything's going to be fine."

In January a grim parade of resolutions march through Natasha's mind. Writing them down or even expressing them would be too much of a responsibility. She desires universal change for her non-life, beginning with her job and her residence, but she procrastinates. She can't bear to think about the revolution that needs to occur. If she lets things continue, perhaps change will come of its own volition.

During the peace of another motherless Sunday afternoon, she's sifting through treasures in a basement trunk. Shirley's wedding dress lies crumpled in the bottom drawer. Natasha tries it on over her clothes and checks herself in the basement bathroom mirror. The dress has turned a sickly shade of yellow. It fits.

She digs through piles of loose photographs, then stumbles onto several boxes of slides. The first is a collection taken at her parents' wedding. The cake cutting, gift opening, getaway in the tin-canned car; her parents are radiant. She marvels at the changes that have taken place since then. The physical changes, like Shirley's grey-blonde hair and Peter's softer shape are, she knows, natural processes of the passage of time, but what, she wonders, what trick of nature could separate two people, once so evidently in love?

"What in God's name are you doing down here? Is that your mother's dress?"

Natasha looks up. "What in God's name are *you* doing down here? Geez, Dad, are you lost?"

"I'm out of shirts. I'm doing laundry."

She watches her father take his dress shirts from the basket on the floor and drop them, one by one, into the washing machine. There's a gracefulness to his movements that she wouldn't have thought possible from him. He dips a cup into the detergent and holds it high above the washer, letting it waterfall into the machine. He turns the knob and the machine rumbles on, the jets coming to life.

"Dad, come here."

Peter shuffles in his slippers to where she's nesting on the floor. "What's that? Old slides?"

"Yes. From your wedding. Did anyone ever tell you

that you looked like Elvis when you were young?"

He chuckles. She passes him a slide and he holds it up to the light. "Well it's one for the money, two for the show...." He does the Elvis swivel. Half his face, the half unaffected by Bell's palsy, seems to light up, and she thinks she sees a moment of the man her mother married.

"Pull up a hunk of cement," she says, slapping the floor. He sits awkwardly cross-legged beside her and together they view history against the bare bulb.

Hours or minutes pass. Natasha opens the last box.

Someone, presumably Shirley, had penned "1961" on the white border of these final slides. Natasha draws one out and holds it up. "Oh, my God."

"What? Let's see."

It's a slide of Shirley in a chair with a young Holly sitting sidesaddle across her. Shirley's wearing a short skirt and heels. Her legs – unbelievably long, tanned and shapely – are swung glamorously to the right and crossed at the ankle. Hollywood legs.

"Let's see," Peter says again. She passes the slide and he frames it against the light. For a long time there's nothing, not even a breath to disturb the air. Then he puckers as if to whistle but nothing comes out except a faint, wheezing sound. He holds on to that thing forever.

First Comes Love

Now.

If she'd have waited one more Mississippi minute to
snatch the keys off the counter and steer the aging Honda
toward Saskatoon it would not have happened. She knows
this, believes in a point of no return and that she was a
razor-edged moment away from hers. Years have been lost
in her father's house where the pair of them lived separately
together, each entertaining their own despair in quiet ways.
Nothing to live for, nothing to lose, she wrote in her journal
during the worst of it, when she'd listen to sad songs and
line up sleeping pills on her pillow or play a blade along the
blue veins of her wrist. Nights when she awoke to a chorus
of weeping children but found only Camille's empty bed,
her Dolls-of-the-World still silent on their shelves. All the
times she heard her own voice urging, "Do it."

It was Saskatoon or death.

She discovers him at a University of Saskatchewan
cabaret, one table over, sipping watery beer from a plastic

glass. Rather old for this crowd, she thinks, but then, so is she. His hair's tossed, as if by wind or a woman's fingers. A burgundy turtleneck sweater and his dark hair create a flattering frame for the well-defined bones of his face. All the right pieces, she thinks, in all the right places. He looks like someone from her past. David? No. Maybe some friend of Holly's whose name is long gone. Ken? Kent? Something like that. Simmering beneath the gallery good looks she intuits physical and emotional strength. A paramedic, perhaps. Someone who remains collected at the heart of emergencies. Or a fireman. Yes. She dresses him in the yellow suit and sturdy boots, hanging off a speeding fire truck. There are sirens. She's not close enough to determine the colour of his eyes.

A woman in his party leans toward him, fingers lingering on his forearm as they speak. He follows her onto the dance floor. Natasha likes the way he closes his eyes and lets the music move through his bones, likes the colour in his face. Her own crowd dissipates in the smoke and noise now that she's noticed him. He laughs easily. He touches people. He's asked to dance often – women are doing that now – and she catches his eye and a shy smile. Her long neck and cheeks blossom with a heat that continues to spread through her chest, down her arms.

"Who's that hunk of burnin' love?" she asks her roommate, Darling, a classified-ad find with an endearing gap between her front teeth, like Madonna, and a waterfall of blonde hair that ends at her belt loops. She's a cosmetologist, and says it kills the other girls in the shop that she's never dyed or coloured or whacked off her hair. They'd happily do it for her.

"That tall guy?" They have to shout over a drummer's enthusiastic solo, sticks flying.

"Yeah."

"With the cowboy boots and black jeans or the other guy, in the turtleneck?"

"Turtleneck."

"That's —"

Darling's tapped on the shoulder by the engineering student she's been ineffectively dodging all night. "Dance?"

She leans toward Natasha's ear. "Brander Mienhart. English major, I think, doing his master's or something equally serious. Nice guy, or so they say."

Natasha nods. Way off, she muses. She couldn't have been further off the map.

A new term. Natasha finds her class and takes a seat on the right side, halfway back. She's become superstitious about where she sits, believing that whenever she can get this preferred spot she'll do well in the class. It's the first time that counts the most. Staking the claim. For all their fierce attempts at individuality, their desires not to lose themselves to the mindless disparity of routine, even university students, she realizes, are mostly creatures of habit.

People keep filing in, slinging themselves into seats. Maybe they have superstitions, too, she thinks. Or maybe they don't care as much about good grades as she does on this, her second shot at university. It's a competition this time, with no one but herself. Shirley worries about the way she attacks her work. "You don't have to get the highest marks in class," she'd said, over their last biweekly lunch together, however that fits into their clashing schedules. Shirley'd cut her classes by half, stretching a three-year degree to five. "High seventies are just fine. I worry about you...all that cramming and the hours you owl away in the library. I remember when you were a kid, hiding out in the basement. All you've done is change locations. Now you hide out in the stacks."

Natasha would have liked to kick something. "Most mothers would be proud. What's wrong with wanting good marks?"

Shirley had crumbled her poppy-seed muffin into little bits and pecked at them with a wet fingertip. "It's not the marks, dear, it's why you feel the need to prove yourself through them."

Natasha sank. The heart of it. Only Shirley holds the knife that knows how to cut there. She feared she might cry then, beneath the too-bright lights of the cafeteria, against the busy till's tired ring.

"You're intelligent. Always have been, honours student or not. Your dad knows that, your sisters. Tasha, everyone knows but you. Ease up on yourself. Live a little."

Again, Natasha heard the faint chord of regret in her mother's speech, but that's all she's ever had. That minor chord, better underwear, fresh lipstick. No hard evidence that would connect Shirley to anything indecent.

"What are you doing after convocation, Mom? I mean, you've only got a few months left."

"What do you mean what am I doing? I'm going home." Her voice turned wire tight.

"To Dad?"

"Why do you say that with a question mark? To be with Dad, or course! What in the world did you expect?"

Natasha folded her white paper napkin in half, quarters, pinched it into a tiny square. "To tell you the truth, Ma, I really didn't know."

A few students are left to lean against the back wall when every desk is taken. There's almost a nervous impatience settling over the room while they wait for their professor. Then Natasha hears the door close and footsteps advancing up the aisle.

"Hello. I'm Brander Mienhart, and this is English 267.3, Western Canadian Literature." He chalks out his name in a dramatic script on the board. "Please call me Brander, and if you never come to class as late as I have today, we'll all get along just fine."

She lives for Tuesday and Thursday mornings, his quick humour and surprising burst of a laugh that accounts – along with his Germanic good looks – for his popularity. There are policies about students and professors, she knows, but he's a thesis and a half away from becoming a full professor and at the end of January they have their first date.

"Bowling?"

"Well there's a bunch of us going. If you'd rather not, I mean, it's not really my thing either. But it might be –"

"Should I meet you there?"

A smile opens his face. "I'll pick you up."

His eyes, she notes, are sapphire.

It has been so long, Natasha wonders whether love will remember her. She feels the virgin again, quivering beneath Brander's striped sheets in her new purple bra and matching panties, bought, anxiously, though not without trepidation, for this very occasion. The stiff lace, uncomfortable on the outer edges of her breasts – she should have gone with the C cup – is all for him. She's grateful for the clouds blocking the moon, the only light to poke fingers through the window. A vague recognition of traffic sounds on Clarence Avenue.

Brander slides under the sheet beside her, the first touch of his skin already making her warm and wet. "Your feet are like icicles," he says, rubbing hers between his. They hold each other tightly, kiss the details of each other's face – eyelids, earlobes, cheekbones – before their tongues meet and explore throughout the midnight hour. She closes her eyes, mind-travels down the snow-packed streets, crosses College Drive, takes the escalator in the Arts Building to the third floor and sees these parts of him as if from her desk. She's just the admiring student again, like any of her classmates, but this is how he tastes, she thinks. This is his breath in my hair. Her lips are warm and swollen, as if all her nerves have made their home here. He moves down her neck, his lips grazing her skin, to the hollow between her collarbones.

"I can hardly breathe in class," he whispers.

"I know," she says, catching herself; she has almost called him, already, *my love.* "It's the same for me. Absolute torture."

He floats his fingertips over her stomach, kissing her there. "This is a dream."

She winces. For her, it's anything but a dream. It is only good. She reaches beneath her back to undo the bra. He lifts it away and buries himself between her breasts, taking his time to appreciate this soft, new territory between his fingers, in his mouth. He pinches and pulls one nipple while he sucks the other, and she can't wait now, begins grinding against his thigh until she comes, still in her panties.

She kisses a trail down his chest, runs a finger along the top of his shorts, then feels him, thick and ready. She pulls his shorts back slowly, slides her mouth around him, loving the "uh uh" sounds he makes, like he can't find his breath. After a minute she tucks her falling hair behind her ears so he can watch.

Later, when he's inside her, thrusting slowly, rhythmically, up on his elbows so he can see her eyes, she has her second orgasm of the night, loud again, and he follows by seconds.

"Whew. I didn't know girls could do that," he says, wiping the hair away from her eyes as he slides out of her. Her thighs are slick with the results of their mutual pleasure.

"Do what?" She worries for a moment that she's done something unnatural or wrong. Did she make too much noise? Dorion had always liked that. She lights a cigarette, passing it from her fingers to the V of his, though he's not a regular or even a particularly competent smoker, and she intuits that she'll soon be buying her last pack.

"Have orgasms while a man's inside them."

"Oh, that," she says, relieved. "Well I guess the prof's still got a few things to learn after all." She kisses his nose, bites his chin, amazed at the comfort level, the familiarity she feels with this man she knows little better than her Spanish prof, her geology prof. Jude had told her that it's like this. The best sex she ever had was with the men she hardly knew. She felt free then, to experiment, lust leading her down previously uncharted paths. Sex with pornographic movies playing, bondage in hotel rooms, sex with toys, the pinch of anal sex, and once – in a cabin before a cinder-spitting fire – a *ménage à trois* with two brothers from Quebec.

She gently squeezes Brander's penis, testing him for another go, and feels him grow in her hand. "It must be true what they say."

"About what?"

"Big feet."

He laughs and she climbs on top this time, rocking while his hands climb to her breasts. She lifts her arms, crosses them behind her head, scooping her long hair up in a centrefold pose.

"You're beautiful. You know that, right? Beautiful." Brander pulls himself up so that they are both sitting, his arms on her ribs helping to balance and bounce her. "I knew it would be like this. This good."

That word, beautiful. She recalls David using it on that long-ago night in the truck. The moon slips out from behind the clouds. In the dresser mirror a sweet bar of light, of bliss, has fallen on the reflection of a woman. That's me, Natasha thinks. This is us.

"Promise me you'll be here when I wake up." Brander says this after they're both luxuriously weary from the half-night of lovemaking.

She rolls him to his side and curls into him, her knees tucked against the sweaty pockets that are the backs of his, her arm snug around him, his hand clutching hers to his chest. A good fit. "Kid, you couldn't get rid of me if you tried."

The wedding's to be in June. There was never any doubt about the event itself but the date has leapfrogged back and forth across the calendar. Tom and Camille are marrying and moving to Alberta where there's more work, better opportunities. Tom has extended family there, an uncle with a construction business or something, Natasha's not hearing clearly.

"Where in Alberta?" she asks Camille, almost dropping the phone as she butts what she decides, again, will be her final cigarette. She hopes Brander won't smell it on her. She's really trying.

"Edmonton. Hopefully after the baby's born we'll be able to find a place somewhere outside the city. An acreage would be nice. Or maybe one of those small northern towns...Athabasca, or Lac La Biche. Maybe even Fort McMurray. Depends where the work is."

Natasha doesn't know how to feel, except left behind,

as though she's the youngest and her sisters, laughing and running ahead, have given up on her. What the hell is this? she thinks. Marriage had never even occurred to her before this conversation.

"You really think you're ready for this? You're still not that old, you know. You guys don't have to get married just because of the baby."

"Tash, I know you're concerned. I think you see Tom as this roughneck who —"

"I do not! I like Tom. Really, I just don't think you need to rush into marriage."

"So who's rushing? We've been together since we were fourteen. Oh! The baby just kicked."

"You're right. I'll shut up now. Hear that?"

"What?"

"The sound of me zipping my lips."

Holly rings her almost immediately after she says goodbye — and good luck! — to Camille. "We're having the stagette in three weeks."

"Have you even asked Camille about it? It doesn't sound like her kind of thing."

"It's tradition," Holly says. "I had one, she'll have one, you...whoops. I'll just pull my foot out of my mouth again."

Natasha doesn't know why Holly's become snarky toward her as of late. Perhaps it has something to do with their parents. Peter, abandoned husband and father, has Holly's sympathy, but whatever the cause, Natasha knows where to bite back. "I know this will come as a major surprise, but getting married is not going to be the highlight of my life. In fact, I actually feel sorry for anyone whose wedding day *is* the highlight. Incredibly sorry. God. Can you imagine?"

"Sounds like sour grapes to me."

"Whatever. Believe what you want. I don't have to be involved in organizing anything, do I?"

"No," Holly says flatly.

"Okay, I'll be there. I haven't seen Dad for a while anyway. Are you inviting Mom? It's weird. Somebody actually thought we were sisters in the college book store. How's Dad these days?"

"Not bad. He puts on this happy face for everyone, but I know he's desperately lonely. I get over every week to clean the house up for him, and Nels is wild about him. They actually spend a lot of time together. You still think Mom's doing the right thing?"

"She seems happy."

"At Dad's expense," Holly says quickly.

Natasha hears her sister swallow. "You've got to make yourself happy before you can be any good to anyone else. Anyway, she's only got a few classes left, then she'll be right back in the kitchen where Dad wants her."

"Sociology. What's *that* going to get her?"

Natasha doesn't answer. "So, the 14th. I'll put it on my calendar. Is Mom invited?" she asks, repeating the earlier question.

"The mothers usually are," Holly says. "Most have the good sense to decline –" There's a crash in the background of their conversation. "Damn!"

"What happened?" Natasha thinks about windows,

a baseball through glass.

"I've got a mess here. We had some friends over last night. I made strawberry margaritas...there was a little left...I just knocked my glass over. Gotta run –" She sounds winded, as though she has, actually, been running.

"Give Nels a hug for me. And tell Dad hello. Is he going to be home during this thing?"

"Nope. He's got his AGM in Winnipeg," Holly says.

"What luck." Natasha hangs up, aware once the dial tone's in her ear that she's neglected sending greetings to Everett.

Brander knows about things. They go to plays: one a powerful two-hander about urban poverty written by a local playwright, the other a rambunctious musical revue with a large cast and numerous set changes. Her lover introduces her to Handel and Schubert, and she tries not to be shocked whenever she finds him alone and reading, not books for his classes but contemporary Canadian fiction, just for the fun of it. He's unlike anyone she's ever known, the antithesis of the men she grew up with. She is falling fast. She is mush.

Darling prowls around the kitchen. "Hey, want to do something tonight. Go to a movie or something?"

Natasha's been seeing less and less of Darling, of her own apartment, and has only popped in this late afternoon to grab a change of clothes and check her mail.

"Sorry, I've got plans. We're going to an art opening, someone Brander grew up with."

"Well la-de-da," Darling says, lifting her little finger while she slurps her coffee. "Getting pretty serious all of a sudden, aren't you?"

Natasha pours herself a cup of the strong coffee, slides a bag of hair supplies out of the way and sits at the table. "It's working."

"Well, he's sure a looker," Darling says. "Not my type, exactly. I like 'em a little more down-to-earth, if you know what I mean."

"Brander's down-to-earth. He loves camping and the outdoors. Bugs, bears, sleeping on the ground...can't get much more down to earth than that." Why, she wonders, does she need to defend him?

"I'll give you the benefit of the doubt." Darling checks the calendar above Natasha's head. "My turn to work a Saturday tomorrow. I've got a dye job scheduled first thing. Streaking always gave me trouble in school. If you think being a cosmetologist is easy, you've never had to squeeze a streaking cap over someone else's head. It's one of those skinhead rubber jobbies with the little holes in it."

"I can picture it. I think my Mom used to get that done." Natasha tries to surreptitiously check her watch, a thin gold gift from Brander.

"The worst part is we have to use a thing like a crochet hook to pull the hair out and it hurts like hell. Some of our clients, usually older ladies, they start out holding their lips together tight but then one big tear rolls down their wrinkled cheek and it's followed by another and another, so pretty soon it's like they've been watching a

Walt Disney movie where all the animals die."

"Hmmm."

"It's like your dad always said before he whacked the shit out of you – 'this is gonna hurt me more than it does you.' That's exactly how I feel when I'm streaking."

"Your dad whacked you?" It's the first phrase that's captured Natasha's attention.

"Didn't yours?"

She tries to recall Peter ever raising his hand against any of them, sure that each of them had deserved it more than once. "Nope. Never."

"Wow. An exception."

Natasha gets up to rinse her cup. She bets there's more to Darling's story. She checks her watch. Time to go.

"Hey, should I be looking for a new roommate?" Darling asks from the table.

The words are little jabs between Natasha's shoulders. "I don't know yet," she confesses, "I don't know."

They're in the gallery, and as Natasha pans the room she realizes she's chosen right – the black, Jackie O dress, midnight nylons, and pumps stand up well in the crowd of unfailiar and mostly older faces. "There's a lot of white hair and good jewelry in this room," she notes, and Brander nods in agreement. She hadn't known what to do about her hair, so at the last moment she swept it into a ponytail with a black, velvet barrette. She hopes it makes her look sophisticated.

The patrons stand in clutches all about the large room,

lined with huge acrylics – landscapes, mostly – in heavy gold frames. An appetizer buffet with several bottles of wine and strawberry punch is laid out on a long table. She and Brander gravitate toward it.

"Wine for the lady?" Brander's already pouring.

She accepts the glass and they clink to finding each other. "And to great sex," Brander adds, lifting his glass to the sky beyond the window. "Thank you."

The artist, a slim fellow in a blue silk shirt and black leather pants, spots them and stops by to shake their hands and thank them for coming. He's antsy and looks past them several times. Natasha doesn't have much to say to him before he's quickly called away.

"He looks undernourished," she says. "I had the strongest desire to feed him."

"Ah, but he's a happy man," Brander says, spearing a square of cheese onto a toothpick. "He's already sold three quarters of his pieces. Should keep him in paints for another year or two."

She breathes in deeply, through her nose. "So this is what culture smells like," she says. "Come on, let's take a closer look."

They refill their glasses, then Brander takes her elbow and they move to examine the nearest painting, a forest scene with roots like long, searching fingers, twisting up trees. "This one's rather unnerving," she says. "What do you think?"

"Not one of his best, but let's stand here for a few moments. That's what people do, you know. They stand before art and expound."

They pause, then proceed to the next painting, pause

and proceed again, like window shoppers on a Sunday afternoon stroll. "I'm going to pop into the washroom for a moment," Brander says. "Be right back."

She smiles after him, and moves on to the next painting. How unusual, she thinks. It's a prairie scene, which is common enough, but the top two-thirds feature a cobalt sky in passionate turmoil, a scene rendered so realistically she can smell the moment before rain. A spring pasture fills the bottom third. There's the shape of a barn, and a row of rundown outbuildings in the distance, barely visible. In the foreground, three black bulls turn their large heads skyward, and a hawk's just released her grip on a fence. She steps closer. In the right-hand corner, leading her eye away, the unmistakable grey scar of a highway.

There is no denying now that something has gone awfully wrong. They are beyond hunger, beyond tears, beyond complaining about their thirst in the choking air. They are mostly beyond words. "Hail Mary," Kent mutters beside her. He takes her left hand and holds it hard. Her hand feels small in his. Natasha squeezes her sister's hand. They are all linking, all preparing in their own ways. "Full of grace..."

"Where in the world did you get him?" Natasha whispers to Holly when the doorbell rings. Ten minutes ago she was warned what to expect. She doesn't have her head around it yet.

"He's a friend of Gina's, from Regina. Hardly costing

us anything." Holly smiles at Natasha's reticence. "Close your mouth, sister. You'll catch flies."

"Since when did Gina start hanging around with strippers?"

Holly clucks. "Don't be a prude, Tash." She checks over her shoulder to see that everything's ready, a full beer in her hand. "Did you add the vodka to the punch?"

"As ordered, Herr Commandant." Natasha feels queasy, believing this night will not end without disaster, or at least the dull brown pain of heartache.

Gina joins them in the doorway. "Here's the tape."

She passes the cassette to Holly. "Crank it."

Holly pushes Natasha back toward their guests. "Don't worry. He won't take it *all* off." She inserts the tape in the player. *"That's* another hundred bucks."

The Stensrud rumpus room is unrecognizable with plum and black balloons dangling from the ceiling, a shroud of smoke above everyone's head, the throbbing music and now this – the entertainment – about to begin.

The room hasn't seen action like this since Camille's twelfth birthday party, which ended in a fist fight between her two best friends, and Camille sobbing: "This is the fuckingest birthday I've ever had!"

They've slid the ping-pong table to the wall where it supports beverages and food – mostly junk, but someone has taken the time to cut up carrots and celery and make a low-calorie dip for the weight conscious. Camille, reluctant guest of honour, is tied with extension cords – all Holly could find – to a straight-backed chair and plunked in the middle of the room. The dozen or so women, including Camille's long-time friends, Tom's sisters and mother, Shirley, the new, female pharmacist, and a few women Natasha's never seen before and has immediately forgotten the names of, sit or stand or wander in a broken ring around Camille. The extension cords add a kinky, almost obscene element to the night, Natasha thinks. Surely her sister didn't have to go this far. Only Holly could orchestrate a night like this, and even *she'd* have to be drunk to do it. Brander wouldn't believe it.

The alcohol's kicking in; the younger women are beginning to loosen up. But not Camille. Holly's painted huge lips in blood-red lipstick on their younger sister, tied her hair in pigtails with condoms and strung a plastic phallus around her neck. Occasionally someone remembers the bride-to-be, passively strapped in her chair, and they give her a sip of coke or ask if she's sure the cords are not too tight around her belly.

Holly claps to get the crowd's attention. "Okay everyone, have a seat. The show's about to begin. Direct from Regina —" There are titters. " — for your personal viewing pleasure, we're pleased to bring you —" she looks at Gina, leaning against the door frame in a pair of too-tight jeans and a low-cut top that shows off her considerable cleavage.

"Oh my God," Natasha says to the pharmacist, who's closest to her and is, if the amount of time she spends swirling the ice in her glass is any indication, equally uncomfortable. "She doesn't even know his name."

"Ricky D!" Gina yells.

Holly, Gina, and Tom's sisters start clapping with the

beat of the music, and Tom's mother, a sixty-three-year-old nurse who's seen it all anyway, quickly joins in with a "When in Rome" look on her well-creased face.

The stripper bunny-hops out in leather chaps and vest, one leather-gloved hand slapping his ass, the other swinging a lasso. "Yahhooo!" He pivots on the heels of his cowboy boots and the women squeal at his exposed, plump buttocks, which remind Natasha of the dumplings her grandmother used to make. He's fresh from the farm, she thinks, brought up on steak and mashed potatoes, one-inch slices of white, homemade bread, four fried eggs every morning, and perogies with white gravy. He has thick, rather unpleasant legs but his broad, well-defined chest and rippling stomach muscles suggest a gym membership.

He throws his lasso around Camille, who squirms and twists away. Holly hoots. Already drunk, Natasha thinks, or well on her merry way.

The beat changes. Ricky has some difficulty dancing and pulling off his boots at the same time and he stumbles into Tom's mother, who pushes him away like he's diseased.

"Take it off, take it *all* off!" Holly chants as he bumps and grinds his way around Camille's chair, the bulge in his gold sequined G-string inches from her nose. Natasha suspects Camille's quietly raging. I should put a stop to this spectacle, she thinks. I should do something now.

She's always thought that if one of the stumbling drunks on Main grabbed her, she'd kick him so hard in the *balls she'd lift him off the ground. If one of the dark-eyed Maloneys cornered her in the bushes, she'd tear his ear off with her teeth. There's a small part of her that hoped it would happen, so she could prove her might and flaunt her quick thinking. She's always believed the urban myth about the adrenalin-rich woman who lifts a car to free her child from beneath it. She believes in adrenalin, period.*

"We need a plan," she says, her voice tight and choked. "Does anyone have a knife?"

A few of Camille's friends are also clapping and moving with the medley of Top 40 music now. Natasha opens another beer and slides over to Shirley, her hands folded demurely in her lap. "You okay with this?"

Shirley adjusts an earring. "It's like a traffic accident. Horrible, but I can't stop myself from watching."

Ricky pulls the bandana off his neck, runs it under Camille's chin. He wings his cowboy hat, Frisbee style, at Gina, then turns around and shakes his fleshy buttocks. Natasha fights the urge to charge across the rug and slap him hard enough to leave a red handprint on his butt cheek. When he hooks his thumbs in his G-string and does a bull-legged, honky-tonk step toward her, she freezes. The pharmacist paws in her wallet, spilling coins, and comes up with a five dollar bill. She gingerly stuffs it in his G-string. "To make him go away," she whispers.

"Thanks," Natasha says. "I'll pay you back."

For a finale, Ricky drags Gina and one of Camille's

friends inside the circle to dance to "La Freak." He runs his hands along the lengths of their bodies, two inches from touching them, and does the dirty dog. He's sweating profusely.

"This is too much," Shirley says.

Natasha checks to see how Tom's mother is taking it. "Elva seems to be having a good time."

There are two more numbers, but Gina was right. Ricky D danced and hobbled himself out of a cowboy suit, a Spiderman getup and a top hat and tuxedo, but he never once took it all off.

"She didn't do this for me," Camille says as Natasha wipes the clown cheeks off her sister's skin. They've escaped to the bathroom. "It was a vendetta. Do you remember Everett's stag? Apparently he had a stripper and Holly was livid. This, tonight, that's what it was about. Holly's getting back at him."

"Oh God, that can't be true. Is it?" Could Holly be a bigger bitch? Natasha wonders.

Camille slips the condoms off her hair and throws them into the toilet. "I swear it." She soaps her hands and arms up to the elbows, as a surgeon might, as if the condoms had been soiled by strangers in an alley.

For all the years they shared a room, Natasha realizes that they've rarely talked about anything that mattered. She's had just enough to drink now to say anything. She wants to ask: Camille, are you happy? "So...back to the party?"

"Not bloody likely! I'm going to pull a Holly," Camille

says, and gently taps her temple with her middle finger. "Headache."

"What are you really doing?"

"Meeting Tom, of course. He's expecting me."

"Ah." Natasha gives her sister the briefest of hugs, but it's a momentous act, and they are both surprised by it. Their family does not hug.

Casual Conversations

The first time Natasha knows for sure that there's anything wrong with Holly's marriage is when she tells her about the berry incident. They're in Holly's impeccable white kitchen. Natasha's mesmerized by the muscles in her sister's forearms as she rolls pie dough to a perfect one-eighth inch. She's mesmerized by the fact that Holly knows how to *make* pie dough. Their mother certainly never taught her.

"I have a good sense of humour," Holly says, as though she's trying to convince herself. "No one can say I don't have a good sense of humour."

Her cat, Mrs. Brown, listens intently. A shorthair, Natasha notes. Cat hair strung throughout Holly's house like tinsel would never do. Mrs. Brown is spayed and declawed. In fact, there isn't much of the original left in the poor thing.

"You have a good sense of humour," Natasha agrees. She's sitting on one of the round bar-type stools at the island, home from the city for a quick visit – there is no other kind – and she wonders if she'll ever have an island, or even a kitchen, to call her own.

"Remember how I used to crack everyone up at the supper table?" Holly places a glass pie plate on top of the dough and jerks around its edges with a paring knife.

"Yeah. You really used to slay us." Natasha pinches a stray bit of dough into a ball, finds two more and makes a yeasty snowman.

"And what about Camille's stagette? It was my idea to buy those wacky gifts." Holly opens the cupboard below the sink and Natasha spies the cluster of empty forty-ounce bottles, waiting to be returned to the liquor board store for a refund. It likely won't be long, she thinks. Holly's getting worse.

"You're a card," Natasha says, struggling not to blurt that Camille wanted to melt into the floor. "A card, and you should be dealt with."

The cat wraps itself around Natasha's leg, a furry leg warmer. She snaps her fingers near its face. It hisses and backs off.

"I mean, I can take a joke like the next person," Holly continues, cutting out her second crust, "but that was uncalled for."

All Natasha knows so far is that Holly, Everett, and Nels went on a late summer camping holiday. They'd returned just before school started. Holly should be glowing. "What happened?"

"We were out for a walk, with Nels riding along beside us. Since the training wheels came off I can't get that kid off his bike. I think it's the speed and sense of freedom, though of course I never let him out of my sight."

Natasha remembers that freedom. The wind fanning her T-shirt, the sun a healing balm on her face as she pedalled...where? Anywhere she wanted. To the Dairy Whip for the icy pleasure of a rum-and-butter shake. To her father's grocery store for a quart of milk. In the spring she slithered through mud, clogged her fenders, and had to dig her tires free with a stick. In the summer she snapped clickers on her spokes and rode hands-free to the end of the block. All that was so many seasons ago. Has she even been on a bike since? No, she doesn't believe so.

Holly snaps her fingers and makes a sour face. "Hey, are you listening? I'm telling a story here. We stopped at one of those park washroom/laundromat places and I went in for a pee. I can't hold it like I used to. I think I need surgery down there. Anyway, when I came out Everett had a handful of red berries. He asked me to try one. He said they were great." She pinches the crust into the pan, spinning it round and round with her other hand. "I said no, but he insisted. He popped a berry into my mouth and I bit. I swear to God I've never tasted anything so vile in my entire life. I spit it out. Dark red. I kept spitting as the taste got stronger and stronger. More red, like I was bleeding. Of course, *he* thought it was hilarious, nearly coughed up a lung he was laughing so hard. I bet the damn thing was poisonous."

"But here you are," Natasha says, "alive and well."

"But that's not all. Then there was the hamburger thing." She fills the pie shells with canned blueberry filling. Thank God, Natasha thinks. She's a Stensrud after all.

"We're back at the campsite. Nels is feeding sunflower seeds to the rodents, Everett's making the burgers, and I'm reading a good book."

Holly's definition of a good book is not Natasha's. "Harold Robbins?"

"How'd you know? Anyway, Everett says, 'Did you see that new handshake they're doing on TV?' I told him no, and I didn't care. Then he says, 'They go like this' and he sticks his hand out for a traditional handshake." She extends her hand to Natasha. "I take his hand, then realize *my* hand's now coated in hamburger grease."

"That's kind of funny." But it's also a tad mean, and unusual, Natasha thinks. Everett's a straight arrow. Practical jokes are not his forté.

"It was uncalled for." Holly pops the pies into the oven and sets the timer. They have an hour before Nels comes home. An hour and ten minutes before Everett. She wipes the cupboard and washes the dishes. Natasha follows her into the front room, fingers laced around a cup of coffee. They take opposite ends of the couch. "The whole thing was a bad idea, anyway."

"What? The holiday? At least you got a tan," Natasha says, noting her sister's bronze legs below the hem of her walking shorts. She pulls a cigarette from a pack in her purse. "Do you mind?" Holly shakes her head no. Natasha opens a window and lights up, half hoping the air won't clear before Everett returns. He hates smoking in general and doesn't tolerate it in his home.

"Yes, the holiday," Holly says, "revisiting." She tucks her hair behind her ears and begins describing how she had envisioned the national park of their childhood vacations. She draws the outline and Natasha tries to paint in the details. Holly remembers the store that sold seashells, but Natasha remembers that it had a huge tortoise shell set against the front of the building. Holly remembers roller skating, but Natasha recalls tightening the skates onto their shoes with funny-shaped keys.

"The roller rink and shell store live on only in the memories of the children who once knew them," Holly says, pushing her glasses up. "The breakwater's still there, but the waves are not nearly as impressive as they used to be."

"You were shorter then." Natasha drops ashes on the carpet and grinds them in with her foot before Holly notices.

"Remember the paddlewheeler bumping us across the rough lake?" Holly asks.

"Vaguely. I pretended the lake was an ocean because I couldn't see the other side. I was so easily amused."

Holly recalls the antagonizing chore of setting up the tent trailer; Natasha's memory includes rain and how the wet walls wept if you ran your finger down their sides.

"What about the golf course?" Holly asks. She's rubbing her temple, and Natasha doesn't know if this is a reflex now or if her sister is in fact currently suffering.

"We weren't allowed to caddy for Dad. Remember the outdoor theatre?"

"Park personnel dressed like elk and put on bad skits." Holly laughs, and the hand falls away from her face. "But it was fun. No, it was *magic*. I thought it would be magic again, you know, like it was?"

With her legs tucked under her on the couch, Holly seems far younger than her age, Natasha thinks, and her blonde hair camouflages the grey that's appeared like a surprise and unwelcome guest. Darling could fix her up. Natasha stubs out the cigarette. "The park or your marriage?"

"Both, but I was talking about the park. Do you know what I mean?"

Natasha knows. She knows every time she returns home and sees their town's thin line of lights on the horizon, and every time she races back to the city and expects butterflies in her stomach like when she was a kid, travelling to Saskatoon for shopping or dental appointments.

Holly explains about the precursory sprint around the campground to select a site, Everett controlling that decision, and the setting up of their tent. She complains about the frogs that never shut up at night, the chickadees and squirrels that attacked her during the day. After Nels went to sleep, Holly and Everett played cribbage on the picnic table. Moths banged against the lantern and flung themselves stupid in her face.

"The lake was friggin' freezing, and the people in the next campsite let their Rottweiler run loose. You should have seen this dog. It was taller than Nels!" Between rants she takes drags off Natasha's cigarette.

"Okay, I get the pathetic picture, but did Nels enjoy the holiday?" Natasha worries about her nephew, a slight, well-behaved boy with excellent table manners. She sees

Everett push him into things, like swimming lessons and ball games that she guesses he would much rather observe from the sidelines. He keeps a cardboard box of crafts and drawings and Natasha's amazed at his considerable talent. Not your usual juvenile fare; he creates complicated, multi-media forests with long-limbed shoestring trees. Elves poke their painted green heads out from behind terrycloth stumps and bushes. The creations remind Natasha of those busy posters they used to have in doctor's offices to keep patients' minds off where they really were. So much going on in his forest, she thinks. She needs to hear that he had a good time.

"Sure, he had fun. He's a kid." Holly picks lint off the couch. Kneading, rolling, pressing, pinching, washing and now picking: Natasha realizes that her sister's hands are always busy. "Everett didn't really lose it until the last day. There were some bigger kids, maybe nine or ten-year-olds, down the beach. Nels was dragging his shovel back and forth along the wet sand, close to where they were building a castle. He must have overheard them. When he wandered back Everett wanted to take him in the water. It was Christly cold, and Nels didn't want to go in. Everett tried pulling him toward the lake, but Nels dug his heels in and wouldn't budge. I was too mortified to move. It was one of those movie moments; you don't believe it's happening for real before your very eyes. It would have been a scene if anyone else had noticed. Nels twisted out of Everett's grip and said, 'I'm not going in that son of a bitchin' water.' Everett marched him to the change room. I didn't think he would do it there. I didn't think he'd wash his mouth out."

"My God, Holl."

"With industrial soap. Someone must have seen." She takes another drag off Natasha's cigarette, then leaves to brush her teeth and rinse her own mouth out. A whole hour has been eaten by her angst.

The door flies open and Nels races in, waving a crayoned self-portrait. "Hi, Auntie!" Natasha kisses him and holds his wiry little body close to her own.

"How was your first week at school?"

"Good! Mrs. Murray's nice. She gave us cookies!" He lets the backpack slide off his thin arms.

Natasha checks the clock. Everett will be home soon.

"Auntie's got to go, honey, but show me your picture first." Nels hands her the self-portrait. She looks at it, then at him. "There's no mouth? How will you eat?" She hands the picture back just as Nels turns to chase after Mrs. Brown. The picture slips out of his hand, landing face down on the floor.

"Gotta go," Natasha says, jingling car keys at Holly.

When Everett arrives, Natasha has no doubt her sister will have lunch on the table, and maybe just one quick nip from her favourite frosted glass.

She drives back to the city that afternoon. She'd told Holly she'd call later and they could talk more about it. Holly hasn't said there is an *it* yet, but Natasha senses there is and she cares. Somewhere along the line her sister has become her friend.

By the time she reaches her apartment, two hundred and fifty miles of single-laned highway later, she feels distanced from Holly's pain but she can't shake the stray dog of discomfort that's followed her all the way home again. Before today she'd secretly mocked Holly's life, personified by the priscilla curtains she's sewn herself, the floor mat that spells Welcome, her sister's Tuesday and Thursday aerobics class. Natasha might have been the one to fall in love and have it stick, perhaps marry Dorion and have his twins. Early marriage was certainly the popular path, and if it was the path she was also meant to take, she wonders at what moment her life took off in its own zigzag direction.

As a child, stuffing her mother's bras with rolled socks and dreaming about becoming a woman, Holly's life was the one Natasha expected. The trips to the moon, the escapes to undiscovered lands – she knew all along that was play. The real world would unfold like the rhyme: First comes love, then comes marriage, then comes Natasha with a baby carriage. She has a telescoped view of what might have been, a vicarious domesticity lived through Holly's experience. It occurs to her that she's forever been the voyeur, spying through peepholes to see how other people live.

There's also the other side, uprooting Holly and placing her, like a miniature doll, into the comfortable disorder that is Natasha's life. Living in the city, rarely going home. Meeting a few odd, interesting people – friends of Brander's mostly. She's keeping the secret of Brander to herself, not wanting to get anyone's hopes up, least of all her own.

Ultimately, Natasha doesn't think her big sister would last in her world. The city would chew her up. From her dim cave of memory she recalls an early excursion to Saskatoon, to Eaton's on the corner of 21st Street and 3rd Avenue. The girls clutched their mother's hands as they rode the city's first escalator, made of wood. They'd wandered through the maze of dresses, followed another family into the elevator's cage and ridden down. They found the bubble gum machines on the main floor, then spun around the turnstile and out onto the street while their mother, pregnant with Camille, tried on maternity clothes behind the curtains upstairs.

On the street every parked car was not theirs. Eaton's disappeared when they weren't looking. "We have to find a policeman," Holly had said, her voice cracking, "or we'll never see Mom and Dad again." Natasha wonders now how it was that so many grown-ups could have passed them, indifferent to two little girls with matching navy sailor coats and mufflers, alone on a city sidewalk. They walked for blocks, staring into store windows, searching for a policeman. Holly was weeping and cold and begged to turn around, but Natasha took her hand and kept moving them forward until they found the big, black car with the silver wings that belonged to their father, and there they stood, hand in hand, until their mother miraculously found them safe.

Yikes, Natasha thinks. No wonder Holly keeps a keen eye on Nels.

Natasha's not able to make it home for two months after her visit with Holly, but they talk often on the phone.

Sometimes, when Brander's over, his head beneath the covers, it's hard not to giggle on the line. But these are not laughing times. Everett's laid off when the mall's construction is completed; Holly is looking for work.

"I might have something in an insurance office."

"Would you like that?"

"No."

"You could go back to work for Dad. Even Everett —" She bucks at Brander, who's trying to enter her from behind.

"Don't you think I haven't suggested that? He wouldn't hear of it. Said he'd sign up for welfare before he'd take a job from Dad. Frankly, I feel the same way."

"He hates Dad? This is news." She pinches Brander's thigh.

"No. It's...Dad doesn't know we're having financial problems. Everett's too proud to admit it, even to himself. Would you believe he actually parted with his golf clubs so we could pay our power bill this month? He says he'll even let the boat go if he has to. He really is making sacrifices."

"It's this damn recession. Everyone's feeling it."

"Yeah. Oh boy...I think he's home. I better get off the phone. Another expense." She hangs up without a goodbye.

"Your sister again," Brander says, flipping her over.

"Yep." She shimmies down the sheets beneath him, tasting skin as she goes. "That is not a healthy house."

Natasha's glad she and Holly had a face-to-face hour in September, beginning with the telling of the berry incident. Holly was right about the aftertaste. More than bitter berries, it signalled the downward spiral of her relationship. She's equally glad for their follow-up chats, during which her sister confided that she and Everett were members of the once-a-month-missionary-club and then, three drinks later, confessed that they'd stopped making love altogether. Everett, still unemployed, is a caged and pacing wolf.

Without this knowledge, Natasha would never have known how it really was before everything changed again.

The front page of the *Marvin Chronicle* announces: *Tragic accident takes one life,* and then, in smaller letters: *Marvin man survives.* A sidebar's relegated to the number of highway fatalities caused by impaired drivers.

A drunk driver barrelled into Everett's car. His legs are crushed. The doctors say it's unlikely he'll ever walk again. "But it's not impossible," Holly insists.

Everett retreats inside himself after this, and what a dark place it must be, Natasha decides, for the man loses every stitch of civility he ever had. He spends hours in front of the television, barking when he needs Holly's help, acknowledging guests with a grunt. Nels and his friends find other homes to play at, and even Everett's old buddies, blue-collar clones of himself, stop coming around.

Holly rallies. This tragedy appears to be just what she needs, for reasons Natasha cannot yet understand. Her sister takes charge, and in time, even grows square-shouldered and harder, to look the part.

"For better or worse," Holly says often, like a perpetual prayer.

Darling moves out, Brander moves in. It's no longer a secret. It also gives Natasha an excuse to stay in the city, but the sisters continue sharing the shreds of their lives over the phone. Holly calls at odd times: before breakfast, late at night. Natasha doesn't know whether this is because of the cheaper rates or because she doesn't want Everett to hear. Or both.

The phone rings at midnight. Natasha's asleep but she's been travelling again, on the highway beneath a storm purple sky. She has soaked through her T-shirt. She's just an ear on the phone.

"Don't feel sorry for me," Holly says, "I have something now that few people ever have."

"And what's that?" A ball and chain locking you to your husband's wheelchair?

"I know what to expect from life. God's given me my big surprise. There'll be no more children, no fancy new house. My life will be rooted in this home with my husband and son. One day I'll wake up and I'll be old. Nels will have moved away and maybe given me a few grandchildren to spoil. And then I'll die, and when I'm finally face to face with God, I'll say 'You gave me a heavy cross to carry but I did it. I carried the son of a bitch every step of the way.'"

She doesn't raise her voice, doesn't sound bitter, but Natasha hears ice chink against glass and she knows her sister is drunk. She hangs up and snuggles against Brander.

Their child is conceived that night. Like Holly, Natasha will have a son. He'll have the traditional Norse blonde hair, almost white at birth, and cornflower blue eyes. She knows this. When the doctor confirms her pregnancy, she finds herself leaping forward to her unborn baby's first smile, first word. She wonders about a crib. Can they get Nels', paint it a pale, summer blue? She laces her baby into walking shoes and he stumbles through her imagination, down a slide, shakes a handful of grass over her hair, and laughs with his four teeth showing. The three of them on a carousel, Natasha holding their son steady on the white stallion with the golden mane, blowing out birthday candles, stomping in Christmas wrap. She wills him three in a sandbox, four on a trike, and finally, five, hair slicked down for his first day of school, when he'll come home waving a crayoned self-portrait with none of the important parts missing.

Johnny Dead Bed

Brander slides the question to her in their lazy, Sunday-noon bed. It's a dull day beyond their blinds; why rush into it? They've been awake and acting silly as circus clowns for hours. "Ill-way, oo-yay, arry-may, e-may?"

"Hmmm. I don't know, let's see the ring first." She raises herself on one elbow and digs a pebble of sleep from her left eye with her little finger.

Brander pauses. "One minute." He rolls out of bed, dragging blankets and sheets, and stumbles out of the room, beautifully loose and naked. She hears rummaging in the kitchen, then his big feet slapping down the linoleum hall. He somersaults onto the bed – his feet narrowly missing her head – and idly opens his hand to reveal a most unconventional ring.

"Garbage bag twist-tie?"

He nods fervently.

"I most definitely do!"

Future in-laws. Their first meeting is at a pretentious, overpriced restaurant where everything that isn't bone china or crystal is silver, or linen. The waiter knows them by name and seats them away from the other patrons, in an alcove. Natasha survives the initial, detached hug from Sterling – her own father would have known better – and takes the cold, slender hand Edith offers. She feels like she's shaking a pickerel. Wine is ordered, swirled, sniffed and approved. Their small talk has the same sort of perfunctory air to it. "And you have two sisters? Younger and older?"

"Yes. Holly married a man from Marvin, near our hometown. Camille lives in Edmonton." Natasha hopes she won't have to get into details. She doesn't.

It's only a minor interrogation. The food arrives. Natasha'd let Brander order for her; he knows the ropes. What's set before them looks less like food and more like a centrepiece: tiny cabbages, a shellacked piece of roast, brown rice topped with a sprig of some weed or another. Edith's vulture eyes catch Natasha's split second of indecision over which fork to begin with, and Edith nudges her, gently, with an elbow, and taps the correct fork beside her own plate.

Edith's one virtue, as far as Natasha can see, is that she's instilled a zealous work ethic in Brander. Instilled or demanded. Either way, he's a roll-up-the-shirt-sleeves, give-it-my-all kind of guy, whether he's marking papers, scouring the toilet, or making mad love.

She also gives Edith points for Brander's name. At a time when the big names of the day were veritable bookends like Robert, Michael, Christopher, and Jonathon, she bucked the trend with her only child.

Just a few shades out of the ordinary. It fit.

Although Sterling punctuates his conversations with authoritarian 'hrumphs' and 'hm hmmms,' Natasha doesn't feel threatened. He's a jellyfish, with age spots decorating his high, shiny forehead and spongy hands; a jellyfish whom Edith moulds into whatever shape she needs.

The in-laws frown on the younger couple's musty apartment near the university, with its oven-like hallways and communal laundry room. Mostly Sterling, an aging oncologist, frowns. Edith's disappearing lips are cast in a permanent scowl, so Natasha never knows what she's thinking. Clearly, however, the older woman disapproves. Their friends and associates are mostly renting, like them, but Brander's parents believe that with the baby on the way they simply must inhabit more permanent surroundings. Fences will become increasingly important. A crib at the end of the bed won't do; a proper nursery is in order.

"You're not very charitable when it comes to your mother-in-law," Shirley says, holding a pair of tiny corduroy overalls in a practical teal that can be worn by either sex. She's dropped off two boxes of Nels' old baby clothes. "Your father's noticed it, too."

"Nope, I'm not," Natasha agrees. She puts the kettle on for tea. "But tit-for-tat. She always makes me feel nowhere near good enough for Brander. I think it's a doctor's-wife complex. Maybe she can't help herself."

"Still, she's family now. And you shouldn't be thinking bad thoughts with a baby on the way."

Natasha laughs and rubs her stretching belly. "It isn't so much the things Edith says, or doesn't say, as the way she watches and waits for me to flounder, to flop on shore like a screwed-up fish. It's pretty much been a toboggan ride since that first meal together."

Shirley's examining a miniature T-shirt for stains. "All downhill?"

"And fast." Natasha hooks her foot around the leg of another kitchen chair and slides it over so she can put her feet up on the seat. She's tired today, and her feet are swollen. "So where's Dad? What's his excuse this time?"

She perceives her father's discomfort around Brander, a relatively young man with initials behind his name, and more to come. Peter's a self-made, not a textbook, success. He worked his way up from stock boy to district manager without so much as a high school diploma. She knows he doesn't trust academics.

"He's meeting with sales reps and other hotshots at company headquarters. It's not an excuse...it's business."

"I remember going there with him once. That place has less ambience than a morgue. But I suppose he's more comfortable there than here."

"Really, Natasha." Shirley has dug a pair of sturdy brown baby shoes out of the bag. She sets them pigeon-toed on the table. "If you haven't got anything nice to say —"

"Nice shoes," Natasha says, smiling into her cup.

The wedding itself will be a surprisingly small, justice-of-the-peace affair between the weeping willows in her in-laws' park-like backyard. She's asked Jude to be her lone attendant, but with a third baby on the way and the distance between cities, her friend has reluctantly declined. "I still can't believe you're doing it," Jude says, "if you don't mind me saying, and I know you don't, you're just not the marrying type. Kevy, put that down, now, before you break it." Natasha pictures Jude with a toddler on her hip, phone wedged between ear and shoulder as she simultaneously tries to keep an eye on the older boy and work the younger's fingers out of her irresistible red hair. Kevy, first-born, is the bad seed.

"Well, I'm not into the whole traditional thing – I'm certainly no Cinderella – but I don't believe I ever said I wouldn't marry. Did I?" She's embarrassed to admit, even to Jude, that she never did get a real diamond and her proposal was uttered in pig Latin.

"So what does your...Kevy! Put that back! I swear to God, Tash. You might want to rethink your pregnancy. Are you showing yet?"

Natasha knows she's joking. "It's a little late now. Yes, I'm starting to show, but I think I can disguise it for the wedding, for Brander's parents' sake. I personally don't give a flying fuck."

"Oooh. You *like* that word, don't you? What does your family think, about Brandon, I mean?"

"It's Brand-*er*. Actually they don't know him that well. Mom's met him half a dozen times, maybe. Dad and Holly twice each. I guess I'll have to ask Holly to stand up for me now –"

"Like I could feel any worse."

"Camille's still never laid eyes on him. What do they think? Beats me. My family's not into divulging their feelings. Any time things get heavy, everything's shuffled back into the closet. The door's locked, the key thrown away. This is my life."

"Kevy! Shit, Tash, I've got to run."

"Sounds like it. Good to talk to you, friend."

"Good to talk to you, too."

She replaces the phone in its black cradle and is struck by a rogue wave of melancholy. *Hope you're not afraid.* She spins, expecting a stranger in her kitchen. The quick action makes her dizzy. It's the pregnancy, she thinks, I should expect this. She rides the spell all the way through.

Edith makes up for the skimpy ceremony with an elaborate reception. All the finest matrimonial accoutrements are unveiled and a caravan of strangers are introduced, but, save her own family, the bride hardly knows a soul.

Then begins the grand search for accommodation. Edith wants to get her grubbing paws in on the action, but, Natasha's determined to find their first home alone. She looks for an agent in the Yellow Pages. She lives by the Yellow Pages. From pizza parlours to chimney sweeps, all are as close as her fingertips. Let your fingers do the walking, she says to herself, that's what they used to say, and perhaps still do. An indispensable book, she thinks, all those people with all that diverse knowledge, or, more appropriately, know-how, packed into a cupboard in her kitchen. Knowledge is different from know-how, she believes. She understands know-how. It, and the Yellow Pages, are much more useful, as she sees it, than any of the knowledge or classics that Brander feeds intra-venously to his students. They'll take it no other way.

She pores over the real estate companies, recognizing some because she's seen their signs, their helium-filled balloons in the early morning sky. One phone call, one awkward explanation of what she's after, and they're hooked up with Graham, their skittish agent, a ferret with too many small, clicking teeth. He has the annoying habit of tagging his sentences with "most probably." "You'll want the extra room for when that little one's born, most probably." His eyes slide to Natasha's belly, like she's storing an egg in there which he can't wait to devour in his ferret way.

"Most probably," she says back, and Brander smiles at her with his eyes.

They traipse through a diverse inventory of houses, some of which will always remain lock-boxed in her mind: the corner dollhouse with its arched doorways that led into other rooms; the grey stucco with its mysterious star-shaped stain on the basement wall; the yellow barn with the purple linoleum; the 1950s bungalow with the rusted fridge that emitted toxic fumes and sent them bolting for fresh air. The lonely ones, the discarded ones, the well-loved ones that left her feeling as inadequate as any new parent. The ones that didn't feel right, or look right, or, as in the one with the squeaky floorboards and wind whistling through the attic, sound right. The divorce houses, the promotion houses, the recent death houses, where the air was palpable with grief, like the gathering after a funeral over Nanaimo bars and tea.

Graham rings again. "He's got another one, Brand," she says, cupping her hand over the mouthpiece.

Brander throws his papers into the air like Mary Tyler Moore. "Let's go!"

It's love at first bite. It's a two-storey brick, within walking distance to the university, city centre, the river and a hospital. Who knew when she might need one or the other?

"What happened to the owner?" Natasha asks. She wonders if he was a recluse; he'd wallpapered over many of the windows.

"Mr. Kovach? He's dead, now," Graham informs them. "The relatives want a quick sale."

The down payment's a gift from Brander's parents. Peter and Shirley give them a washing machine. Brander carries all one hundred and sixty pounds of pregnant wife across the threshold, but needs help with the major appliances.

The house holds its own in an eclectic neighbourhood favoured by poets and painters, students, the unsuspecting elderly who would never have thought that their neighbourhood might one day be considered chic – and who would probably never have bought there in the first place had they suspected – a few riff-raff, a grab bag of professionals, and some, like the man with the Hitchcockian belly and thick, one-armed glasses who shuffles past at five o'clock every day, who refuse to be defined.

When Holly phones, Natasha lists her home's virtues like one might their child's accomplishments. "It's got white shutters, maple floors, a pantry that gave me déjà vu, four bedrooms, a claw-footed bathtub, a red brick fireplace which we broke in on the first night, a garage and a reasonably large yard. Oh yeah, and we also got the old man's wrought-iron bed, a seven-foot dresser that must have been built in the room, a plum couch, various curtains which we immediately yanked and replaced with venetians, a winter's supply of firewood and one wooden crutch."

"Dad said it's a carpenter's delight," Holly mono-tones. "I'll see it soon. I'm coming in next week for a meeting. I'm taking part in a study...on migraines. A research project."

"That's great." Migraines; you should be coming to an AA meeting, Natasha thinks. "The house needs a little work, but we're young and we've got lots of energy. It feels right, you know? As soon as I saw it I thought: This is the house I want to grow old in."

She has five keys cut and tries them all. For the first week the newlyweds can't help tossing "home" clichés back and forth. Home is where the heart is. There's no place like home. Home is where you hang your hat. Not until the cows come home.

It's a silver-lined time. Nothing she has to do except take care of herself, eat right, put her house in order.

Brander lectures to bored eighteen-to-twenty-year-olds when he isn't working on his thesis. He puts too much of himself into his lectures which are, ultimately, unappreciated by the flippant kids. Try as he does, he's never nominated for one of those 'outstanding professor' awards. He puts even more into the thesis.

The pie should be sliced into three equal pieces, but these weeks Natasha's is only a polite sliver. She forgives his imperious idiosyncrasies, like correcting poor grammar.

The true story about Johnny (aka John J. Kovach) comes from Ann Louise in the clapboard behind them, the only person on the block who might be described as normal. She delivers a carrot cake shortly after they move in and gives Natasha the goods on Johnny.

"He died in the house. Tumbled off the broken-down cellar steps to the concrete floor, to his demise. More cake?"

Natasha thinks the cake's a nice touch, a rural touch, reminiscent of small-town courtesy. She likes Ann Louise immediately.

Funny, Natasha thinks, considering Johnny's story after her new friend leaves. It doesn't smell like a death house.

They burn Johnny's wood and hack up the dresser, but the bed they keep. Once Natasha touches up the ornate Victorian frame with black paint and throws a handmade quilt on it, it passes even the Edith test. "But you must do something about those carpets," she urges, referring to the once fashionable but now dowdy and worn patterned carpets in the upper rooms.

"Yes, we're going to lift and replace them as soon as

Brander has time," Natasha reassures, but Brander never has time and she rather likes the tattered things, mouldy as they are.

After her husband leaves in the mornings she wipes his breakfast dishes, then clambers back into that old bed under inches of blankets and the lumpy quilt. The room stays dark with the blinds closed, and there's rarely noise from the street below. A womb of her own, she muses.

She safely drifts in and out of dreams.

The baby in her own womb is restless. Natasha chooses the room with the slanted ceiling at the end of the hall for a nursery. It has a window seat and looks out onto the backyard, splattered with rusty leaves which cover the consequences of the neighbourhood dogs. The room next to theirs has more light, but that might be startling to his newborn eyes.

"You're so sure it's a boy?" Brander asks, rubbing her shoulders as she lies against him, between his splayed legs in bed.

"Look how low I'm carrying him. Yes, I do think it's a boy. I probably shouldn't say this, but I want it to be."

Brander stops rubbing and pushes her up and away from his groin, which is sore where she's been leaning against it with all that extra weight. "It's supposed to be the guy who wants a boy."

Natasha rolls to her own side of the bed. "I know. I don't know why I want a boy, maybe it's because of all the things that can happen to little girls."

"Things happen to little boys, too," Brander says in a low and serious voice.

"Of course, but you know the stats as well as I do. Girls are much more likely to experience something nasty in their lives. Anything can happen anywhere –"

"To anyone," Brander finishes.

No one *has a knife.*

"What about shoelaces? Maybe we could knot them together and –" Natasha feels her heart beat faster.

"And what? Lasso him?" Rosco scoffs. He's on his back, arms X'd across his chest, as if he's already dead.

"Hey jackass, that's my little sister," Holly says, also on her back. "At least she's got some ideas."

Natasha feels a lump build in her throat and she's afraid she might start crying again. She stretches out, feeling all her bones against the vibrating floor. The hip bones, new this year, are two small tents of crushing pain. Back to side, side to stomach. Her arms, crossed beneath her head, become a pillow, her nose to the semi's wood floor. She licks her lips. It's easier to breathe when they're wet.

Five bodies, spent with hunger and fatigue, tuck in for a nap beneath the communal blanket of fear. Gina and Rosco succumb quickly. Kent is somewhere between the two worlds, whistling, though he barely makes a sound.

Natasha thinks of her father. He can whistle, birdlike, in several keys, and once he was on television with his act. He looked like a real celebrity, she thought, tall and steady beside the accompanist while his cheeks fluttered and the camera closed in on his profile. He looked like a success. Someone you could trust with your life, someone who could save it.

She and her sisters were each asked which tie he should wear for the appearance. His tie collection, a brilliant cluster of wagging tongues down the back of his bedroom door, is unmatched by anyone. Paisleys, stripes, solids, polka dots, checks, ties with flecks of gold, ties that made her dream of jungles and cold lakes and faraway places and leaves. She judges, by his ties, that whatever it is he does in that office, he is extremely good at it. He'd gone with her choice for the television appearance: wide navy and white stripes in a diagonal.

A moment of awkward silence passes, then Brander turns out the light. "Well, I still think we'd better discuss a few girls' names, too, just in case."

"Okay," Natasha says, exhaustion dropping on her like a heavy cloak, pulling her down toward sleep.

"Mañana."

She can't wait to fill the sunroom with plants, with green, with life, but she'll have to, because it's not insulated and already it's too cold in the evenings to watch the sun set through these windows. She puts "Buy Boston Fern" on her mental to-do list.

The daytime house is hers alone. She wallows in the space and quiet. The apartment block had rocked with music and voices, sometimes deep into the night. There were several students in the building, doing everything but studying.

When Brander and Natasha learned that she was expecting, he suggested she defer her degree. The baby'd need her at home. She agrees.

"Seems like a waste," Holly says during another late-night, alcohol-induced chat. "All that time, all that tuition."

"Education's never a waste," Natasha counters. How could she do it? How could Holly continue to get smashed after a drunk had stolen their future from them? "And besides, if it weren't for university I'd never have met Brander and set sail for a new life."

"Well, good night then. Happy sailing." And her sister hangs up. This is how it is.

Natasha ambles around the house in her rocky gait, exploring and imagining scenes in each room like a little girl with a brand new dollhouse. Except this is better. She presses her palm against the cold brick fireplace. "Mine." The stained glass above the bay window. "Mine." The oak, battered banister; the lazy Susan; the failing back steps. Mine. Mine. Mine. She forces herself into the cellar. There's no sign of an accident, not a hint of blood, but she feels better after the inspection, knowing what isn't there.

There are occasional visits with Ann Louise and a persistent Avon Lady, but mostly she's alone. She half-heartedly tries to conjure the ghost of John Kovach, but there's nothing there. Apparently he'd had Alzheimers' disease. Perhaps he doesn't remember where he lived, she thinks, then smirks at her own cleverness. It would be wrong to say his presence has vanished completely, however, for each night she and Brander sleep in the dead man's bed.

Natasha never forgets this. They laugh about it, even make jokes to disguise any discomfort they suspect the other might be feeling. And she truly does sleep while the baby turns inside her, a blessing tied to the pregnancy and the presence of her husband's arm slung across her, his chest snugged against her back. Brander's much better at wordplay than Natasha, so it's he who comes up with Johnny Dead Bed.

In October, when the snow dusts everything and contemplates whether or not to stay, Natasha sits in Brander's office facing their impressive collection of books. Her contributions to the shelves are mostly geography and sociology texts brightened with colourful photographs to hold the students' attention. There's also the requisite first-year English reads, and a few Western Canadian classics – *As For Me and My House, Wild Geese,* and *Fruits of the Earth* – from her class with Brander. Between the chapters of these she tumbled into love.

She pulls out a text from one of her final classes, Spanish. Her high school French teacher, a *monsieur* with woolly white hair who was mooned and tormented by Dorion and his gang, had told her she had an aptitude for languages. It was offhand compliments like that, morsels, really, which stuck in her brain and saw her off on unlikely tangents. She blows the dust off the book and decides to brush up, or rather, to keep brushing, because one year of textbook Spanish has not made her fluent.

After rediscovering the text it's never far from her reach. She's consumed by the language, basking in it for hours at a time. "Brander, you're home already? *¡Caramba!* Where did the time go?"

She begins to think in Spanish. When the phone rings she has to check herself to be sure she answers hello and not *bueno* or *hola*. Numbers are *números. Necesitamos leche,* she tells Brander when he's making up the grocery list.

"What?"

"We need milk."

She's always skipped from passion to passion. This is nothing new.

"Natasha, where are you?" Brander asks, often, when there are long, quiet moments between them, or in the last breaths before sleep. Natasha rubs her belly. Natasha *no está. Regresa más tarde.*

They eat late, sometimes in front of the fire, then Brander leads her up the carpeted stairs, down the hall with the faded runner and into their bedroom, where the white moon's framed in their window, and they crawl into Johnny Dead Bed, though sex is now too much effort for them both.

The nights grow longer and colder. The house's wood-chip insulation is insufficient, especially upstairs. Their bedroom.

"Brander, let me call someone about the insulation," Natasha tries. "It's going to be too cold for the baby."

"We can't afford it right now," he says, without losing his place in a book. He almost always has his nose, in fact the better part of his face, buried in a book. The tips of his ears are red. *Rojo.* She could say something about his wool socks.

"Your parents will help."

He looks up from the book, sets it down, the spine arching in protest. "My parents. Why is it always *my* parents? The crib, the change table, the downpayment...now the goddamn insulation? They're shit to you unless you need something from them."

"I'm sorry. It's just...the baby...any day now."

He returns to his book. With a hrumph.

Jameson is born on a winterlike, late autumn morning when the sun cuts diamonds in the snow. The same hour of the same day, an earthquake in Mexico kills hundreds. People are hacking up their brothers and sisters, even babies, all over the world. There's a gas war. It's also the birthday of Fernando Valenzuela, the famous pitcher.

She'd suffered through back-wracking hard labour all night but sleep now is impossible. Brander was present for the whole birthing, spooning her ice chips, mopping her head. When the pain ripped her apart and she begged for drugs, he squeezed her hand and said in a calm, professorial voice, "You don't need them, you can do this." He was wrong. She did need them. She didn't get them.

She's rolled into the recovery room where an angel with a gold stud in her nose brings tea and toast. "I've never been closer to God in my life," she tells the nurse, whom she assumes is accustomed to postnatal raving.

She keeps Jameson in her room, a ward, with three other new mothers. She glows when one of the young nurses says, "I like this one best," behind the pulled curtain. Brander's parents want to pay for a private room, but Natasha's glad she opted for the ward. The indignities of having her episiotomy stitches examined, an enema, her breasts, big and hard as coconuts, kneaded, are far less severe knowing that three feet away another mother's enduring the same indignities.

They bring Jameson home, where the heart should be, but Brander's never is. It's Natasha's house, has been since Brander lugged her up the front steps and in, and he seems to sense this, as if the walls have a will of their own and the furnace conks out to spite him.

It's a pleasant shock that her husband's at immediate ease with the baby. He's adept at clipping the tiny white fingernails and swabbing Jameson's ugly navel. He'd been the one to go in during the circumcision, while Natasha cried into her hospital pillow. He's a natural at bathing Jameson in the plastic tub, at burping him over his shoulder. Natasha's primary role, as she sees it, is to feed the baby. It's something she does well.

The baby shower's at Edith's. Natasha doesn't know the silver-haired women with painted-on lips and cheeks and glued-on eyelashes who coo over her baby and ask to see his little feet, white and plump as rising dough. Holly arrived with another garbage bag of Nels' baby clothes, a night light in the shape of a rocking horse, a new highchair, and rye on her breath. Still, Natasha's glad to know at least one of the guests. The other women present Natasha with layettes, bunting bags, overall sets with snaps along the inseams, white sweaters and bonnets, teddy bears, a plastic bowl and a cup that won't spill when tipped, and a curious mobile with heavy pieces of copper cut into clouds and a sun.

"Like I'm going to hang *this* over his crib," Natasha whispers to Holly, who won a cut-glass candy dish for being the first to unscramble all twenty infant-related words on the sheets Edith had done up at the printers.

"It could take an eye out."

Holly pops a slice of salmon roll into her mouth. "Ugh. Tastes like matches." She discreetly spits it into her linen napkin. "Which way to the john?"

Jameson peeps and Natasha feels her milk let down.

She hopes she remembered to stuff pads into her bra. "One up, one down. Up's fastest. Go back out to the foyer and turn right."

"Foy-ay. So that's what that was," Holly says, not caring which of Edith's smart-suited lady friends might hear. "A foy-ay."

Camille, of course, is too far away to attend the shower, but she sends a newspaper horoscope from the momentous day of Jameson's birth. Shirley could only send her love and a generous cheque. She and Peter are in Toronto on a business/pleasure trip.

Later, when Natasha's alone again with her baby nuzzling at her engorged breast — like a watermelon, she thinks, marvelling at the size she's become — she unrolls the horoscope she hadn't had the nerve to examine earlier, with all those proper ladies looking on. She reads: "Your baby born today will excel at keeping secrets – both yours and his own. He (or she) will have faith in his own judgment and rarely ask for advice. Luckily, the child's instincts are excellent. Do not expect your deep thinker to be the life of the party: chances are he may not even attend the party. Content with his own company, the child will prefer solitary nature walks to crowded gatherings."

What more could she ask?

She sets it aside and pulls the sleeping baby off her nipple. He is new bread, a good, warm sack over her shoulder as she gently pats his back. She carries him into the bedroom they all share, his crib at the end of Johnny Dead Bed, and covers him with the lemon-yellow blanket that she'd given Nels when he was born. Before she also tucks in for a nap, she returns to the rocker for the horoscope. She rolls it, slides an elastic band around it, and sets it in the closet in a box she'd labelled "Jameson's Treasures" a week before his birth. What goes around, she thinks. Somewhere, in her parents' house, "Natasha's Treasures," are similarly stashed.

Life settles. Jameson's a good baby, which means little except that he sleeps and eats well and occasionally, by coincidence, turns up the corners of his pink lips at the right time so that Brander, Natasha, Sterling, or Edith think he's smiling.

Natasha bundles him tight and stuffs him into a Snugli, throws the lemon blanket over top and sets out for long afternoon walks. Edith approves; says fresh air is good for the baby. Why, she pushed Brander in a stroller every day, and anyone can see how well he turned out. Ann Louise says motherhood looks good on Natasha; another morsel for her jar.

Her stitches have healed and she's eager. Natasha slides her hand over Brander's nipples, which are almost more sensitive than her own. She pushes her hips toward him and scissors one leg between his, then reaches down and strokes.

"It's too soon," he says, lifting her hand off his penis. "You should have a checkup first."

She has the checkup, gets the okay, and they fumble through, but it's not like before. Brander is extra gentle with her, but it pinches. "Am I hurting you?" he asks. "I can stop."

"No, it's okay," she says, though her back teeth are clenched and she exhales with each of his thrusts. "They said the first time would be rough."

Brander lifts her a little. "Who said?"

"They said."

"Who are *they?*" he says, losing his rhythm. "Oh shit, I'm losing my erection."

"Just *they.* You know, *them!*"

It doesn't work. She's still bleeding, and her breasts leak milk onto the sheets or squirt onto Brander's chest and he hates this. Time. *Necesitamos tiempo.*

Spring comes, as it always does, even after those wretched winter days when the sky's a naughty child holding its breath and no one expects to ever see the sun again – it rides in on the wind.

Natasha starts tomato plants from seed and sets them in flats in the sunroom. At night she carries them to the bay window in the living room, the nights still quite cool in the uninsulated sunroom. It's too early to trust them, gentle things, entirely to nature.

She reads to her son. Jack *y el* Beanstalk. Snow White *y los siete* Dwarves. She measures the quality of each day by the number of ticks she makes on her to-do list.

Usually, the ticks add up to a pretty good day.

Jameson bounces in a Jolly Jumper. When he gets too heavy for that, it's into the walker. "We have a good arrangement, he and I," Natasha tells Holly, who's in Saskatoon for another session at the hospital and only has time for lunch. "While he bumps from table to couch, I clean windows, polish wood, scrub, paint, fill holes in plaster, change wallpaper, tile my washroom, make my house my own."

"You're lucky," her sister says. She's wearing her hair long again, with waves in the front that soften her face but also make her look vulnerable.

"Why?" Natasha sets a bowl of sliced bagels on the table between them. "You've got a house and a son as well."

Holly selects a bagel. Natasha notices that her sister's eyes are welling. She can see them better now that Holly's converted to contact lenses. "But you've got a home."

Oh boy. Natasha doesn't know how to respond.

"Listen, I've got to get to my appointment," Holly says without meeting Natasha's eyes. She kisses Jameson on the top of his head. "Bye, sugarcane. Stay sweet."

In the summer Brander and Natasha carry Jameson's playpen outside. He marvels at the butterflies and stuffs grass in his mouth while they attack the dog-plagued yard.

They dig a small garden plot. There will be radishes, and lettuce if the bugs don't get it first, peas, and of course, Natasha's tomatoes.

Brander constructs a fence along the back lane. His parents bring an anniversary gift. A barbecue. Natasha picks up a patio table and chairs at a yard sale, and a paddling pool, from Ann Louise's husband, Ken, who works at Canadian Tire. The pool is for later. Natasha and Brander often look out their back window to see what they've become.

But day and night are just that. Night and day. "Is it me?" Natasha asks, after Brander rolls away yet again, mumbling something about an early morning. Natasha pulls the sheet to her chin.

"No, it's no one. I'm just tired."

"You've been tired for three weeks. This isn't natural."

"Who says?"

"I say."

"Look, our sex life was bound to drop off a bit. We've been married over a year. We can't go on screwing twice a day. It happens to everyone."

Natasha knows it doesn't. Ann Louise tells her, and Jude. She knows that Sterling and Edith sleep in separate beds, and she can't fathom ever ending up like that. She's come to depend on Brander's warm body at night. If he's up late working in the room next door, she watches the moon until he joins her. He emanates heat and more than that, he embodies a quality she can't name, although *sanctuary* comes close. *Safety*, too. She curls into him or he into her. Then, and only then, does she sleep.

Natasha suggests counselling. Brander suggests a party. They string patio lanterns along the clothesline, send witty invitations to Brander's colleagues, and spend too much money on vodka, rye, good wine and beer. This isn't like a college party, where everyone's expected to BYOB. They're homeowners now, responsible, parents. They're not throwing a party, they're *entertaining*.

Jameson's to spend the evening with Ann Louise's kids, but Natasha's more than reluctant to let him go. She's terrified.

"Come on, Tash. Darcie's got her babysitting course," Brander says as he opens lawn chairs, creating a circle for conversation. He sounds tired, she thinks, or maybe just impatient. "Besides, they're just a stone's throw away if there's any trouble, real or imagined."

"I know, but I've never been away from him. What if

something terrible happens? What if he picks something off the floor and chokes? What if they forget to lock the door and a pervert walks in and –"

"Oh, Jesus," Brander says sharply. "Come on now."

"But anything can happen anywhere to anyone, remember?" She rubs the goosebumps off her arms. This was not a good idea.

"He's going and that's it, and if you can't handle it, maybe you should go over there with him too!" Brander storms past her into the house, barely missing her.

She feels like she's been slapped again. The long arm of Mr. O'Brien, reaching across the years.

It isn't a huge crowd, but there are several strange faces. They barbecue steaks and eat Caesar salad with three-quarter-inch croutons that could break a tooth. Natasha's relieved that Ann Louise and Ken have agreed to come. The three of them hover near the barbecue, making themselves look busy. "Would you like more barbecue sauce on that?" This is where we fit, Natasha thinks, with the barbecue tools and lighter fluid. The animated conversations about dead English poets and post-modernism are conducted in another language. Much further out there than Spanish. When the barbecue cools down, the trio gravitate to the punch bowl. *¿Tienes sed? ¿Tienes hambre?*

After the meal there's an uncomfortable pall. *Incómodo.* People work harder at conversation without the scrape of plates, the jangle of falling cutlery to fill in the gaps. Natasha knows she's expected to aid this process, and waltzes from conversation to conversation, adding little more than a presence and an occasional chuckle. She knows enough to laugh at the right times, a lesson learned with Sterling and Edith.

She ducks away from the party to check Jameson, and returns lighter, having found him safely asleep. The beverages have mercifully taken effect with many of their guests and no one notices whether she laughs at their clever jokes or not.

Hours later, when everyone's well-lubricated, the music's louder and the lawn chairs have picked up and deserted their original positions, another guest arrives with her own bottle of wine. She wears a black turtleneck and a skirt that hugs her ass. Her hair is dark and full, like Camille's, and appears to float just above her shoulders. Her short skirt emphasizes long, tanned legs and black Grecian sandals with long straps that crisscross up and over her ankles. She holds a jean jacket, and her small handbag's slung sideways across her chest, as is the fashion. If she had breasts this would emphasize them, Natasha thinks. It would emphasize hers. "Hi," Natasha says, extending her hand. "I'm Natasha...Brander's wife."

The latecomer's gaze slices right through her. "Hi. God, I'm so late. Oh! Sorry, I'm Roxanne —" She takes Natasha's hand and shakes her fingers. Ivory and jade bangles jingle on her wrist. "Roxanne Eklund." She pans the other guests.

"Can I get you a glass of punch?"

"I'd like that." She hands Natasha the bottle of wine, which she sets on the makeshift bar, unopened.

Ann Louise watches with interest. "She might be

twenty," she whispers, as Natasha whisks past her.

Brander hasn't noticed the late arrival yet; Natasha pounces. "So are you in the English department, Roxanne?" The girl seems to gather up her shoulders and pay attention then.

"No, well not really. I'm in my second year. I had Brander last year –"

A strange, even comic choice of words. Brander would be amused, Natasha guesses.

" – for English. I'm working at the university this summer. Just filing and stuff."

Ann Louise crunches beside Natasha with a palmful of potato chips. After the introduction she ducks out under the pretence of obtaining more pretzels. Roxanne and Natasha watch her disappear into the bright lights inside.

"Great house," Roxanne says. "Would you mind if I had a tour?"

Natasha's pleased to show off her house at every opportunity, and takes her in through the back, narrating as they move from room to room. "Of course it wasn't like this when we bought it," she says, her voice light. "We've had to do a lot of work."

"Was the mantel like this?" Roxanne runs her hand along the carved oak, Natasha's wood.

"Yes, but it was painted over and I stripped it."

Roxanne's impressed with the nursery, with its blue-striped wallpaper and border of green and blue trains. Natasha isn't particularly crafty but has managed to sew the letters of Jameson's name together, stuffed them with batting and pinned them to the wall. She thinks that they spell other things, too, like *contentment, family, life as it should be,* if anyone cares to look that deeply.

"And last but definitely not least," Natasha says, swinging the door wide, "the master bedroom." She follows Roxanne in, so is unable to gauge her initial reaction. A sudden intake of breath? A giveaway sigh?

"It's all antiques," the strange girl says, looking at her reflection in the oval standing mirror. She skims over the slippers on either side of the bed, the framed photos of Brander and Natasha, and the two of them with the baby. Natasha thinks she'd like to be able to skim over the bed, as well, but she can't, and Natasha knows what that's like, thinking something so hard, so secret, that you're afraid you'll say it out loud and then you surprise yourself by doing exactly that. "Johnny Dead Bed."

If she were less of this world and more of the world of spirits and other good ghosts, Natasha would say that it was the house looking after her that night. Or maybe old Johnny himself. Of course, all that dirty laundry comes out in the months to follow, complete with many hollow promises, the suspicions, custody threats, meddling in-laws, and, finally, arrangements they can all live with.

The wrangling leaves her limb-heavy and sore, as though she's been run over by a heavy vehicle. Parked on. One night, when Brander has Jameson at his new place, she follows her feet down the creaking steps to the basement, to the dark, and creeps barefoot across the gravel that's crumbled off the eighty-year-old foundation. The coarse stones and shards of cement split the soles of her feet. Centipedes scurry. She worries the small ears of mice.

After her nocturnal tour's complete she sits on the bottom step, Johnny's final step, and begins picking her feet clean. Still looking for the body. Still not found.

In spite of the wrangling, Brander continues to be a wonderful father. His thesis is accepted, and he teaches even more classes to even more unappreciative students. Jameson – like the tulips, the lilacs, the undemanding pink and purple petunias that bordered their home – blooms.

Natasha realizes that the maze of her life neither began nor ended in the two-storey brick. She comes to realize, too, that some of Brander's knowledge, which she's so often scorned, has rubbed off on her, and that knowledge and know-how can hold hands.

Her passions turn, and turn again. She loses herself in morose books, follows the various paths of human destruction and horror through the nightly news. She rents movies in which the characters' lives are desperate, impossible.

Peter and Shirley frequent the city. They take Natasha and Jameson out to dinner or for drives along the river, where Shirley exclaims over the grand homes, Peter wonders about the taxes the owners must be forking over, and Natasha gets queasy from the twists and turns.

"There are worse things," Shirley tells her. "Think of

Holly." Natasha knows she's being selfish with pain. It's not hers alone.

"When the going gets tough," Peter says to the windshield, still severing any possibility of deeper conversation with his back pocket clichés.

And so. With the poets and painters, the dropouts and drug addicts, the Hitchcock-bellied man and the rest, she accepts her dishevelled life. She files divorce papers, finds an apartment, feeds her boy, gets the new university calendar, starts looking for prospective daycares.

She kisses Jameson and sings him to sleep, the two of them washed in the protective glow from his rocking horse night light. How did Holly know?

She *is* afraid of the dark.

Intermezzo

The driver of the half-ton – this is her *second* move with hired help in the last five years – is beginning to look good. *Too* good.

The rented duplex is certainly several rungs up from the modest, intermediary apartment, although those rooms will be ever remembered in soft focus as the site of first steps, first sentences, first tricycle rides around and around and around, but it will never become home. The duplex will suffice until she squirrels enough money away for her own house. Until she gets the eggshell bits of her life into something resembling order.

"Bad," Natasha thinks aloud as she unwraps a glass plate from layers of newspaper, "I've got it bad."

"What?" Ann Louise pushes her hair – peppered with grey – off her damp face. She sets a glass salt shaker on the shelf above the sink. The matching pepper could be any-where. "Did you say something, Tash?"

"I said, 'wow.'" Her eyes are fixed on the window-framed image of the young mover, his muscled arms beneath rolled sleeves. At even the tongues of his unlaced workboots, hanging like the tongues of large black dogs on summer's hottest day. "God, what a vision."

Ann Louise asks, "How'd you find him?"

"I got his name off the Employment Wanted board on campus. He can't be more than twenty-one, but he'd do for an erotic escape." She moves away from the window, afraid to get caught. "Even his helper, that unfortunate, slow-moving creature with a head like a torpedo, even *he* holds a certain, primitive appeal."

Ann Louise laughs and snorts, making Natasha laugh, too. "You need to get laid, girl. Oh, here he comes."

The muscled driver backs into the room at one end of a small deep-freeze. During the split, when they were well into that grown-up game of "This is mine, That is yours," she'd considered leaving it with Brander, in case Jameson ever crawled in and got trapped – these are the things that she thinks about – but she buys bread and meat in bulk, so here it is, wedged in her doorway, following her like a big, dumb ox.

"Would you like some more water?" she offers, stepping over splayed cardboard boxes that release little poofs of air beneath her feet.

He sets his end of the deep-freeze down. "Thank you, ma'am." He has a deep voice that reverberates in her chest and sends pings of heat to the backs of her knees. She bets he can sing. Louis Armstrong, maybe. Or "Mack the Knife." The top of his head is hidden beneath a red bandana, a style popularized by Hispanic street gangs in Hollywood movies. Long waves stick to his neck, and sweat blossoms above his thick upper lip. She draws in his blended scent of sweat, cigarettes and what? Horses? He chugalugs his water. "Thanks. That was great."

She takes the cool glass from his hand, his fingers touching hers briefly. "You're very welcome."

"Better get back to it," he says, looking left of her eyes. "A few more loads should do it."

He leaves.

Natasha steps over a box to get to the window again. "Is he hot or is he hot!" It's not a question.

Ann Louise turns the tap off, shakes her hands beneath it; she has yet to find any towels. "Girl, if you met him in an alley you would scream."

It's stifling. She frees Jameson and Ann Louise's two, Dylan and Darcie, from unpacking and they scatter: the boys to the front, where a third boy in long shorts is doing figure-eights on his bike, and Darcie, eighteen, to the backyard. She flops in the shade of the mountain ash.

"Jameson's already made a new friend." Ann Louise has brought in the final box marked *kitchen*. "Jordan something or other. They want to ride their bikes to the park."

Natasha recovers. "I don't know. He's barely off his training wheels. We don't even really know –"

"Dylan can go with them."

"He'd want to?"

"Sure. It'd be a break. Besides, it's only a couple of blocks from here. Darcie'll stick around with us."

Natasha shakes her head. "You're teaching me lenience, Ann. I'll let them know it's okay."

The outside air has an oven-like quality. Sweat trickles behind her ears and meanders between her breasts. She dabs at it. "You guys can go, but keep an eye on the time, okay? I want you back by five. God," she wipes her upper lip, "I'm losing weight just standing here. Remember, five o'clock."

"For pizza?" Jameson weaves around her, still wobbly on his new, big-boy bike.

"Yes, for pizza."

"No pineapples," he squeals.

"Or mushrooms," Dylan adds. "Or anchovies. Yuck!"

The two younger boys wheel over the curb. "Watch for cars!" Natasha shouts to their backs.

"Uh, excuse me," the mover in the bandana says. "Where do you want this thing?" His voice is an ice cube slid along her arm. She feels her nipples rise, blood rushing to roses in her cheeks.

"Um." She forgets herself. She's supposed to be directing this little drama and she's completely forgotten who she is, what she's doing. They've rolled the piano – a Yamaha purchased by Brander's parents for Jameson's sake – down the ramp and await instruction. "Just a sec." She skirts past them to prop the front door open with a rock the size of a grapefruit. "Against the north wall," she says, pointing, as though they're incapable of comprehending directions. "Right there."

It's a slow navigation, like a difficult birth. The thighs of her favourite mover look about to burst as he squats and forces his end of the piano around, then pushes it back against the wall. He unties the ropes and Natasha helps pull the quilted covering off. The piano's found its new home with only one ding – a three-inch scrape on the left side – to mark the passage. She instinctively runs her fingers over the keys, like a birthday child who yearns to get her fingers on the toy she's just unwrapped. Only a little out of tune, she thinks. She plays the simple introduction to Elton John's "Daniel."

"I love that song," the driver says, staring at the keyboard, her fingers, as if in disbelief. He plays an A-minor chord, surprising her. "My girlfriend used to play it."

"She doesn't any more?" Natasha asks.

"She died."

"Oh," Natasha says, solemnly closing the lid on the keys and her fantasy of splashing in a bathtub with him. Now she sees him weeping over a coffin, and curses the kind of day it's going to be.

At three o'clock Natasha decides she doesn't like the neighbour, a man in an off-white cotton shirt – not unlike something her father would wear on a casual day – with buttoned flaps over each breast pocket. His pants stretch across a bottom that reminds her of a puffball, and he doesn't so much walk as he lurches, with his upper body angled as though he's forever walking uphill. With his tan cap, red beard, and sturdy shoes, he looks like he belongs either in a lighthouse or in the woods leading a Boy Scout troop through the brush. He's the type who would know which mushrooms are the good ones and which could kill you like that. She watches him watching Darcie bend for another box. The girl should be wearing a bra, Natasha thinks. And longer shorts.

"Darc!" she calls. "Come have something to drink."

Darcie's there in a minute, setting a box of books on the floor. "Oh, my aching back," she says, rubbing it.

Natasha hands her a glass of water. "Cheers." They clink and finish their drinks quickly. She runs the tap again, testing the water with her fingers until it's cold. "Darc, have you talked to the neighbour?" Over the fence she sees him watering his garden. With the angle and height of his hands on the hose he appears to be urinating on his herbs. Where are those boys?

"No. We've just said hi," Darcie says. "I think he's kind of a goof. His name's Freddy. Do you believe that? Not Fred, or Frederick, like a regular adult, but Freddy. Like Freddy Krueger."

"Freddy Krueger," Natasha repeats.

"*I saw* his name," Natasha blurts. "*It was on his shirt. Freddy.*"

"*I saw it, too,*" Rosco says. *They are resting now, even their shoulders sore from the physical effort it takes to have a truly good cry.*

"*Me, too,*" says Holly, sounding far away.

"*That's good,*" Kent says, "*that's something.*"

"*Comfortable?*" Holly snuggles into Natasha, little girls again.

"*Mmm.*"

Everyone returns to their private thoughts. Natasha rests her head on the floor. The rumbling against her ear could be a distant train. She imagines boarding it, waving goodbye to her parents. She has lunch on her lap. A peanut butter and banana sandwich, a perfect apple, a bottle of orange juice, two Dad's oatmeal cookies wrapped in cellophane. Where is she going? To the ocean. Why the ocean? She wants to see where the world begins.

The train leaves the station – ch ch, ch ch, ch ch, ch ch – speeds through the back sides of towns, over pennies squashed flat on tracks and past cows that don't have a hot clue. It cuts a fast, iron trail across fields, then foothills. It snakes through the Rockies, over glorious bridges, and gorges where water appears frozen.

"*Thy kingdom come, thy will be done, thy kingdom come, thy will be done.*" *Kent's desperation snaps the thin walls of her reverie.*

"*His record's stuck," Rosco whispers. "On earth as it is in heaven.*"

The hours of the afternoon long jump toward four o'clock, four-thirty, five. Natasha hopes to be settled inside a week, then it's back to work at the Education Library on campus. She's grateful for everyone's help – the promise of pizza does wonders, she thinks – but where are those kids? She pulls herself off her knees. She's covered the drawers with Mactac; now the utensils can go in. "It's after five. I'm getting worried."

"I already called in the pizza," Darcie says. "Tough luck if they're not back."

Natasha rinses her hands. She'll line the sill above the sink with African violets, something that will bloom all year. Something, she realizes, her mother did, once upon an unusual time. "God, I could use a beer. A beer and a cigarette."

"I thought you quit?" Darcie pulls a strand of her hair to test its length. It's easy to forget that she's a teen, Natasha muses, until she pops a bubble or throws her hair over her head, shaking it out to give it more body and a wild, runway model look.

"About ten times already. I'm back and forth."

"The bathroom's done," Ann Louise interrupts. "Darc, go see if your brother's out there yet."

"You asked me to do this." She sets another can in the lazy Susan, spins it, puts in another, spins again.

"I'll go have a look," Natasha says. "If the pizza comes there's money in my —"

Dylan and Jameson bang through the back door with Jordan on their heels.

"Mom!" Jameson screams.

Natasha's heartbeat doubles.

"Someone stole my bike!"

"Oh God, Jamie. Where?"

"At the park," Dylan answers, gasping. "We were at the paddling pool and this kid took off on it. We saw him take it."

"I know where he lives," the other boy, Jordan, says. "I'll show you."

Natasha's already lacing her bare feet into running shoes. "Let's go." She glances at Ann Louise.

"This way," Jordan says, jumping onto his bike.

Dylan starts after him. Natasha grabs Jameson's hand and they break into a loping run, as though their ankles are tied for a two-legged race. Jordan bends over his handlebars, shirt flapping around his ribs like gills.

"How far?" Natasha asks at the end of the block.

"Not much farther," Dylan says, slowing for them.

They cross the street, turn left, hurry down another quiet block of homes with potted red geraniums on the front step and Nanking Cherry shrubs growing through fences.

Jordan skids to a stop. "There! That big house." He points to a one-and-a-half storey in dire need of paint or a tornado. There are toys in the yard but no bike, no people.

"I gotta go now," Jordan says, and speeds off.

"You guys stay here," Natasha orders. *"Right* here. I'll check the back." She takes the dirt path between the ominous house and an unruly caragana. There's a rusted Mustang up on blocks, a pyramid of Pilsner beer cases and a boy, about three years old. Oh, Jesus, Natasha thinks. There's a face that likely hasn't seen soap and water since a nurse cleaned it off at birth. "Is your dad home?"

"Home," the boy says, picking at a scab on his heel.

"Yes, is your daddy inside?"

The child sticks a filthy finger in his mouth and Natasha wonders if he's slow. She returns to the front. The boys are still waiting on the far side of a fence with many of its pickets missing. "Nothing yet," she says, thinking of missing teeth.

She knocks, hears television voices inside, then footsteps. One Mississippi, two Mississippi. A man with one eye opens the door. The other eye is a milky marble, the same colour as his ribbed muscle shirt. A tightly-wound package in jeans with a slash across the thigh and a pocket showing through, and high-top, laceless runners.

He doesn't say hello.

"Excuse me, but these boys said they saw your son take my son's bike in the park." *Tight.* She tries not to stare into the white eye. "It's new."

"Robert, get over here," the man calls, his single eye steady on her. An unhealthy-looking boy of about nine appears from the darkness behind the door. His hair's been shaved very close to his scalp, and his T-shirt sports a decal of a large screw and the letter U. "Do you know anything about this kid's bike?"

"No," Robert says.

Natasha looks back at the boys. They're frozen: twin stalagmites. "They said they saw you take it. At the playground. Just a few minutes ago."

The one-eyed man steps from the doorway, a foot from Natasha now. They're the same height. "No bike."

"It's new," she repeats. "We just bought it."

"Listen lady, you heard him. My kid," he cocks a bare shoulder toward her, "didn't steal no fuckin' bike." He's become much louder than necessary.

A woman turns up behind him. She's possibly three hundred pounds and wearing a tent dress. A family could camp beneath it, Natasha thinks, shifting her own weight. "But they saw him. They wouldn't lie." She wants to add, "They're good boys," but that would sound like another attack. More fuel.

The man steps closer, face inches from hers. "You've got no right to come over here and accuse my kid, ya stupid bitch!"

"Hey," the woman in the door says.

Natasha's immobilized. The boys are immobilized. She wishes for magic dust to blow off her hand, some potion to make this go away. Shit! She spins and storms down the three steps. He's right behind her on the sidewalk, toes on her heels.

"What the fuck gives you the right to come over here and call my kid a thief? Huh? What the fuck makes you think you can do that?" He jabs her between the shoulder blades.

She snaps around. If he's going to hit her she wants to see it coming. Facial bruises will look better in court than the damage he might inflict on her back. "Listen, you son of a bitch. You can deal with me or you can deal with my husband, and let me tell you, I'm a hell of a lot nicer than he is!"

"Oooh, threatening me now." He waves his fingers in her face.

They're nose to nose. Go ahead, she thinks, nail me. He dekes around her and lunges toward Jameson and Dylan, a spellbound pair in the spot where a gate should be. "Whicha you little fairies is spreadin' lies?"

Natasha jumps between them. "For God's sake!

They're just kids!"

The man claws around her to reach her boy. She grabs the arm, sinking her nails into skin, and hisses, lips grazing his ear: "Don't even fuckin' think about it."

Our father, who art in heaven, hallowed be thy name. Our father, who art in heaven, hallowed be thy name. Our father, who art in heaven, hallowed be thy name. Our father, who art in heaven, hallowed be thy name.

She pushes Jameson to get him started down the sidewalk. Dylan jogs ahead.

"Who the fuck do you think you are?" the one-eyed man yells after her. "We don't have your fuckin' bike!"

All this trouble over a bike, she thinks, but they're doing it, they're getting away with it. She half hopes the creep will charge after her. She's certain her adrenalin would give her superhuman powers; she could kill him with her own rage. "You're gonna be fuckin' sorry!" she yells back, wondering what boulder she could drop to crush him completely. What comes out stuns them all: "My husband's a cop, you son of a bitch!" She yells it again. "My husband's a cop!"

Jameson doesn't miss a step.

She listens, waits for the jump from behind.

Nothing.

"Well, that's over." She grips her son's bony shoulder and keeps striding toward home.

It's not getting any cooler.

One day we'll laugh, she thinks, putting her head down, getting to it. Going home. She's aware that she's plowing through the heat, plowing through her electrifying rage. She's done it. She's done a man's job, a father's job, Brander's job, and it's over now. She plows past tidy bungalows with their window boxes spilling petunias. She plows past the elderly woman sweeping elm seeds off her steps, the roofing crew pitching shingles into a disposal bin. She plows up her own driveway, where Ann Louise and Darcie wait with their hands pasted over their mouths, the news preceding her. She plows into the house, into the bathroom, bends over the unfamiliar toilet and lets everything go.

Through the next two years, she plows.

The City *Becomes* Her

"*Grandma won* how much money?" Jameson's perched on the kitchen counter, legs swinging over the edge, while Natasha irons the fussy shoulders of a blouse for work.

"Twenty-five thousand." Water spurts from the iron and she rides over it, hoping it won't leave marks. Now she'll have to wear it to work damp. The history side of her double degree – history and Spanish – has opened the door to the local history department of the public library. It's a pleasant job but she works just enough, having resolved that there's more to creation than chasing after money like it's a slick panacea for life's problems. Because the library's a magnet for both rich and poor, the educated and illiterate, she meets all types.

The boy tries to whistle. "How many zeroes after twenty-five?"

"Three." She slides her arms into the sleeves and arranges her long hair to see if it will cover the wet spot. "Three fat ones. Now you'd better get ready for school, young man."

Jameson scoots off the counter. He's wearing Ninja Turtle underwear and nothing else. "Did you do laundry?"

"Your jeans are in a basket in my room. And put on a sweater...it's thirty-two below."

Her boy. Jameson's a mature child with a razor wit; she keeps little from him. Despite the see-sawing between Brander's home and hers, he's turning out just fine, he's a peach.

"You'd better wear a sweater, too!" he calls from his room.

He returns for inspection. He's slicked down his cowlick and his cheeks shine. She hands him his knapsack, his lunch already inside, and pushes a toque over his golden hair.

"You know I kinda don't think it's fair," he says.

"What's that?" She could squeeze him and never let go; he's that perfect. The clock could stop here. She forgets that she's been trying to stop the clock every year since he was toilet trained. They're a good team. They're more than managing.

"I don't think it's fair that only you, Grandma, Auntie Holly, and Auntie Camille get to go to Venezuela and the kids have to stay home."

Home is a 1940s bungalow in an aging neighbourhood. A *real* home this time, with only Natasha's name on the mortgage. Her kitchen's a soft, nuzzly yellow and her rooms, though small, bear her stamp. There are photographs, seashells, rocks, plants. The old area rugs – salvaged from the two-storey brick – now cover Natasha's hardwood floors. There are two wingback chairs and a walnut dining room suite – also leftovers from her marriage – and an antique desk she acquired for a pittance at an auction. Rolled behind the desk, out of sight and mind, is a map of the world containing circled destinations she's never explored. There's a deep bathtub with a row of scented candles on the shelf behind it, for this is travel, too. With the lights off and the lace tablecloth/shower curtain pulled, she looks up to the ceiling's flaking paint and makes believe she's soaking in a quaint flat in Paris.

Like Goldilocks, she's finally found a bed to her liking. She sleeps soundly, completely, and wakes raring to begin her days. When Jameson wakes he sees constellations on his ceiling; a sun rises over his window. Natasha bought him a telescope for birthday number seven. There's lots of light, and a fence around the yard. There may soon be a dog.

"We've been through this," she says, her voice unruffled. She twirls a blue scarf around him so that only his eyes show, like a ninja. "It's just two weeks, and besides, you've already had a big holiday. Dad just took you to Disney World! I've never been anywhere, and Mom wants to do this with her daughters before she gets too old."

"She's old already." His voice is muffled beneath the wool.

"Sometimes," Natasha says, "you'd never know."

Peter.
All her life, he's been such an important man, sitting up in his office before that long row of windows, his oak

desk slathered in papers, invoices and files, his phone ringing and ringing. A decision-maker. A mover and shaker.

"Hello, Mr. Stensrud."

"I'd like to apply for the job, Mr. Stensrud."

"Our budget's up by half this quarter."

"The renovations are well underway."

"Hello, this is Natasha. Can I speak to my dad?"

All the conventions across the country, the frequent staff socials, the visits by other men in equally impressive suits and polished shoes.

And then it's over. Three hundred people, including the mayor, attend Peter's retirement party on a breezy, late November night. There are speeches and jokes, gifts and surprises, the usual fare. A long-time hardware employee gives a moving account of Peter's managerial virtues, a tribute that leaves both men dabbing at the eyes beneath their glasses. Navy-suited men from every sector of Peter's life are eager to raise a glass in his honour. Even the United Church Women, with their rational hairdos and serious mouths, take a nip or two in the kitchen. The ucw put on an excessive spread: ham, turkey, cabbage rolls, perogies, scalloped and mashed potatoes, sauerkraut, vegetables of all colours and flavours, potato salads with pimiento sprinkled on top, garden salads, jelly salads, lemon meringue, apple, and raisin pies. A country band – local, of course – provides the entertainment. When they break into "Roll Out the Barrel," Natasha has a spin around the Civic Centre with Holly.

"Dad's proud that even his newest employee, that

eighteen-year-old gas jockey with the red eyes, had the good sense to show up," Holly says. Their feet tangle and they bump into another couple. "Are you leading, or am I?"

"I am. God! Did you burp? Don't even breathe on me," Natasha says. "You smell like a beer factory."

"What's the matter, your friend over there doesn't dance? Or maybe he only pirouettes." Holly laughs from her belly.

Natasha has been dating, but good friends are closer to the top of her list of favourite things than good sex. It's hard to imagine a time when she couldn't buy a friend, when she was a girl who played both sides of the *Scrabble* board. She has real friends now, people she's chosen and who've chosen her, like Myles, whom she met through the library and has wrangled into joining her at this farewell. And Isabelle, from Montreal, who occasionally turns her words around and makes them smile. Ann Louise is a lifer, and Jude, though she never has made the trip to Saskatchewan. There's Eun Jung and Andrew, who cycled across Canada before their daughter was born, and Stell, who works for the Human Rights Commission. Zack's a jazz musician who keeps busy with gigs, Amelia teaches deaf kids, and Robin, well, Robin can't find a job that sticks. Natasha and her eclectic gang mull over life's vicissitudes and try to make sense of the times. None claim to have definitive answers and none believe in definitive answers anyway, so it works out.

"I didn't know you were a homophobe," Natasha says. "Congratulations. His partner – the other half of his life

tell me Everything – 269

and his mortgage – left him for a lawyer. He's mourning."
She was worried about how her father would receive
Myles – he has an earring and, worse, a goatee, which by
Peter's standards is even more unscrupulous than a beard
– but he's too preoccupied with well-wishers to react.

The next day they drive back, dropping Myles at his
townhouse on the exploding northeast corner of the city.
"Does Grandpa know he's gay?" Jameson asks.

"No," Natasha says, "and neither do you."

Camille is having babies like crazy. She's up to number three, and talks about four, even five. Holly believes
she's doing it to make up for the abortion. Natasha hopes
not, this one of three Stensrud daughters whom she
believes has a life that resembles normality. Holly and
Natasha don't see their sister often, stuck as she is in a pre-
fabricated house somewhere north of Edmonton, near
oil. Holly and Nels tagged along with Peter and Shirley
for one visit. "It's a nice house," Holly'd said, drinking her
pre-dinner beverage out of a thick glass, "but like everything else in that godforsaken place, it's not built for per-
manence. I could put my fist through a wall, easy."

Natasha likes the woman she's becoming. She envisions
a strawberry plant whose runners stretch out and out, covering new ground each day. Times are ever changing. New
Age philosophies have become almost as popular as Jesus
once was, but unlike Robin, who hangs crystals in her win-

dow, is heavy into incense and meditation and wears a little leather pouch of seeds around her neck, Natasha finds herself turning back to what she already knows. She's recently begun attending church, where she likes the choir, the stained glass, and the architecture. She thinks maybe she even likes God – the Creator, the Almighty – as her woman minister is fond of inclusively saying. Sitting in her pew with her hands in her lap makes Natasha feel very small, like a little girl with her whole life ahead of her. Jameson's still young enough to be keen for Sunday School. They made a piñata there once. He lives in hope they'll do it again.

Two hours a week she volunteers with the Open Door Society, teaching immigrants English. She's a parent helper in Jameson's class. She watches foreign films. She's become a voracious reader, a passion that began with the books that lined Brander's shelves. She pays attention to her body, stabbing out her final cigarette when Jameson started withholding hugs and she could no longer stand the smell on herself, the taste of her tongue. She does crunches in the morning; long walks evolve into brisk winter runs. She feels herself growing taller and stronger. Her phone rings and rings; sometimes she answers, sometimes she doesn't.

The doors have been opened, light and a sweet dream let in.

The semi stops.

Everyone rises but no one dares a word. The lock is unlatched, the doors swung open. Yellow light pours in like syrup. Natasha strokes the pins and needles from her legs and leaps to the ground. It's clear that the sun has been queen again but her kingdom is cracking in the western sky. She stares at the blinding light.

Flights are booked, childcare arrangements made. The Stensrud women will soar out of Edmonton in two weeks thanks to Shirley's scratch-and-win lottery luck. Hawaii was Shirley's first choice – several friends recommended it – but Natasha talked her into Margarita Island off the northern coast of Venezuela, where Canadian money goes further and there's little possibility of running into a neighbour. She calls Holly to double-check flight times. Her sister answers immediately, as if her hand was already on the phone. There's country music in the background.

"So you're driving, right?" Holly asks, though this has already been decided. For each of them, discussing the holiday details again and again adds to the total experience, as if the holiday began with the decision to go. "Picking up Mom, then me?"

"Yep. Camille will meet us in Edmonton, and I'll leave the car with Tom. His mom's going to stay with the girls and help out. God, I can't believe this is really going to happen. Are you excited?"

"Totally."

"Me, too. Nels will be okay with Everett, won't he?"

"Ha! If nothing else," Holly says, "I've taught the boy how to cope."

God help him if he copes like you, Natasha thinks. "Something's been bugging me a little."

"Hmmm."

"Don't you think this vacation is kind of a payback?"

"What do you mean?"

"I think Mom harbours a long-standing guilt for not having spent more time with us when we were girls. And more of her heart on us."

"Oh, I don't know. She did the best she could."

"You think? I never felt she was there for me, not like she was for you, or Camille."

"Why are you so bloody needy? Can't you just be happy that we're all doing this together, now? God, Natasha! Mom's being extremely generous."

Natasha flushes at the scolding. "I know, and I'm thrilled about the trip, but –"

"I wouldn't slam her if I were you. What a bitchy thing to do." Holly spits the word *bitchy* out.

"You're right," Natasha says, but this time she's sure of it. Her sister's deliberately cut her off.

"I'll see you soon," Holly says.

Natasha hangs up and her phone rings. She thinks it's Holly calling back, not to outright apologize, because she doesn't do that, but maybe to share some humorous anecdote about work or Everett that she forgot to mention a minute before. Natasha picks up. "What'd you forget?"

"Oh good, you're home," Shirley says, huffing. "I've got some bad news." Natasha hears a beginner plinking out the C scale. "Camille's not coming."

"What?"

"Tom's mom slipped on the ice. Broke her hip."

"Well, can't Dad go and stay with the girls?"

Shirley sighs. "If they were older, maybe, but he doesn't have the patience for little ones. I don't know what to do. Everything's booked, and –"

"That really sucks. Camille needs this more than anyone. Is Dad taking her place?"

"South America's not high on his list of priorities. He's planning our spring beds. Can you believe he's taken up with flowers? Plus, he's heard it's not clean."

"Like that should bother a man who's never washed a floor in his life."

"I'm just saying –"

"That's okay, Mom. We'll have more fun without him."

They briefly discuss which medications they'll take for air sickness, diarrhea, sunburn. Natasha hears "Chopsticks" in the background.

"I hope you've kept your Spanish up," Shirley says. "We're counting on you."

"Actually, I'm a little rusty."

"Well, it's probably like riding a bike."

"I haven't ridden a bike in years, either." She looks at her watch. "I've got to run, Mom. Brander's bringing Jameson home soon and I haven't even started dinner. Myles is joining us, too."

"Is that the man you brought to the retirement party? The man with the tuft of hair on his chin?"

"Yes. He's a good friend."

"Well, your father wondered."

"I'm sure he did."

Now impatient little hands are crashing on the piano.

"Mom, you'd better get back to your student."

"She probably shouldn't be travelling anyway," Shirley's saying, apparently oblivious to her student's digression.

"Who? Camille?"

"Yes, Camille. She's pregnant." There's a long pause. "Again."

Natasha falls in love with the sky. "I should have married a pilot," she tells Holly, in the middle seat beside her. "That was my big mistake. No, screw that. I should have *become* a pilot. *That* was my big mistake."

They're above Puerto Rico. Shirley's asleep beside Holly, who's drunk on peach schnapps and finds the inflight movie much funnier than it should be. Natasha's drunk with the view, and the air that's already changed. The ocean's more amazingly blue and magnificent than she'd even hoped, with sparkles where the sun catches the cresting waves. From this perspective it's hard to fathom that this serenity also swallows airplanes and ships, that it's home to man-eating sharks and lashes hurricane fury upon unsuspecting coasts. If she looks closely she can see cruise ships moving like tiny toy boats across the water, pushed by an invisible hand. She can imagine herself on one of these ships, standing with her hands on a golden rail, her long hair flying behind her like some character on the cover of a Harlequin romance. I can die now, she thinks, and then changes her mind. No, I can die on the way home, after I've had my holiday. And then she thinks of Jameson and decides she can't die at all, but expects to anyway. She drafted a will before leaving.

When the plane lands and they step into the sweltering Caribbean breeze, Natasha thinks she might faint. Holly's struck immediately sober. Shirley's outrageous, orange sun hat – she's been wearing it since the snowy, changeover flight in Toronto – flies off her head. They chase it down the tarmac, laughing like schoolgirls.

"Hey, let's ask someone to take our picture," Natasha suggests. Maybe this will make it real, she thinks. She still expects to drop dead at any minute. The three of them stand beside a palm while a man with a Texan accent leads them in "Cheese" and snaps their picture.

Their hotel's a thirty-minute drive from the airport on a small, crowded bus. They see green hills shrouded in mist, palms with their leafy arms waving, Spanish billboards for high-rise accommodation. The highway is good. Then they're entering the city, Porlamar. "It means 'by the sea,'" Natasha explains, but her mother and sister are rapt with the fruit stands and shanties, the brown faces and haggard dogs.

At the hotel they're further entranced by the dark, smiling, exquisite men who hold open doors in the lobby.

"*Hola,*" Holly says, getting into the spirit. She pronounces the 'h.'

"*Buenas tardes,*" they answer, one after another.

The hotel staff speak miserable English, or none at all. The desk clerk appears surprised when Natasha begins in

Spanish, but is less impressed when the Canadian *turista* asks her to repeat a reply and slow it down to half-speed. Her Spanish, also, is miserable.

"What'd they say?" Shirley asks. She's sweating profusely, and dabs under her arms and beneath her neck with a handkerchief.

"The room's not ready yet," Natasha says. "They'll let us know."

"We have to *wait*? We've just travelled halfway across the world and now we have to sit here with our suitcases! In this heat? For crying out!"

They're directed to the courtyard. "This is gorgeous," Natasha says of the large swimming pool, fringed with chaise lounges. "Better than the brochure." There's a thatch-roofed bar and umbrella tables. The smells are coconut oil, grilled chicken, water, flowers, and oranges.

"The music's kinda catchy," Holly says, taking one of the stools at the circular bar where Latin pop underscores the reality of where they are.

Natasha orders each of them a rum from the wide-smiling bartender with phosphorescent teeth. "Eighteen hundred bolivars!" Shirley cries. "Can we afford these?"

Natasha explains the exchange rate, and Shirley, who keeps forgetting that she's just won the lottery, settles down.

"Ask him his name," Holly whispers, her eyes on the bartender who mixes each drink like he's creating art.

"*Perdón,*" Natasha begins. "*¿Cómo se llama?*"

"Orlando," the man replies, extending his warm hand. His black hair is very short, and he has a small gold hoop in his left ear.

"*Hola* Orlando. *Me llamo* Natasha."

"Holly," Holly says, next in line for the exotic hand, which she holds a few moments longer than necessary.

"*Y nuestra madre,* Shirley," Natasha says, worried about using the proper possessive.

Shirley reaches across to shake, but her right breast catches her drink and knocks it over. "Sorry!"

"*¿Eres alemán?*" Orlando asks, mopping the spilled rum.

"No! *Somos de* Canada. *De* Saskatchewan." Natasha turns to Holly. "He thinks we're German!"

"*¡Ah...claro!*" The next round's on the house.

A porter arrives; their studio apartment is ready. They follow him through a tiled corridor and up a flight of stairs to their suite: two bedrooms with double beds, one with patio doors and a balcony; two bathrooms, both with bathtubs and showers; a sizable kitchenette; and a bamboo furnished living area, with yet more patio doors and another balcony. "Pretty swanky," Shirley says. She opens cupboard doors, checks the air conditioner, tries the key in the safe-deposit box.

Holly walks to the patio doors that look onto the pool, opens them wide, letting the sound of water and children in, the scent of paradise. "If this is a dream, don't you dare wake me up."

"Come on you two, let's hit the beach. Surf's up!" Natasha's already made the continental switch into a black two-piece, with blue jean cut-offs pulled over top. "I've always wanted to say that."

Holly's on the left balcony, sizing up the pool and courtyard, maybe more. Natasha joins her. "Come on, kid, let's find us an ocean. Always wanted to say that, too."

"Right away," Holly says, dreamily. It's ninety-two degrees in the shade. They hear French and Spanish and languages they will later identify as Norwegian, Danish, German, Italian.

"Good Lord!" Shirley says, breaking the spell from the adjacent balcony.

Now what? Natasha wonders. "What's the matter, Mom?"

"They're not wearing any tops!"

Natasha and Holly follow their mother's gaze to the sunny side of the pool, where two women on the far edge of fifty are engaging in boisterous conversation. The brown nipples on their languid breasts are like wide, incredulous eyes.

Shirley directs her disgust at Natasha. "What kind of a place did you bring us to?"

By day seven Natasha's spent so much time in the ocean that at night, in bed, she continues to experience the push and pull of the current, but other than that there's no movement in her sleep. They've travelled to the top of the island and back, eaten fish *empañadas,* meat *empañadas,* and Natasha's favourite, *empañadas.* They've toured a seventeenth century castle whose complacent stone walls and towers witnessed centuries of religious persecutions. They've seen more bare breasts than a whole lifetime of locker room skin, and three iguanas. Natasha and Holly have bad burns tattooed on their noses and foreheads. They are forced to admit that Shirley's hat was a good idea, even though they made her walk behind them in the Toronto airport because of it.

While Holly and Shirley opt to fill the day with souvenir shopping at the flea market, Natasha hops a ramshackle bus with the locals and two chickens. They drive north, to a fishing village she's starred on her map. *Pinch me,* she thinks, as they pass a man leading a donkey. *Pinch me,* the red bursts of flowers. In the coastal village of Manzanillo, fishermen with skin as thick and brown as bark mend their nets on the beach. Natasha walks up to one of them and asks how to say *nets* in Spanish.

"*Redes,*" he tells her, smiling with teeth white as bone. She takes his picture, thinking, already, that it'll be worthy of enlarging and framing for her wall.

She eats fish so fresh it might have been alive only moments before. She finds a large, derelict conch shell on the beach and wonders how she'll smuggle it home. Six-foot waves smash very near the shore – too risky for swimming – but she cools her legs and arms in a glassy tidal pool and passes a pleasant hour conversing with an Argentinean family who don't mind her turtle-paced Spanish. After they leave she lies on her towel, face to the sun, while two young Venezuelans caper nearby. She picks out words: *casa, abuelo, trabajar.* There isn't another Caucasian for miles. This, she thinks, is as good as it gets.

When she returns to the hotel, just before nightfall, she's surprised to find Holly fiddling with eyeliner. "Orlando's taking me dancing."

"What?" Natasha brushes sand off her feet and sets down her tote bag, heavy with the contraband conch shell which has spilled salty sand.

"We're going out for lobster, then to a club in town. Does this dress make me look fat?" Holly spins to give Natasha a view of the sleeveless shift. Purple flowers as big as pancakes stop just above her knees.

"It looks great." She peels off her T-shirt, her back to her sister. More sand. Grains bounce across the floor. "Where's Mom?"

"Out by the pool," Holly says, "making friends."

Natasha patters to the balcony and steps into the sun's final act. She scans the deck for her mother's orange hat, locates it. "Who are those men? Holly...get out here! Who are those two men? Who's that guy in the Speedo?"

"*Un momento,*" Holly sings. She swipes a lipstick across her smile, then pours herself a rum and Coke before joining Natasha. "Mr. Speedo there is a former Olympian, Olav. Man, some men really keep it going, don't they? Mom says he runs backwards to stay in shape."

"Now there's a picture," Natasha says. "Does he run in his Speedo?"

Holly laughs. "The bald guy is his brother. I can't remember his name. Guess where they're from? Norway!"

"Olav looks like the man from Glad," Natasha says, "you know, that TV commercial?"

Holly sips her drink. "Not tall enough."

Natasha doesn't recognize the woman out there who's impersonating her mother. Even her laugh has changed. It seems to start from her knees and rumble out of her. It makes her double over, then she throws her head back when she straightens. "What's gotten into our mother? She's become a veritable butterfly."

"She's always had...friends, if that's what you mean. She's a flirt. She's good at it. It's basically harmless."

"But what about Dad?" Natasha slides her sunglasses to the top of her head.

Holly bends to buckle a new leather sandal. "What *about* Dad?"

"He puts up with this?"

"You think *he's* innocent?" Holly says coldly.

Natasha is stunned. "You've got something on him? My God, Holly, don't hold out on me!"

"I promised Mom I wouldn't – Tash, there are lots of things you don't know."

"Mom knows?" Natasha feels dizzy. She grabs Holly's arm and sits her down so they're knee to knee. "Talk."

"It's ancient history, Tash. Long dead."

"Talk," she says, louder this time.

"Remember that year Dad went to Switzerland for two weeks and Mom didn't go with him?"

"He had a fling with a Swiss woman?"

"No," Holly says, looking at the floor. The maid had done a poor job of sweeping up the sand. "He took Arlene. Someone he'd met at a conference somewhere, sometime. A Canadian. Mom thinks it'd been going on for about a year, and that Arlene gave him the big ultimatum in Switzerland. Close your mouth, sister —" Despite the severity of the news she's breaking, she can't help smiling "— you'll catch flies."

Natasha does close her mouth, but now that the initial slap's been delivered she begins to feel the pain. She feels cheated. God, so much going on all around her and she knew nothing about any of it. Why? "Am I even part of this family? No one tells me anything, ever! I swear you and Mom talk in codes around me."

Holly puts a hand on her sister's knee. "You don't need to know everything." She pauses, and the sounds of splashing children reach Natasha ears. "Hey...he chose Mom. He chose us."

But people respect him, Natasha's thinking. People have always respected him. And now Mom, out there, acting half her age. Little kids look up to her. Jameson. She's rattled right to the bone.

"I'm leaving now...Orlando will be ready to go any minute." Holly goes to steps away but Natasha catches her by the wrist, her hand closing on gold bangles.

"Do you know what you're doing, Holl? These South American guys...I mean...anything could happen." Damn, why's *she* giving this lecture? It's a mother's job.

Holly looks across the pool to the bar. Orlando spots her and waves. She lifts her drink; the bracelets on her other arm tinkle. "Look at me, Natasha. What do you see?"

Natasha sees that the humidity has done wonders for her sister's hair, that there's a blush beneath her skin that has nothing to do with the tropical sun. And then she recognizes that in this moment, on this edge of an island in a country that may as well be the moon, her big sister has a heart that's finally happy.

No one has phoned home yet. No one has thought to. They're each building for themselves the holiday they need most. Natasha's leads her to another coastal town, Juan Griego, and Playa el Carmen, the beach where she meets Manuel and Ana, and their preteens Celso and Nina. More than anything she wants these new friends to take her into their home. Only this will make the circle of her holiday complete.

She finds herself in the back of a taxi between the young husband and wife. They're all slightly loaded from drinking away the afternoon on the beach, but still she melts with shame when Manuel slings his arm around the back of the seat and begins rubbing her neck, just below the hairline. As if Ana doesn't know. As if she doesn't deserve better.

Natasha doesn't think she's been sending signals, can't imagine what's brought this so suddenly on.

They're dropped near a barrio of cinder-block homes. In the next house an old woman with skin shined like leather sits in the doorway, pulling on a pipe. Two men in a beaten Pontiac — the driver holding a bottle out the window — leer as she follows Ana into the house. She feels conspicuous in her own skin, in her sandy hair in Heidi-like braids. She's thinking that this may not have been a good idea.

The house is dark and close, like a storm before it breaks. She smells chickens, straw, grease. Her heart flutters. There are only three rooms, two of which host beds and nothing else. No pillows. *Almohadas.* No blankets. *Mantas.* In the larger room, the room they walked into, there's a black-and-white television, a hammock, two mismatched chairs and a copper-feathered chicken. Manuel keeps pushing Celso at her, speaking to his son in fast Spanish that Natasha doesn't like. She needs out. She needs air, and light. They've been gracious, but –

"Ow!"

Rosco and the driver rush to Holly, who's splayed on the ground. They're lifting her, helping her slowly to her feet.

"What happened?" Natasha asks Gina. Only now does she realize that they're again at the Highway Esso, although the registration table's long been whisked away and no one's around.

"She jumped and fell," Gina says. "You didn't see?"

"My ankle!" Holly's sobbing. "I think it's broken."

She keeps one arm around Rosco while the driver kneels to inspect her injury. "Just a bad sprain I think. Look...it's already turning purple. A sprain can be worse than a break."

"Lady, lady," Ana is saying. She has Natasha's arm and she's shaking it. Natasha explains about the bus, having to return before sundown, her mother and sister, waiting. People are always waiting for her. She presses

bills into the children's hands. Ana gives her directions to
el centro.

"*Voy contigo,*" Manuel says, but Natasha insists he
needn't come, she really must hurry, and she thanks God
she's had the sense to wear running shoes, not sandals.
Thanks God she's quit smoking and can run, hard.

"*Gracias,*" she yells behind her, and, because that does-
n't seem enough, because they seem to require more, she
adds: "*¡Buena suerte!*" Good luck.

As the bus bounces her back to the city, she weeps.

"*Come on,* Tash, it's a riot! These guys are fabulous
dancers. My God, what they can do with their hips.
Orlando's friends want to meet you."

Holly's almost unrecognizable in a short skirt and high
heels. In a kind light she could pass for the ubiquitous
twenty-nine, Natasha thinks. "Thanks, Holl, but I'm
hanging out here. I'll take in the house band. Relax."

"Mom, tell her to come with me." Holly pouts like a
child who can't get her own way, and suddenly Natasha
experiences an overwhelming wave of guilt for leaving
Jameson. Is he okay? Is Brander's wife being good to him?

"You might as well," Shirley says. She's painting her
toenails to match her hat. "I've already made plans. You'll
be alone all evening."

They've forgotten who they are, Natasha thinks. What
ever will become of them when Air Canada dumps them
back on the prairies and they're obliged to return to their
mundane lives in the snow and wind? What, in the cold

that freezes motors and snaps power lines? "So I'll read. Sit on the balcony. Count the stars."

"You're not being a poor sport, are you?" Shirley finishes with her toenails and stands to buckle her belt, which matches the chunky gold knots at her ears. She's lost eight pounds to diarrhea and, Natasha expects, hasn't looked this wonderful, this *radiant,* since 1956, her wedding day.

"I'm exhausted, Mom. I've seen more of this island than both of you put together. And let's not forget all that translating. That's work! And I'm whipped. Really. Go!"

A little pushoff is all it takes, and then she's alone. She peels off her clothes, her top slightly stiff, as if salt water's dried in the fabric, and stands beneath the shower until the water runs cold. She leaves the patio doors open; the house band is playing "Guantanamera" on the pool deck. Dorion, she thinks, crawling into bed in her panties. Whatever happened to Dorion?

A light breeze stirs the sheers. She can't sleep.

One o'clock comes and goes. Two.

Shirley returns. Natasha hears her undress, then the light beneath her door flashes out. God, why can't I sleep? she wonders. She thinks about Holly – is she safe? – then gets an unbeckoned slide show of disturbing images featuring Peter and a woman who's not her mother in some Swiss love shack. She's homesick for Jameson and wonders how it's been for him, staying with Brander, Marlene and the kids, *their* kids, for this length of time. Another part of her is ashamed for her mother.

But mostly she can't sleep because she's reliving what

happened the night Myles came for dinner and the night shawled around them. They'd watched "Damage," a passionate movie about obsession and loss, with lots of skin. They'd both seen it before. They drank one bottle of wine – each. Near the end of the movie, where Jeremy Irons' affair with his daughter-in-law is found out, Myles got drowsy. He'd close his eyes for a few minutes, then blink them open. "Shit, the best part is coming up and I'm crashing."

"You shouldn't drive," Natasha'd said, lifting the empty glass from his hand.

"I'll be fine," he murmured. "I just need to rest my eyes for a bit."

"Come on," she said, pulling him up. "You take my bed, I'll take the couch." She walked him to her room and snatched a sports bra off the headboard. It was the way he was looking at her – not smiling, not showing her anything in his eyes – from his post at the end of the lonely bed.

They both knew.

He held her fiercely. They'd hugged like this before, in the way that friends can when there's nothing at risk, but this time neither was letting go. Like the blind, his fingers travelled slowly, as if trying to commit to memory every curve, every scar and muscle she'd earned. "I'm a virgin with women," he'd admitted, embarrassed when they began, and so she helped him, her hand over his.

"Here," she said, "and here." No one had ever spent more time learning her body. She learned what he needed, too, and gave it to him. And it was fine. And when it was over, she tucked into him, her arm around his ribs, knees snug against his. And this is how they awoke.

It's snowing in Edmonton when they land, but it's storybook snow: fat, light flakes that blow off like powder. Camille's waiting with Tom and the girls. "You're so dark!" she exclaims. "How was it?"

"*¡Fantastico!*" Holly answers for all of them.

Shirley promises a treat – a hotel with a waterslide – for Camille's daughters. Tomorrow the Saskatchewan crew will take the Yellowhead Route east.

Later, while Tom plays with the girls in the pool, the women linger over mochas in the hotel restaurant, telling their tropical tales. Camille's quiet, even distant, Natasha thinks. She doesn't radiate with the proverbial glow of pregnancy.

The next morning Natasha witnesses a payoff. Shirley uses an automated teller, then surreptitiously feeds her youngest daughter a handful of bills. Camille hands the treasure to Tom.

"What was that?" Natasha asks Shirley on the highway back to Saskatchewan. "That thing with Camille and Tom."

"What thing?" Holly asks, poking her head between them from her seclusion in the back seat.

"The money...Camille and Tom," Natasha says. "Mom gave them some money."

"That was her share, equivalent to what I spent on you girls. A little extra, too. They're having some money troubles, and with the new baby coming..."

Broken hip. A lie, Natasha realizes. Their mother has lied to them. "I'm not just talking about the money, Mom, I'm talking about your daughter, your *baby.* Didn't you see how –" she searches for a strong adjective, " – how despondent she was? My God, she looked older than any of us!"

Now Shirley looks stricken; she loses most of her tan in three seconds. She turns her face to the passenger window, absorbs herself in the flat white fields. "She's tired. Cripes, she has a right to be."

Natasha tries again. "Holly?" She looks in the rearview mirror. "Did you notice anything?"

"Noper," she answers, still reverberating with holiday bliss. "Everything seemed peachy to me."

Natasha was missed. Jameson whoops into her arms and coats her with kisses. She wonders how she could have ever left this precious, precious human being, risking life and limb on a vacation and a chance to exercise her Spanish. Or it might have gone the other way. Jameson might have taken ill, seriously ill, and she wouldn't have been able to reach him. She prays. A quick thanksgiving. Even Brander looks relieved that she's returned in one piece. He's a tinge less stuffy, a trifle less scholarly. He gives her cheek a perfunctory kiss.

"Tell me everything," she says, when Jameson finally lets her breathe.

"You first!"

She begins to convey this other world but finds words

can't do it justice. "Wait for the pictures. Then you'll see."

They pile Jameson's bags into her car and wave good-bye to his other family. At home she's alarmed to find the front door unlocked. Isabelle was supposed to be watering the plants and making the house look lived-in with the pretense of lights and shovelled walks, but her car's not on the street. Natasha pokes her head in the door. "Hello?" She asks Jameson to go back and wait in the car until she's certain it's safe.

"But it's a surprise!" he shouts, pushing her forward. "Surprise!" And then a golden retriever pup skids across the floor and jumps at her knees.

"What the...did Daddy buy you this dog?"

"Uh uh. His name is Finnigan."

"Surprise again." It's Myles, stepping around the fridge where she can see him, and Natasha, who's anticipated the inevitable reunion and tried to make it right while riding through clouds and waves and towns without rain or hope, is purged.

Jameson, *Swimming*

How rapidly time evaporates, Natasha thinks, her eyes on the barefoot children splashing in a puddle across the street. First you're a girl in knee-highs, face to the sky, wondering at the impossibility of gravity, of an invisible force so strong it anchors factories and great cathedrals to the ground. You're spilling lemonade tea into the birthday cups of your ponytailed sisters, or disbelieving your ears the first time you hear your father weep. You can't remember why, there's only the terrible sound of his tears.

You close your eyes and when you open them again it's to take the bundled package that is your own child from the nurse's outstretched arms. You can't imagine what she expects you to do with it.

Soon you're flailing in the quicksand of lost mittens and sand shovels, of half-eaten apples discovered between couch cushions, broken crayons stashed beneath beds. There are bee stings and needles and feverish nights that leave you whirling. There's hair that disagrees with the school's photographer, baseball games, and track meets lost to the rain.

Now it's the sound of doors – yawning open, protesting against the wind, rattling in the middle of the adolescent night – that define Natasha's days.

Hours, and her front door hasn't uttered a word.

The frames of her life have led to this: Jameson is thirteen and she has no idea where he spent the night, had no inkling he was even gone. These are the moments when good friends are not enough. She wonders if she should worry Brander, who exists in an excessive Cape Cod across the murky ribbon of water that separates their city. His family's growing. He says he needs the room. Certainly their son wouldn't be there, but it's a beginning.

She dials the number penned inside the cover of the phone book, imagines Marlene running to the phone. It used to please her that Jameson disapproved of his father's wife, but Natasha's warming to Marlene. She's got her own cross to carry.

"And you haven't heard from him since when?" Natasha asks.

"Monday, I think." She almost hears Marlene flipping back the pages of memory. "No, Tuesday. He stopped by after dinner."

"Just for a visit?"

"For money."

Her voice has changed since the third baby, Natasha decides. A voice that's resigned itself. She imagines how Edith and Sterling must have struggled to maintain their cultivated calm, learning that this fourth grandchild, too long in the birth canal, would never walk, would never, likely, learn to tie her shoes.

"How's Callie?" Natasha asks, a deliberate detour around any more discussion about her errant son.

"She smiles," Marlene says, "lots."

If the hours could be peeled back to the morning before, the day would begin with this: a seventy-two-year-old motorist in Lelystad, Netherlands, was run over and killed after stopping on a highway to give first aid to a rabbit.

"Weird," Jameson said, his mouth full of toast. He flings the crust to Finnigan, now a wise and full-grown dog whom they have to spell certain words in front of. *Car. Walk. Cheese.* "What else?"

Natasha cherishes these moments before their mornings and lives fork in opposite directions. "A tiger killed one man and mauled another at a Calcutta zoo after the men tried to put a marigold garland around the tiger's neck in a New Year's greeting."

Jameson thinks about this. "Why don't they just sing 'Auld Lang Syne,' get smashed, puke their guts out and wake up January first with a massive hangover, like normal adults?"

"There's no such thing as normal," Natasha says decisively, as this is among her recent revelations, "plus, they have different customs."

Jameson bolts his orange juice and pushes his chair back from the table with his heels. His fine, straight hair, once white as clouds, has deepened to a colour he says he can live with. "Gotta fly, Ma." His kiss is a butterfly, winging off her cheek.

"Your face! You've got jam on your chin."

Jameson spins and she hears the bathroom door close. He never forgets to close it anymore.

She flips through the rest of the paper. Scientists have discovered evidence of life on Mars; new, unpronounceable countries are being formed daily; the forecast is for a mix of sun and clouds; only one number's a match on her lottery ticket; the horoscopes are too general to be of any interest; a twenty-two-year-old boy they know and admire has died as the result of an asthma attack.

Scott.

The obituary lists his accomplishments, his travels, his dog, who's in mourning along with the family. The funeral will be on Monday.

It must be the look that sweeps her face, a countenance of disbelief and ineffable sadness, as if it were her own son smiling off the obituary page, never to smile again.

"Mom?" Jameson creeps toward her, one hand ready to grasp her shoulder. "What's up?"

Scott was still a kid, her son's swim coach, his friend. He will never again push her laughing son into the pool. He will never give Jameson another high five after a fast fifty metres of back crawl. *Never* is the one word that pushes itself into the centre of her thoughts.

His death is unfathomable.

"Not true," Jameson says, and pushes the paper away.

"I'm sorry." It's all she knows how to say.

Jameson has two best friends. She likes that fact and

she likes the boys. They're not the type who'd roughhouse at the back of a city bus and release a rosary of obscenities, regardless of who might hear. They don't shave their heads bald or pierce anything. She suspects they've tried smoking but have no experience with sex or drugs.

Clint, whom her son's known the longest, is another swimmer. Four days a week, Clint's mother drops the boys at the pool and Natasha arrives early to pick them up. She sits on the cement bleachers and remains amazed that she's the mother of a streamlined athlete, or of anyone at all.

When Jameson was nine, she learned there was no finer line than the one his body made; freestyle was the stroke he was born for. A little fish, just like she'd once been. His skin shimmered in the reckless water, every molecule of light sang his praise. He'd reach the pool's edge, search for her among the parents, and she gave God thanks in the holy moment of one thin arm, waving.

Jameson worshipped his swim coach. When there were meets out of town, Jameson buckled into Scott's Toyota and the two barrelled down the highway, wailing to Scott's alternative music, the ever-popular teenage themes of death and desire. Scott encouraged and challenged Jameson and the group of swimmers he called "my boys." He was a character, hair always in his eyes, and a broad, chip-toothed smile, earned, not ironically, through a miscalculated dive of his own.

Her son's right. There must be a mistake. Scott? Dead? But he epitomized exuberance! He reminded her of Dorion in that way, the way Dorion was in the beginning, when she lost her heart to him. Now a boy like Scott, too young to be a lover, strikes a mother chord in her.

She looks at the obituary again. How can a photo be tender, beautiful, and awful, all at the same time? *Survived by his mother.* Natasha bets that she spent her share of time on concrete bleachers, too.

She hardly knows where to begin, but there must be more to it than sitting on the couch and willing the phone to ring. Should she collect recent photos of Jameson and rush them to the police station? Call everyone she knows? Everyone *he* knows? It's Saturday, so at least she doesn't have the complication of work adding to the weight of the air.

Clint hasn't seen him. She tries Terry, but he's at his father's in Calgary for the weekend; his mother put him on the bus alone.

She's desperate for clues. In the mess of his underwear drawer she finds a jackknife, four dollars in change, a folded Hustler centrefold and a wrinkled scrap of paper with two phone numbers on it, no names. The first proves to be a comic shop. The second belongs to Tessa, a fourteen-year-old with a private line.

"I saw him in the hall at school," she says. She sounds like a nice enough girl. "We have French together, last class."

"Was he alone?"

"Yes, er, I think so. I'm sorry Mrs. Meinhart, I don't know where he could be."

Natasha doesn't bother to correct the girl. She's still a Stensrud, her father's name. She'll always be just that.

"That's okay, Tessa. Thanks."

She rings everyone she can think of, except her parents. Why terrify them before she's certain there's an emergency? There might still be a logical explanation. Kids do this, they take off. Didn't she at thirteen? Yes, she seems to remember it. And she wasn't alone, either. Off with a few friends? No, not likely. She didn't have friends then. She wore out cards playing solitaire, crawled around the musty basement acting out life-and-death dramas. Perhaps she *had* wandered off alone. It wouldn't have been unusual. No, she remembers others. Touching. They were in some kind of trouble. But she was just fine. And Jameson will be just fine, too. Late, maybe, but fine. *Jameson!* He'll be home soon. And after she stops hugging him she may ground him for life.

She realizes that she's shaking and pulls an afghan around her shoulders.

That long-ago time, were there cops at the door? Or are these vague recollections, something she's dredged up from one of those recurrent games of make-believe? She was a chronic pretender. Too late to separate fiction from fact, but she knows something sent her mother into a canyon of gloom. There's a sense of unconscionable guilt. An old emotion? She's not sure, but it's hers here and now, in this house with walls painted in contemporary colours inspired by African landscapes. *I've lost my son!* She *must* call her parents. But her gut says no, you're wise not to alarm them. Where does that come from? Instinct? Some scrap of memory? And what could they do, anyway?

She waits until the last possible moment. Mississippi four...Missippi three...Mississippi two; the grenade's about to blow. "Hello, Mom?" She recounts the terror and Scott's death that may have set it off.

"God, no!" Shirley cries. "Is anything missing from his room?"

"I can't tell. It's a mess. No, wait! I didn't trip over his skateboard. He must have taken it."

Her father picks up the extension. "Who died?"

"His swim coach. A young man. Jameson adored him." Admitting this does not make it any more real. "I've called the police. I'm so bloody scared!"

"I'm coming in," Peter says firmly. "You shouldn't be alone."

Natasha hears sirens inside her head – *Jameson's missing!* – but understands she must find control. "You're *driving* in?"

"I haven't learned how to fly."

"Mom, is he okay to drive?" She hates that she has to do this in front of him, this man who catapulted through life, but she doesn't need two disasters. She knows he's on the downhill slide; his eyesight, hearing, memory. He falls asleep in his kitchen chair. Church is an all-out write-off.

Her mother hesitates. "Oh God! I've got Brianne Vanderzalm's wedding to play for this afternoon. I'll get someone to take it."

"No, Mom, that's okay. I'm sure he's just –"

"I'll be there by five." And Peter hangs up.

Holly phones. A very long distance.

"No leads yet," Natasha says, "but I'm sure he'll

be home any minute." *Jameson!*

"I'd be freakin' hysterical."

"Believe me, I am. I *am* hysterical! This is me being hysterical. Inside I'm screaming. Even the dog knows something's wrong. What the hell's taking the police so long?"

"Oh my God, remember when Mom and Dad did that to us?"

"No. God, I wish I still smoked."

"We were sixteen and eighteen and one measly hour past curfew. The cops found us in the pizza parlour on Main...we were buzzed."

"And this is supposed to make me feel better?"

"He's a teenager, Tash. Just sewing his oats. Get used to it..." Holly says, drifting. "There's something else. This may not be the time – you've got enough emotions to deal with already –"

"What are you talking about?" *Jameson!*

Holly pauses. Natasha feels blood rush to her ears.

"Actually, it's Camille," Holly says.

"Pregnant again?"

"No. She kicked Tom out."

"What?" Natasha sits down.

Holly coughs. "She and the kids are staying in the house and Tom's getting his own place."

"My God. When did this happen?"

"On Tuesday. You should call her."

"Of course. As soon as Jamie's back home." She hangs up. Great, she thinks. Even more disturbing images for her mental gallery. Jameson's body in the river, Jameson's body in the trunk of a car, Jameson hitchhiking to Vancouver or Montreal. All that, and Camille dragging cardboard boxes – Tom's stuff – into the front porch while her kids tug at her limbs, angry that something's taken their mother's attention from them. She'll be decent about this, Natasha thinks. She'll give Tom whatever he needs, the brown couch, extra bedding. All this she has to assume, because what she knows of Camille could fit into a thimble. She knows Meryl Streep better than she knows her own sister.

At three she's set to call the police again when she hears the scritch of a key in the lock. Finnigan beats her to the door. "Jameson?"

The door closes, shoes are kicked off. "Hi, Mom."

She wants to run to him and crush him with her love. She wants to slap him silly. She wants to gather his long arms and legs and rock him as if he were still a child.

"Where were you?"

He sets his skateboard down. "Nowhere, really. Alone. Thinking."

She steadies her voice. To lose it now would be dangerous. "Where?"

"I slept under the bridge."

My God! She knows what lurks under the bridge, has seen the graffiti on her morning runs. "Children against Christ." "Boys only sex club." She's been flashed by old men and a huge, slow-moving creature with a moonlike face who rolled his penis between his hands the way a child rolls a Plasticine snake.

"It's not fair, Mom," Jameson says, and he lets her put her arms around him, and he breaks. They break, together.

Jameson bathes, then climbs into his bed for a sleep that will carry him to the fish-and-chip smell of supper.

He'll get over this, Natasha convinces herself. She'll take him to the funeral, they'll face it head-on, as a team. She won't hide death from Jameson like her parents did with her, refusing to allow her to attend the services for grandparents who looked more dead than alive even when they were still breathing.

Her son will heal.

She checks on him, sees his ribs rise beneath the sheet, his face to the wall. She closes his door, pads down the carpeted hall to the front room. The police have come and gone but Peter's not arrived, and she's reminded again how life's like a child's game of connect-the-dots: from stress point to stress point.

She consults the time on the VCR. Quarter to five. She can't bear another fifteen minutes of sitting alone with her thoughts. She opens a book of short stories by W. D. Valgardson and a passage leaps out with the startling clarity and truth of an epiphany: "In life there are no real beginnings or endings. There are so many moments where one can say, 'That's where it started,' and, in most cases, it is both true and false. Life is nothing if not untidy."

Where it started. She slides a scrap of paper between the pages and closes the book. Wedged within her wall unit are dozens of videotapes. "Jameson's first birthday." "Summer Camp." "School plays, grades one to six." She believes it's important to capture the scenes of her son's life, and, in the process, the periphery of her own.

Trembling again, she pulls "Jameson, Swimming" off the shelf. Before the image fades in she hears the slap of water, the distortion of voices above the pool's din. She watches Jameson dive off the block and swim and swim, flip turn and swim, and she wonders, not for the first time, what drives him. With a daughter, she thinks, she would know.

Brander's in the next clip, his arm slung around his wet son, moments after Jameson's heaved himself out of the pool.

"Hi Jameson!" She hears her own voice. Shaken images of water, a stranger's arm, the back of a head as she walks across the deck with the camcorder, trying to get closer. "Over here!"

He turns, his hair a wet cap against his skull. "Hi Mom! Did you catch that?"

Then Scott's there, and Clint, a white towel draped around his neck. Scott slings his arms around the two dripping swimmers, pulls their heads close to his. "These are my boys," he says, walking toward the camcorder, every inch alive.

She never learns who or what Jameson encountered that shivering night beneath the bridge. She never asks. In the cloud of her unknowing she can only imagine the hours her son poised like a diver on the concrete girder, contemplating the temptation of water. A piece of her stood there, too.

Thunder

She rolls over, a spanking new forty-year-old, and smells smoke. "Wha-what?"

"Happy Birthday, Mom-o!" Jameson vaults onto her bed with his fourteen-year-old weight. Finnigan follows suit, slapping her across the mouth with his tongue. "I burnt breakfast."

"Thanks. I'll get up." She pushes the affectionate dog off the bed. "What time is it?"

"Eight fifteen. And sunny. Looks like it's going to be a scorcher. Me and Clint are going to head down to the mall, if that's okay. I mean, I could stick around if you want. You only turn forty once."

"Thank God," she says, slipping into the man's pale yellow dress shirt that hangs on the bedpost. The shirt's several sizes too big – it hangs just above her knees – but it's soft with many washings and just right over bare shoulders on lazy, summer mornings. It was Peter's shirt, one of the dozens that hung in his closet while she and her sisters were growing up. After he retired, he thinned

305

out the mélange of formal shirts Shirley'd never have to press again, and Natasha helped herself before they went to the Salvation Army. Now the pale yellow's become her thin robe, the robin's egg blue a beach cover-up. She uses a white one with an ink stain on the left breast pocket for painting projects, the brown-striped on days when she doesn't want too much sun in the garden. Five others hang in the back of her closet, still waiting assignment.

The phone rings and rings. Myles, Ann Louise, Holly, Isabelle, Zack, someone wanting Horizon Computers, Jude, Shirley. Her mother repeats what she's been saying for years: "Life begins at forty."

"Did you get my cheque?" her father asks, taking his turn on the phone.

"Don't believe her," Holly says, visiting her parents and on another line, "hemorrhoids begin at forty. And menopause. How much did you send her?"

"I didn't know this was a conference call," Natasha says, wondering if her new lover's trying to call while her family's tying up the line.

Camille sent a sympathy card, which was supposed to be funny but fails to amuse Natasha, who feels, today, like she just might die.

After she cleans bacon and egg spatters off the stove and whole wheat toast crumbs off the floor the day is hers to play with. Jameson has his afternoon mapped out.

The boys are busing downtown. Later they might get up the nerve to call two girls and see a movie at a discount theatre, but the odds are against this.

Davis, the man she's sleeping with and likes very much

even with his clothes on, is in Vancouver for a Telefilm conference. His company's pitching a documentary series on aging and its effects on women who care for both aging parents and their own children. The sandwich generation. God forbid it happens to her.

Davis is eight years younger. She met him at one of Zack's jazz gigs; she'd smelled a set-up, but upon meeting Davis didn't mind. What's to mind? Her lover's an articulate and compassionate man who's already enjoyed a life well-lived, including a six-month trek across Israel and Egypt, during which time, he says, he grew into a man. He has a condo, an ex-wife, and a four-year-old daughter in the suburbs. He's proven to be comfortable, even adept, at playing Frisbee with Jameson, shaking hands with strangers at church, running along the river beside her – even with his bad knees – or giving a well-received presentation to film students at a conference they attended together in Edmonton. There he met Camille, who pulled Natasha into a restaurant washroom and gushed, "My God, he's gorgeous! Got any brothers?"

He's fun and he adores her. In bed he spends hours touching and tasting the skin over collarbones, ankles, wrists. He licks her fingers, sucks her toes, rubs peppermint lotion into her sandpaper heels. His lovemaking's reminiscent of her fleeting encounter with Myles, who has since found love with an architect.

"So what are you going to do, Mom?" Jameson has one hand on the door, his shoes on. Ready to dash, but hanging back, making sure.

Natasha threads her fingers around her pottery coffee

cup – one of Shirley's new endeavours – and walks out onto the front step, regardless of who might see her in the long thin shirt and bare legs, her tangled morning hair. Jameson stands beside her, taller by an apple, looking at the cerulean sky above the sweeping elms.

"I'll go for my run before it gets too hot, then –" She smiles at him, at his wanting her to be okay on her birthday. "I think I'll go garage saleing. You know me, I love other people's junk. Or maybe I'll walk down to the Farmers' Market."

Jameson relaxes, the worried lines on his forehead – barely visible beneath ultra-blond bleached bangs, a shade he once couldn't wait to grow out of – disappear. She touches the back of his head. "You need a haircut, kiddo."

"Yeah, yeah," he says, kissing her cheek. "I love you, Mom. I hope your birthday's really great. I'm picking your gift up at the mall."

"I love you, too. Now go have fun. Next year at this time I'm going to be on your back about getting a job, so enjoy your freedom while you can."

He goes, and before the thermometer can climb another degree, she changes into grey sweat shorts and a black running bra, the Nike running shoes she reluctantly paid for with three fifty-dollar bills.

Finnigan howls when he sees her lace into them. He knows.

"Sorry buddy, it's too hot for you already. I'll take you for a w-a-l-k tonight. Promise." She stretches her Achilles tendons against the front step, touches her toes, twists left and right, then begins her run toward the river.

She flies past Kinsmen Park's miniature Ferris wheel, the multi-coloured train, the frightening faces of the carousel horses that used to make Jameson cry, then along the paved trail that takes her through poplar trees which volunteer a sweet, nostalgic smell.

There's life on the river already – rowers, Sea-Doos, a solitary waterskier in a black wetsuit. Soon she's down town, in front of the Delta Bessborough Hotel, past the Vimy Memorial, beneath another bridge, then running across a fourth bridge, a freeway. She nods hello or lifts a hand to the runners who also favour morning runs along the brown sash of the South Saskatchewan. An English woman with a spaniel tells her she's getting a nice tan. Two boys, not much older than her son, whistle past her on bikes. They do a double take.

I could be your mother, she wants to yell. *I'm forty years old! Forty years old, and I can do this, I can run!*

Perspiration trickles down her neck and between her brown shoulders. A good feeling. Her arms and face glisten beneath the intense sun, and her hair swings in a wet tail. She could go and go. Her energy is at once both alarming and miraculous; at twenty, she couldn't have run one block.

She doubles back, but zags off her usual route to run past the house she once shared with Brander, the two-storey brick near the hospital. After they split, the house was purchased by another professor in the English Department, maybe the dean, she can't recall now. Later it was broken into suites and now – she sadly notes the cardboard crushed into a window frame, the half-shingled roof and weeds poking out the eavestrough – it's regressed into a place that nice girls avoid.

Back at home she bathes, combs out her long hair, slips into a sleeveless dress. She decides that although it's late and the best bargains have likely already been snatched, she will go yard saleing. Already this spring she's bartered for an ornate plant stand that she painted forest green, crystal glasses so thin they'd draw blood on a lip, a seventy-five cent copy of *Gray's Anatomy* in excellent condition, and a pair of antique lamps that appealed on a makeshift table in someone's front yard but failed to impress once she brought them home.

She doesn't know that the five-foot woman with the fried hair is his wife, the child with the bandaged knee, his daughter, the black labrador guarding the door, his faithful dog.

He steps from the dark of the garage, looks up and stops short. "Natasha? Oh my...is that you?"

She turns from the table of kitchenware to the doorbell of her name. There's a split-second delay where memory rides to the surface. "My God...Kent?"

He embraces her harder and longer than would seem necessary, and she breaks away, embarrassed. Time, distance, and surprise make people reach out, she realizes, these conditions permission enough for two people who've lost years between them to hold each other. "I didn't know you lived here!"

"Four years," Kent says, displaying the number on his

fingers. "I'm an engineer with a small firm, and Julie," he nods toward the short woman, "teaches school. Grade three."

Natasha glances at Julie, who's watching a knot of teenaged girls paw through her paperbacks. They're tittering and making fun. Of what? Natasha wonders. *Joy of Sex?* Or a decades-old copy of something she might have thumbed through as an adolescent in the musty basement, *The Happy Hooker?* Julie doesn't look the type.

Kent leads Natasha between the sawhorse tables of knick-knacks and folded clothes and played-out toys toward his wife, his arm still firm on her elbow. "Julie, this is Natasha Stensrud. We grew up together."

If it weren't for that unfortunate hair, Natasha thinks, she'd almost be pretty. "Well, Kent was actually more a friend of my sister Holly's," Natasha begins, shaking Julie's tiny hand. It sounds like a denial, she thinks, and instantly regrets the remark. "But we hung out a little bit, too." Did they?

"Nice to meet you," Julie says, with the everywhere-at-once eyes of one who spends much time with children. "Would you like some coffee?"

Natasha notices a sign advertising coffee and a donut for fifty cents and her tongue gets stuck.

Julie catches it. "It's on the house. I'll just –"

"That would be lovely," she hears herself saying, although another part of her doubts this is wise. She should just shake Kent's hand and leave. She's getting a vibe from this hometown boy – this full grown *man* – that's not altogether unwelcome, and he hasn't stopped sneaking glances since she arrived.

"Who do I pay?" A woman cradling a brown teapot accosts Julie.

Kent smiles warmly at Natasha. "Come on in," he's saying, and she walks with him around the side of the house and through the back door, his hand a shadow on the bones in the small of her back.

They enter a country-styled kitchen with bright blotches of daisies papering the walls, a child's artwork on the fridge. "Please, have a seat."

She sits at the round oak table, and when her host turns to pour coffee she sneaks a look, too. He has a good start on a tan, she notes, and still lots of thick, curly hair. Strong shoulders. He played pretty good tennis, she recalls. Or was it ball? No, that was David Gillespie. Her first kiss. "Cream and sugar?"

It's coming back slowly, like a kite spiralling down from an incredible distance toward the grass. His tenderness, his soft way of speaking, like a song she once knew the words to. He'd been on the thin side as a boy but has filled out in all the right directions. "No thanks."

The back door opens and she hears the scuffle-drag of feet coming up the stairs. "Daddy, I –" A girl in a denim jumper and her mother's highheels stops when she sees Natasha, a stranger in her mother's chair.

"This is Rebecca. She's five." He straightens a plastic blue barrette. "What do you want honey?"

"Mommy needs some bags," she says, her long-lashed eyes glued to Natasha. "For the stuff."

Kent grabs a handful of plastic bags from beneath the

sink and passes them to her. Rebecca shuffles off in the large shoes. "Be careful on the stairs!"

They are now acutely alone.

"It's great to see you, Tash. You look...terrific." He touches her hand.

"You, too. It must be, what, twenty years?" She thinks, briefly, about Davis. He wouldn't do this to her. He wouldn't even feel what she's feeling right now with anyone but her.

"At the very least."

The first cup of coffee takes them as far as college days, Natasha's failed marriage, Jameson's birth, her work. The second cup takes them to the point where Kent's implying his own marital misery. A thread begins to unravel. "Engineer with a small firm" was actually last year's job description, hence Kent's tan, hence the yard sale, the FOR SALE sign on the second car, the fee for coffee and a donut.

"There were personality conflicts at the office," he confides. "I got caught in the crossfire."

It could mean anything, she thinks. It explains nothing. She's suddenly terrified he'll tell her too much about his life and she won't be able to hold it all in. "Do you get home often?"

"Never." He adds another teaspoon of sugar to his cup. "You?"

"Not often, though Mom and Dad are still there, and of course there's Holly, in Marvin. You heard about her husband's accident?"

"Yes," he says, stirring. His spoon scrapes against the

cup. "My brother keeps me informed. Terrible thing. Years ago, wasn't it?"

"Years."

Julie calls from the door. "Kent? Someone wants to know if this toaster works."

"I'll be right back." He touches her arm, leaving a warm fingerprint on her skin. "Don't go."

Don't go? It's clear that he's sliding toward something. She knows that the last thing she needs — the last thing *either* of them likely need — is a common disaster, but it's summer, and her birthday, and there's no denying that something's blooming in her chest.

Peter's stroke is so sudden the surprise never leaves his face. He loses the power of speech, and, as if to make up for it, Natasha, her sisters, and Shirley fill the private white room with flowers that have long names — chrysanthemums, Floral Essence carnations, Queen Anne's Lace. They fill pitcher after pitcher of water, to keep the plants healthy and wash down the cavernous, hospital words.

Peter is sliding.

The grandchildren come to say goodbye. Nels has flown home from Toronto, where he's studying psychology at York University, and learning where it went wrong. He did what he had to, Natasha knows. He got out. "I love you, Grandpa," he says, touching Peter's soft, sunken cheek. Natasha notes that these words are almost easy to his lips, a minor miracle, considering he never heard them from his own father.

Holly weeps. In these last years, she and Peter have grown close. Natasha holds her up, gives her Kleenex, makes her wipe her nose. Everett has stayed home, his heart locked up in its own grief.

Jameson brings his girlfriend and Natasha must accept that there are parts of her son's life that are no longer hers. "I wish you could have known him," Jameson tells the lithe beauty beside him, another swimmer. "Before this."

"There's still time," Kristen says, taking Jameson's hand. Natasha turns away. She's going to have to like this girl.

Camille's four daughters and Jesse, the toddling boy, review their grandfather with caution, their eyes blue mirrors of doubt. Only Sarah, the oldest, bends to kiss him, the others believing he's already dead. They take the elevator to the cafeteria with their cousins. They order french fries and wait for their mothers, but they are a sober bunch. Even Jesse seems to sense the necessity of silence. He is uncommonly quiet.

"I'm not ready to let him go," Natasha tells Davis, and he holds her, lets her weep when they fall into his bed or hers after another night that should have been Peter's last. She doesn't tell him that she doesn't know her father yet. She's still waiting for him to bring a marionette home from the city. She's holding her breath for pennies from his pocket which she'll spend on Mojos and suckers at the corner store. She's willing to help him dig potatoes, even to search out the little ones that are no good for anything except chucking at trees.

Two weeks are crossed off the calendar of graces and the last of the grandchildren leave. Now the nurse stands over Peter, and a knowing passes between this woman and Shirley, who has not left her husband's side.

"It's not possible," Holly whispers beside her father's bed. They all whisper. They have become a family without volume, even in the halls, the parking lot. "I have so much to tell him. *He* has so much to tell *me.*"

Shirley coughs into her hand. "You girls, take Camille out."

Camille's standing at the window that overlooks the park. She's as white as the sleepwalker who knocked on their door when they were children, a neighbour who'd wandered across the street. As a girl Camille had suffered from fainting spells. In this final hour it seems they're all becoming the girls they once were. Your life could have been so beautiful, Natasha thinks, taking Camille's hand, the long fingers that haven't graced a note in years. You could have done anything. She and Holly lead her to the cafeteria where Camille stirs too much sugar into her coffee.

"Stay with her," Natasha tells Holly, "at least for a few minutes. I'm going back."

She sees them through the open door. Her mother, stroking Peter's forehead, singing or speaking.

Don't leave. She knocks softly.

Shirley looks up, registers her middle daughter's face, then nods.

"How's he doing?"

"Shhh, baby," Shirley says, her voice all breath. "He's sleeping."

Natasha slides a chair over and remembers. She remembers that Peter loves Christmas, always has. He becomes the little boy again, letting the grandchildren stick bows in his hair. When she was a girl it was the one day she and her sisters were allowed to touch the gleaming, black crown. He liked to watch them tear into their gifts, and later passed around Pot of Gold chocolates and Mandarin oranges, challenging them to master one long, single peel. He liked them to sing carols, with Shirley at the piano. As a boss he always believed in Christmas bonuses and staff socials. Everyone had the best time. She reaches toward her father's face. When he dies they are almost touching.

"It's Davis. I need to see you. If you're home, please pick up the phone."

"I'm not home," Natasha says to her answering machine. She stares at the television. Talk talk talk. A box full of talking heads.

Myles says, "Natasha, I know you're there. Come on, pick up! People die. We're born, we live, we die. That's the cycle. Answer the goddamn phone!"

"It's work calling. Sorry to hear about your father, but we're just wondering when you'll be back in. Please call as soon as you can."

"Sorry about your dad, Natasha. This is Kent. Listen,

if you want to get together, just give me a shout."

She picks up the phone.

Their third date is linguini and red wine. "Who'd have thought we'd ever be sitting in a pseudo-Italian restaurant drinking cheap wine together," Kent says, "after all these years."

"Not me." She manages a small smile but her voice is as flat and cold as the sky at first frost. The world's become a barren place in the weeks since her father's funeral. She hasn't wanted to spend time with Davis, has shattered commitments with Myles and Ann Louise and Isabelle. She rails at God. *It's not fair!* Her father had a greenhouse. He was growing tomatoes. He'd just begun to pay back his blessings.

Holly's warned her about the darkness, how it was for her after Everett's accident. "But the real world returns," she promised, "you'll see. One night you'll tuck into bed and realize that you haven't cried all day."

Natasha remembers: Holly was a soldier. She got back on her horse. She bucked up.

Outside a mid-afternoon thunderstorm is lashing passersby with arrows of rain. People aren't prepared; umbrellas are scarce, and newspapers folded over heads or jackets scrunched up around ears provide little protection from the downpour.

"Forget cats and dogs," Kent's saying, "that's goats and ponies out there."

Another couple enters the restaurant and shakes the

weather out of their hair. There are only two vacant tables left.

"We just made it," Natasha says.

Kent salts his pasta. "Timing is everything."

They're talking themselves up against a wall, all the safe topics behind them now, the storm a welcome diversion between the stops and starts of their futile conversation. Kent's knees bump and press against Natasha's beneath the white-and-red gingham tablecloth. It makes her think of checkers. Of games of every sort. She's growing tired of playing this one. It's a small city; she's not ready to lose Davis. He has many friends. Soon she and Kent will have to go undercover, if they go anywhere at all.

Kent swallows more wine and she watches his Adam's apple bob. He spreads his large hands on the table on either side of his plate. They look out of place, two starfish, stranded. She's waited for him to take them to the point of no return, for the deliberate words or premeditated action – more than the casual brushing of knees beneath a table – that will send the whole thing into fast motion. She feels it's imminent. He'll seize this moment or it'll pass like a cloud of necessary rain over a freshly-sown field; a near miss. But for now: only talking, talking. She watches his mouth move, doesn't hear a solitary syllable.

The waitress comes. They've been here two hours, waiting out the rain, waiting out each other. Do they want their bill now? Kent sends her off.

"Do you still think about it?"

"Sorry?" she says, realizing she's blanked out and he's

been talking this whole time. "You know...what happened."

Her face is a page of wonder.

"Natasha...the day of the bike-a-thon."

"Bike-a-thon?" She's in another world, dreaming. The family has just driven to the ocean. Water sprays up Victoria's rocky coast. Shirley warns the girls to stand back. A drama is unfolding. Two children, sisters, are being carried out to sea on a paddleless rubber dinghy. Natasha can see the smaller girl's white knuckles clinging to the red-rubber sides. "Do something!" Natasha screams at her father. He turns. His lips move but she can't hear what he's saying.

She starts and knocks her fork off the table. It clatters on the restaurant's hardwood floor. The drama never happened; they never saw the Pacific Ocean together, they never saw it at all. Where on earth did this story come from?

"Surely you can't have –" His thick eyebrows are arched and incredulous. " – when we were kids."

Natasha studies his eyes, the furrows fanning out from the corners. We're getting old, she thinks.

"The bike-a-thon to Marvin. The bad storm."

Yes, she recollects, there had been a violent storm, with thunder so loud it seemed apocalyptic. There was a bike-a-thon. "There were balloons...a big send-off." She's thinking hard, but the ocean's crashing and those girls are screaming for help. "Crazy thunder and lightning."

"That's right. The weather was wild."

"I went with Holly and a group of her friends. Were

you there? First it was really, really hot, then it rained...poured. Something like today. I don't believe we finished the ride."

Her food's cold now. She pushes it around her plate. "Eat up everyone," she hears Peter say. "Everything's getting cold."

Kent's flushed. "That's *it*? That's *all* you remember?"

She sets her fork down, nerves rising to the edge of her skin. "Kent...God...it was almost thirty years ago."

A new waitress passes and notes their empty bottle. Kent shakes his head at her offer to bring another. "It's gone for you. I...I thought –"

She rests her hand on his, hers the first overt gesture after all. She hopes to quiet him so she can return to the ocean and save those kids. It doesn't look like her father's going to do it.

"When it started to rain we said we'd take the next ride." His words are a slow train, leading her into a tunnel. A dark, closed space, walls pressing in. She can hardly breathe.

She takes her hand back. "Who? Who was there?"

"Me...you...Holly...Gina...and Rosco. There was a big truck." His voice wavers and cracks. "A really...big... truck."

"It wasn't a truck, it was a semi," Natasha corrects. She's so tired she may need to sleep right here, right at this table, at least until the rain stops. Maybe forever.

"Yes...a semi. It stopped for us and we got in the back with our bikes."

"The doors," she says, looking past Kent through the

window to the street where rain pings off the roofs of parked cars. "I remember them closing. God it was black in there...empty except for our bikes and bits of straw. We couldn't see each other. You were beside me. I had a crush on you."

"We thought we were being kidnapped...it was taking so long to get home. We had all kinds of crazy ideas racing through our heads."

Yes, the smell of oil, and hay, and the sensation of spiders scrambling up her back. Wondering what time it was. Where he was taking them. Whether she'd ever see her family again.

"And then −" Kent says, leading her.

The semi stopped. *No one dared a word. The lock was unlatched, the doors swung open. Light poured in like syrup. Natasha stroked the pins and needles from her legs and leapt to the ground. It was clear that the sun had been queen again but her kingdom was cracking in the western sky.*

She stared at the blinding light.

Rosco and Kent passed the girls their bikes and the trucker locked the trailer door. "You kids take care now," he said, pulling on the greasy peak of his cap, but Gina and Kent were already long gone and Rosco had spun away to the west.

The semi rumbled to life and rolled back onto the highway.

"Beat you!" Holly squealed, then she and Natasha blasted off in the general direction of Earth.

"*We stopped.* I remember the door opening and the light hurting my eyes, as if I'd been in solitary confinement for months. It hurt like that. I remember. We all got out," she says, "and we were back where we began, at the Highway Esso. You guys passed us the bikes...then we separated and Holly and I rode home."

"No, Natasha." There's water in his eyes, the outside seeping in. He's shaking, breaking on her.

Waves crash inside her head. She claps her hands over her ears, afraid of what might leak out or find its terrible way in.

"Holly fell and hurt her ankle," he says. "She was in serious pain...there was no way she could ride. He said he'd drop her at home, said it wasn't out of his way. He seemed very concerned, so we trusted him. We all trusted him."

"No."

He takes her hands and traps them beneath his. "We got on our bikes, but Holly...she got into the cab. She waved at us when they went by."

"No," she says, louder this time. "That's a lie."

Sand and rock and sea. Why doesn't somebody help them? Her father just stands beside her on the wet rock, useless arms at his sides as the girls are dragged further and further out, a purple speck in the distance. He just stands there, whistling.

"Natasha, the police talked to each of us."

The police.

What did he look like?

Did you see his license plate?

Take your time. What colour was his hair?

She's back at the kitchen table, ringed by the ghostly faces of her parents. Her father is weeping.

"They caught him in Manitoba the next morning, then...remember?" Kent waits. "The police brought Holly home."

She remembers the taste of weeds, as if she was the girl thrown into the ditch with her panties ringed around her ankle. She rubs her knees. Now she understands the scars.

"We should never have left her. I was just a kid...things like that didn't happen." Kent sobs, and conceals his eyes with his hands. People are looking.

"You're lying. You're a liar." She pushes back hard, sending her chair to the floor.

"I saw Gina in Calgary once, on a street corner. She had her arm around another girl –"

She focuses on the door. Everyone lies. And if you don't tell it's just like lying. Her parents. They thought it right to dig a grave? To bury the whole dirty business and roll an entire town over top? And Holly was in on it, too. Holly.

"They were working, I –"

Kent continues, but Natasha's already down the block, skin slick with rain real and remembered.

She is ill. She asks the library for an extended leave of absence. She can't run in the mornings, can't make it to the breakfast table to share those first, unblemished moments with her son. Mornings, especially, are hell. She doesn't yet know that life's begun again, within her, or that she'll name her daughter for the season she's known too little of.

"*We're moving,*" she tells Jameson, "to Victoria."

"You're jerkin' me, right?" He expects a smirk but sees in the steadiness of his mother's mouth that she's serious. "Victoria? As in British Columbia?"

Natasha begins packing. She envisions herself in a small house with large windows, not far from the ocean. She imagines her next universe as a tangle of bougainvillea. Starbursts of pink, green and yellow stud her nights. She pictures herself starting over from here, a thirteen-year-old girl with one shoelace untied, leaping toward anything that gives off light.

Acknowledgements

The author gratefully acknowledges the Saskatchewan Writers Guild for providing the Saskatchewan Writers/Artists Colony at Emma Lake, where this novel was conceived and grew over a number of years. Gratitude is also extended to the Saskatchewan Arts Board for financial support during the writing of this book.

Earlier versions of some of the chapters appeared in the following: "Grief" in *Grain;* "Hollywood Legs" in *The Fiddlehead* and in *Due West: 30 Great Stories From Alberta, Saskatchewan, and Manitoba;* "Johnny Dead Bed" in *NeWest Review;* and "Casual Conversations" (as "First Comes Love") in *Other Voices.*

The author thanks Kris Engstrom and Des Browning for reading early chapters, Jeanne Marie de Moissac and Sandra Birdsell for help with certain scenes, W. D. Valgardson for permission to use a quote from his story "The Cave," which appeared in *What Can't Be Changed Shouldn't Be Mourned,* The Tragically Hip for lending a lyric, Edna Alford for her editorial acumen, and Troy, Logan, and Taylor Leedahl for everything else.

An eclectic writer, *Shelley A. Leedahl* has previously published a short story collection, *Sky Kickers,* a book of poetry, *A Few Words for January,* a juvenile novel, *Riding Planet Earth,* and a children's picture book, *The Bone Talker.*

Her fiction, poetry, nonfiction, and children's literature have been appearing in journals and anthologies across Canada since 1987, and are regularly broadcast on CBC Radio. Shelley's work has been recognized with numerous nominations and awards, and she is frequently invited to speak in schools and libraries.

Shelley was born in Kyle, Saskatchewan, and spent her childhood in small Saskatchewan towns. She now lives in Saskatoon with her husband and their two teenagers.